EASY CHARM

BOOK TWO IN THE
BOUDREAUX SERIES

KRISTEN PROBY

EASY CHARM
Book Two in The Boudreaux Series
Kristen Proby

Cover Art:
Photography by: Kristen Proby
Models: BT Urruela an⸍
Cover Design: Okay Cr   **60923950**

ISBN: 978-1-63350-00

This book is dedicated to women who pull themselves up by the bootstraps and kick ass. Fierce women.

And the men who admire and love them.

OTHER BOOKS BY KRISTEN PROBY

PROLOGUE

~Gabby~

Eight Years Ago

What is he going to say? What is he going to do?
Dear sweetness, I'm a mess.

I'm sitting on the front porch of the plantation house, waiting for Colby to pick me up. He's been my boyfriend for four months, and I love him.

Like, *forever* love him.

He's tall, and handsome, and funny. And he tells me he loves me all the time. And a month ago, we made love and it was perfect.

Just like the movies.

But now my stomach is turning, like there are a million fireflies in my belly, and I can't stop wringing my hands.

I hope he's not mad. I hope he's as excited as I am! I'm nervous to tell him, but Charly says it's the right thing to do, and she's right. Thank goodness for older sisters.

Colby's car makes the turn into our driveway. The older Pontiac is louder than usual today. The muffler must have finally given up the ghost.

Colby is forever working on his car. And I don't mind because that means I get to watch his muscles flex as he works, and hand him tools.

We've made out many times in that car.

I grin as he climbs out of the car, his sunglasses covering his bright blue eyes, that smug smirk on his lips. He's in a Fall Out Boy T-shirt and jeans, and I bounce down the steps, excited to see him.

"Hey, baby," he says as he scoops me up into a hug, then glances around to make sure no one is watching before he kisses me soundly. "You look beautiful today."

"Thank you." I take a deep breath and paste a confident smile on my face. "Let's go sit in the garden for a minute before we leave."

"We don't have time, babe. Scott and the others are expecting us."

"It's just a BBQ," I reply. "I have some news I need to share with you."

He smiles and tucks my hair behind my ear, as though he's indulging me. Sometimes Colby can be condescending, just because he's two years older than me, and at twenty-one, he thinks he's the shit because he can buy beer and stuff. It gets on my nerves.

But then he can be the sweetest thing *ever*.

"Okay, let's go sit for a minute," he says and lets me lead him to the bench in the garden that's hidden from the house. It's summer and it's *hot*, but this spot is in the shade, and surprisingly comfortable. "What's up?"

"I'm…" I bite my lip and glance up into his face. "Can you please take your glasses off?"

He frowns but takes them off, and narrows his eyes at me. "What's wrong?"

"I'm pregnant."

He blinks rapidly, then pulls his hand out of mine and scoots away from me so we aren't touching at all. "Bullshit."

"I took six tests, Colby."

"This is fucking bullshit," he repeats.

"Look, I know it's unexpected—"

"Unexpected?" He laughs and shakes his head. "We were careful."

"Not the first time," I remind him, remembering how he said that he didn't want anything between us for the first time because he wanted it to be special.

"That was *one time*, Gabby."

Why is he looking at me like I'm lying to him?

"I can show you the tests," I reply and reach for his hand, but he pulls it out of my reach.

"I don't need to see them. Get rid of it."

I jerk back, stunned. "What?"

"You heard me. Get rid of it. I'll pay for it."

"No." *Get rid of it?*

Now he stands and paces away, then back at me. "If you think I'm going to ruin my life because you can't keep your legs together, you have another think coming."

"Excuse me?" I jump to my feet and bury my finger in his chest, royally pissed off now. "There were two of us there, Colby. I'm no slut. You were my first!"

"So you said."

My jaw drops. Did he seriously just say that to me?

"We are in love," I say, trying to be the calm, rational one. "We can make this work."

"We're not in *love*, Gabby," he says and rolls his eyes. "Jesus, you're naïve. We're having a fun summer together. That's it."

"Why are you acting like this?" I back away and wrap my arms around my belly. "You tell me you love me all the time!"

"Yeah, I tell you I love you all the time because it gets me in your pants and you clearly get off on it," he insists, then chuckles when I just stare at him. "This is what I get for dating a virgin."

"Stop that. I'm nineteen. I'm hardly a baby."

"You're right. So be an adult, and take care of this issue."

I shake my head and feel tears well in my eyes. "I don't even know who you are right now."

"I'm the same Colby who drove up here. I'm not going to raise a kid, Gabby. I didn't sign on for this. So fucking get rid of it."

He slides his glasses on his face and stalks away. I can't move. I hear his car start, then pull away, and slowly lower myself down to the bench.

CHAPTER ONE

~Rhys~

"It's hot down here," I mutter into my phone.

"I can barely hear you," Kate, my cousin, yells into my ear making me cringe. "What kind of car did you rent?"

"A convertible Camero," I reply with a satisfied grin. "Black."

"Of course it's black." I can almost hear her rolling those bright green eyes, and it makes me laugh.

"Hey, I need a way to get around while I'm here. This inn is in BFE."

"But it's worth it," she insists. "It's so peaceful out there. You'll recover quickly there."

"I'm already recovered," I reply, gritting my teeth. "I feel fine."

"Bullcrap."

Of course it's bullshit. My shoulder sings every time I try to throw a ball, but I won't admit that to anyone, least of all Kate, who seems to think it's her God-given right to mother me.

"It's really far from the city. I could probably stay somewhere closer to you."

"It's quiet there, and it's not that far. Stop whining."

I pull the phone away from my ear and look at it, then

reply with, "Did you just tell me to stop *whining?*"

"Yes." She giggles.

"You're going to pay for that."

"You don't scare me."

She's probably one of the few that I don't scare.

"Go rest," she says, serious now. "Heal. The inn is the perfect place for it."

Being away from the media circus and my coaches, who are constantly on my ass about conditioning my injured shoulder, sounds perfect.

Being off the grid, calling my own shots for a while, without anyone checking on me every five seconds, sounds like pure heaven.

"I want to see you," I tell Kate as I take the exit off the freeway.

"Let's do lunch tomorrow. That'll give you time to get settled and rest from your trip."

"Why do you think I need all this rest?" I grumble. "I'm a healthy almost-thirty-year-old man, Kate. I hurt my shoulder. It's not like I'm coming home from war."

Although recovering from this one has felt like a fucking battle every single day since it happened a few months ago.

"Okay, tough guy, I'll see you tomorrow for lunch." She sounds perky and happy, and that makes me happy.

Kate was unhappy for far too long. Being in New Orleans and with Eli Boudreaux, seems to be agreeing with her.

But I'll save my opinion on that until I see her with my own eyes.

"Call me if you need me," I say, just like I always do right before we hang up.

"Ditto."

And she's gone. I take a deep breath as I adjust my grip

on the steering wheel, loving the way this car handles. It's as smooth as a beautiful woman's bare skin.

Not that I remember exactly what that feels like, given that I've been preoccupied with major league baseball, and doctors, and the very real prospect of losing the sport that has been the only love of my life far too much lately.

Maybe that'll change while I'm down here in Louisiana. It wouldn't hurt to distract myself with a fun woman for a while.

I rub my hand over my lips and quickly dismiss that idea. I don't need any distractions. I need to get my shoulder in top form again so I can return to the team and sport I love in the spring.

The GPS announces that I've reached my destination, and my jaw drops as I slow the car before turning into the driveway and take in my first glimpse of Inn Boudreaux.

A row of enormous old oak trees lead to the front door of an impressive white building with wide pillars and a deep front porch. Porch swings hang on either side of the inviting red door and ceiling fans spin lazily above them.

The trees soar high into the air, the branches heavy with Spanish moss dripping from the limbs. Some of the limbs are so long that they rest on the ground.

I turn into the driveway, still crawling along. The grounds are adorned with different buildings, gardens, a creek—complete with bridge—and beautiful colors *everywhere.*

If there is a heaven, this is exactly what it should look like.

I come to a stop beside a Buick with Florida plates and climb out of the car just as a pixie of a woman with long dark hair steps out of the house, tossing a friendly smile and wave in my direction.

Yes, heaven should have her greet every person to show up as well. Still hidden behind my glasses, my eyes take a leisurely stroll up and down her petite frame, not at all offended by her smooth, bare legs and bare feet. She's in tiny denim shorts and a black tank top, because of the hot weather, I'm sure. Her hair falls almost to her waist, and I can't tell what color her eyes are, but that smile could melt the coldest heart.

She descends the stairs, slips her feet into flip flops, and walks toward me.

"You must be Rhys. I'm Gabby." She holds a hand out and I immediately take it in both of mine, and rather than shake it, I raise her knuckles to my lips and kiss them lightly. Her eyes—the color of old whiskey—widen in surprise, and then she giggles, making my gut tighten. "My sisters warned me that you're a charmer."

"They did?" I reply delightedly. "Did they also warn you of my debonair good looks and giving spirit?"

Gabby laughs again and shakes her head. "I must have missed that part."

"I'm wounded." I reluctantly give up her hand and cover my heart, as though I've taken a bullet to the chest.

"You'll survive," she replies and rests her hands on her hips, pushing her breasts forward, and I rub my fingers against my thumb, instantly wanting to touch her again. "Do you need help with your bags?"

"No." I circle to the back of the car and pull my single duffel from the trunk, leaving my workout equipment there for now. "This is it."

"That's it?" She frowns and shakes her head. "Kate said you'd be here for at least a month."

"I'm a guy, Gabby. A few pairs of jeans, some shirts, workout clothes, and I'm good. It's women who need every stitch of clothing they've ever owned for a weekend trip."

She smirks and tilts her head to the side, sizing me up. Why it suddenly matters to me what the thoughts running through her gorgeous little head are, I'm not sure.

But it does matter. A lot.

"Is he here?" The screen door slams as a little boy comes crashing out of the house and races down the steps. "You're here!"

"I'm here," I reply with a grin. "And you're Sam."

He offers me a wide, toothless smile. "You talked to me on the phone," he says.

"I remember." I also remember the twenty minutes of non-stop intelligent questions from this adorable kid. "How are you, Sam?"

"Good." Suddenly shy, he moves to his mom's side and tucks himself under her arm. She doesn't have to bend far to kiss his head.

"Do you want to help me show Rhys to his room?" Gabby asks Sam, who lights up and nods.

"Sure! You get the best room in the whole house." He walks over and takes my duffel, as though it's as natural as breathing, and with not a little effort, turns to lead us inside.

"I can take my bag, Sam."

"I got it. I'm trying to pay off another broken window." He cringes then climbs the stairs. "Mom says this is part of my job."

I raise a brow at Gabby, who just smiles and shrugs. "He's broken four windows in five months."

"How?" I ask as we follow the little boy who looks so much like his gorgeous mother.

"I'm really good at baseball, just like you," he informs me seriously.

"And sometimes the baseballs end up through my windows." Sam is huffing and puffing from the effort of carrying my heavy duffel, so Gabby takes it from him. "That's far enough. You can mark a dollar off what you owe."

Sam smiles triumphantly and I take the bag from Gabby.

"You're our guest."

"If you think I'm going to let you haul around my sh—*crap*—you're not as smart as you look."

Her mouth twists and I can see that she's trying to decide if she's going to let me get away with being a sexist ass, but she's interrupted when Sam announces, "You can say shit. I've heard it before."

"Sam!"

I chuckle, but hide my smile behind my fist as I fake a cough.

"What? I have!"

"Well, *you* can't say it," Gabby says sternly.

"I can't say what?" Sam asks with a delighted giggle.

"Come on, smarty pants, let's show Rhys his room." She sighs defeatedly, but when Sam turns around, she lets the grin spread over her face, and my heart stills.

She's stunning.

"You get to be in the attic," Sam informs me as he stomps on the stairs ahead of us. "We saved it for you."

"Is the inn full?" I ask politely, bringing up the rear, and trying not to watch too closely as Gabby's ass sways back and forth while she climbs the stairs.

"We're full most of the season," Gabby replies. "Guests come and go during the day. I serve breakfast in the dining room between seven and nine every morning. If you give me a heads up, I can provide you with lunch and dinner as well."

"We just finished cleaning all the rooms," Sam says as he climbs another set of stairs.

"You clean this whole place yourselves?"

"No," Gabby replies with a smile. "I hire two women to come in daily to freshen the rooms and bathrooms. I am the inn keeper, and the cook."

"I'm helping clean to pay off the window," Sam informs me and opens a door. "And this is your room."

"This is the Loraleigh room," Gabby says as she points to the sign beside the door and hands me a key. "Each suite is named after a different woman from the family, and has a unique scent and décor."

"Where is the Gabby room?" I ask.

"Ancestor women," she clarifies. "The bathroom is through there. This is how you adjust the temperature. If you need anything, let us know."

"Let's go play catch!" Sam exclaims.

"Hold it," Gabby replies before I can say anything. Watching her with her son is fascinating. "Rhys is our guest, and he's had a long trip. So we are going to let him be, Samuel Beauregard. Do you hear me?"

"Yes, ma'am." He nods and turns his big brown eyes to me. "Sorry, sir."

"How about if we play catch later?"

"You don't have to—"

"I need to practice, and I could use a practice partner," I reply and smile.

"Yes!" Sam high-fives me, then runs down the stairs.

"Really, Rhys, I don't expect you to indulge my son. He's just really excited that you're here."

"He's a good kid."

Her smile brightens as she looks out the door where

Sam just left. "He's the best." She clears her throat and steps out, pulling the door closed behind her. "Let me know if you need anything."

"Yes, ma'am."

When she's gone, I drop my bag on the bench at the end of the bed and turn a circle, taking it all in. The king-sized bed is covered in a blue quilt, obviously hand-sewn long ago. The furniture is dark brown and heavy. Wide windows are open and look out of the front of the house to the line of old oaks. The shade from the trees has kept the room cool, and a breeze is blowing through.

I saunter into the bathroom and whistle through my teeth. The floor is tile, the shower is big enough for four, and the copper tub in the corner is going to be my very best friend when my shoulder is aching after a workout.

I flop on the bed and let out a long sigh, for the first time in what feels like a long time and let my heavy eyelids fall closed, just for a minute. It's quiet here. Every once in a while I can hear Sam's voice float through with the breeze and his mother's soft response. Birds are singing.

I roll onto my side, and wince when a wrong movement sends a zing through my shoulder, reminding me why I'm here.

To heal. To strengthen my shoulder and get back to work.

Not to think about a certain sexy inn keeper.

***

Bacon. I smell bacon. I bolt upright on the bed and gaze about, completely disoriented.

I'm at the inn. In Louisiana.

Did I sleep all damn day and night?

I frown and check my watch. No, it's only noon.

But I smell bacon. And I'm hungry as fuck.

I descend the stairs, still half asleep, and glance into a large dining room with several small tables and chairs scattered about the room rather than one large table. It's empty.

I follow my nose to the kitchen and stop short at the magnificent view of Gabby bent over at the waist, looking in the oven, giving me a prime view of her perfect little ass.

"Can I help?" I ask, startling her. "Sorry, didn't mean to scare you."

"Oh, there's always someone coming up behind me," she replies and pulls a tray of sizzling bacon from the oven. "I'm making BLTs for lunch. Are you hungry?"

"Starving."

"Good. I made homemade potato salad too." She turns away to dig in the fridge and I don't think I'm starving for food anymore.

I'd rather feast on the gorgeous woman standing in this kitchen. Boost her up on the countertop, lay her back, and make her moan my name until she can't remember her own anymore.

Which isn't ever going to happen, so I shake the thought from my head and take a seat on a stool, watching Gabby bustle about assembling sandwiches and scooping salad.

"Tell me about yourself," I say, surprising myself.

"My name is Gabby, and I'm an inn keeper."

"Tell me more," I say dryly.

She frowns and licks some potato salad off her thumb, bringing my cock to full-alert.

"I'm not sure what you want to know."

"I'm just making small talk," I reply and sigh in ecstasy when she hands me a plate full of delicious food.

"Well, there's not much to tell," she says and takes a

bite of her own sandwich.

"Hobbies? Interests? That sort of thing."

"The inn and my son are my interests," she replies and sends me a look that says *back off*.

So I do.

For now.

"Is it possible for me to set up a makeshift gym?" I ask, changing the subject.

"What do you need?"

"Just a bit of space, and some shade. I don't want to cook in the sun."

She thinks it over and takes a bite of salad. "I have an empty barn at the back of the property. We just emptied it out a few weeks ago. You could probably use that."

"Perfect."

***

"Did you know that it's almost impossible for a human to lick their own elbow?" Sam asks me the next morning as he holds a rope for me. He's been helping me in the barn this morning, getting it set up for my work outs.

"I bet that's not true."

"It is! Look." He bends his elbow and tries, unsuccessfully, to lick it. "See?"

"You proved me wrong," I reply and hand the end of a rope ladder to Sam. "We're going to lay this flat on the ground."

"Why?"

"Because I'm going to jump over the ropes."

"Like hopscotch?"

"Kind of, yeah."

"Okay." He shrugs and helps me spread out the ladder. "Did you know that a shrimp's heart is in its head?"

"I'm learning all kinds of things from you today."

He smiles proudly and adjusts the Cubs hat on his head. "Mom says I'm pretty smart."

"I'd say she's right." I check the time and lead Sam out of the barn. "Let's go back to the house."

"Okay."

The walk doesn't take us long, but we're both sweaty and thirsty when we reach the house. Gabby is in the kitchen, kneading something in a bowl. She has flour on her cheek, her hair piled on her head, and a frown on her pretty face.

"What's wrong?" I ask and lean my hands on the countertop.

"Yeah, Mom, what's wrong?"

"Nothing. I'm just making the dough for tomorrow morning's cinnamon rolls."

My mouth immediately salivates. This woman can *cook*. Her biscuits and gravy this morning made my stomach weep with joy.

"Mom, can I go to Stanley's?"

"No."

"Can I go see if Uncle Beau's home?"

"He's at work, baby."

Sam's face falls, but I can't stop watching Gabby. She looks tense. Something is on her mind.

"Can I go hit some balls around the back yard?"

"Sam, I love you, but you're getting on my last nerve. Go read a book or something."

"I'm going into the city to have lunch with Kate. I can take him with me."

"Yes!" Sam exclaims.

"That's not necessary." Gabby shakes her head. "But thank you for the offer."

"It's really fine," I reply. "He's welcome to come."

"Can I ride in your cool car?"

"Sure."

"No." Gabby stops kneading her dough and stares at me with frustration. "No offense, but I hardly know you. Do you think I'm going to let you take my kid into the city?"

Without replying, I pull my phone out of my pocket, dial Kate's number, and with my eyes holding Gabby's, wait for Kate to answer.

"Do not cancel on me today."

"I need you to tell Gabby that I'm not a kidnapper, and if I bring Sam with me to lunch today that he'll be perfectly safe and well cared for."

Without waiting for Kate to reply, I hold the phone out to Gabby. Sam is silent as he watches the exchange between us. Gabby chews her lip for a second, then sighs and jerks the phone from my grip, and turns her back on me when she says hi to Kate.

I wink at Sam, who winks back at me and smiles that toothless smile.

"Kate, he didn't need to interrupt you—" She stops and chuckles. "I can imagine. You're kidding! That's funny. Okay. If you're sure. Sam will be excited to see you and Eli too."

Sam silently pumps his fist in the air triumphantly.

"Okay, thanks. I'll see you on Sunday."

She hands the phone back to me, which I click off and shove back in my pocket.

"Better?"

"You can take him."

"Thanks, Mom!" Sam launches himself into Gabby's arms and kisses her cheek. "You're the best!"

"Yeah, yeah." She eyes me with the scary eyes of a stern

mom. "You drive safely. Seat belts at all times. Got it?"

"Of course. Does he need a booster seat?"

"I'm not a baby!"

"No, not in Louisiana," Gabby says with a smile. "He's too old for that now."

"Are you ready, Sam?"

"Let's go!"

He runs out of the house, toward my car, and I stop in front of Gabby and tilt her chin up to look me in the eyes. "We'll talk later about what's bothering you."

She raises a brow. "You'll be careful with my son and mind your business."

I tuck her hair behind her hair and grin as I walk away.

"Challenge accepted."

CHAPTER TWO

~Gabby~

"Challenge accepted," I mimic after Rhys closes the door behind him. What is up with all of the damn testosterone-flexing men in my life?

And Rhys has more testosterone to fling around than anyone I've ever met. He's super tall, I'd say just a couple inches shorter than my brothers' six-foot-four, which puts him more than a foot taller than me. His eyes aren't simply green. They're bright green, giving the grass a run for its money.

If grass had money.

I punch my fist into the bowl of dough.

As if the eyes weren't enough, he has that damn cocky half-smile thing working for him that I'm sure reduces most mortal women into a puddle of goo at his feet.

Not this woman.

I mean, sure, he's hot, and when he tucked my hair behind my ear, just the brush of his fingertips sent heat searing down my spine.

But that's just because I don't even remember the last time a man that I wasn't related to touched me.

And that's just damn sad.

"More like pathetic," I mutter and give the dough

another punch before covering it and setting it aside to rise.

And this morning at breakfast, he devoured my biscuits and gravy, that sexy, square jaw flexing as he chewed, and he *listened* to Sam. He didn't just indulge him and pretend to be interested in what he was saying, he *was* interested. He's polite and sweet and sets my libido on fire.

And now I have a sexy, single man living under my roof for God knows how long, being nice to my son, tucking my hair behind my ear, and I'm going to die from sexual frustration.

Because there's no way I'm having sex with Rhys O'Shaughnessy.

Not that he's likely to ask me. This is the famous baseball player we're talking about. He probably has a piece of tail in every city.

And damn if the feminist in me isn't more than a little pissed that I called them a piece of tail.

I laugh at myself and wander through the empty inn. It's rarely empty these days, which is great for business, and my own sanity. Between the inn and Sam, my days are full, so when I finally fall into bed at night, I sleep hard.

There's not time for anything else in my life.

Especially not a sexy athlete with a killer smile and muscular arms.

Of course I noticed his muscles. I'm alive, aren't I?

I glance around, content that the work is caught up for now, I walk out onto the front porch, and slide into my favorite swing. Both swings on either side of the front door are identical, but this one has always been my favorite. It has the best view of the trees, and it's where I do my best thinking.

But my eyes are so damn heavy.

So, I curl my feet under me, brace my face in my hand

and close my eyes. Just for a minute.

It's hot today, but the row of oaks provides a nice breeze. I can smell the roses, fully bloomed and reaching for the sun, in the back yard. I should get up and make sure the two rooms I'm expecting guests for are to my standards. I should order more complimentary soaps and lotions.

I should reply to the email I received this morning that sent my heart into my throat. It's not like me to ignore someone, or to not face conflict head-on, but my gut says to leave it be.

For now.

Besides, the breeze is lovely, blowing through my hair to my neck, over my face, and the blue jays are calling back and forth.

So for just a few minutes, I'll rest my eyes and enjoy the quiet.

***

"Gabs?"

I jolt awake and sit up straight, and there in front of me is my oldest brother, and my best friend, Beau.

"You're home early," I say and stretch my arms over my head.

"It's Friday," he replies with a shrug. "And Eli's the workaholic, not me."

I grin and pat the swing next to me. "Sit."

Like all of my siblings, Beau is tall and dark, with the same hazel eyes as the rest of us. He's strong. Calm. He's been my rock for as long as I can remember. And despite being ten years older than me, he's the one I've always felt closest to.

Which is saying a lot because the Boudreaux family is a close one in general. Mama and Papa saw to that.

"I haven't seen you sleep during the day since you were

a kid," he says as he lowers his tall frame next to me and rests his arm on the back of the swing. "You feeling okay?"

"I'm fine," I reply immediately. "It was just a rare, quiet moment and my eyes got heavy."

He peers at me closely, narrows his eyes, and tilts his head.

"What's on your mind, baby girl?"

He knows me too well.

"Nothing." I shrug innocently. "What do I have to complain about? Aside from the fact that you still live in my back yard, despite me being twenty-seven and able to fend for myself. You seriously need a woman."

"We aren't talking about me."

"Maybe we *should* talk about you," I reply and turn in my seat to face him. "You don't have to stay here to babysit me, you know."

"I like being here," he replies calmly. "It's a good place."

"It's a bitch of a commute to work for you every day."

"It's a good place," he repeats. "I also don't like the idea of you and Sam out here by yourselves."

"I can—"

"Yes, I know you can take care of the both of you. You're one of the strongest people I know, but damn it, it gives us all peace of mind to have me nearby." His jaw clenches, the only sign that he's good and irritated with me, so I lean over and kiss his cheek.

"I love you, you know."

"You'd try the patience of the Dalai Lama."

"He's pretty patient," I reply. "Maybe a different llama."

Beau laughs and shakes his head at me.

"Hey," I say casually. "The last you heard, was Colby

still living in San Francisco?"

The smile vanishes from Beau's face, and he leans closer to me. "Has he contacted you?"

"No," I lie. "I'm just curious."

He searches my face, and finally says, "Yes, he's still in San Francisco."

I nod, relieved.

"If he contacts you, I want to know," Beau says.

"He signed his rights away," I remind him. "What would he want with me?"

"I know, I was there," he replies grimly. "Promise me that you'll tell me if he contacts you."

God, I hate lying to my brother. But nothing has really happened, and there's no need to worry anyone.

Besides, I *can* take care of myself!

"Fine."

"Promise me, damn it."

"Okay, I promise, geez. You should have been an interrogator or something."

I move to stand, but he grips my arm and pulls me back.

"I'm serious, Gabs. You haven't asked about him in seven years. Not since the day Sam was born. Why now?"

"Because I just wanted to make sure there were still several states separating us. That's all."

Just then, Rhys pulls in with Sam, who climbs from the car quickly, running toward me.

"Hey, buddy!" I call as he climbs the stairs.

"Hi Mom! Hi Uncle Beau!" He hugs us both, then turns to me, practically bouncing with excitement. "Mom! Guess what?"

"Slow down. Did you have fun?"

"Yes, ma'am."

"Did you have a good lunch?" I glance up as Rhys joins us on the porch, that half-smile on his impossibly handsome face. He leans his hip against the railing and crosses his arms over his chest and my mind just... empties.

Damn hot man.

"Yes, ma'am, I had a shrimp po' boy for lunch."

"Good. Rhys, have you met my brother, Beau?"

The two men nod at each other as Sam frowns, still quivering with excitement and impatient to share his news.

"We met at the office," Beau replies.

"Mom, I have something really important to tell you."

"Okay, I'm all ears. Shoot."

"So, um..." He shifts his weight from side to side, his big brown eyes on mine, and I feel my heart tug, just a bit. This perfect little boy is *mine*. I made this. Amazing. "Miss Kate has a friend at work who has a dog—"

Uh oh.

"And the dog had puppies—"

Of course it did. Tramp dog.

"And Miss Kate said that if it's okay with you, she'll buy me one for my birthday next month. It'll be an early present!"

His eyes are so full of excitement and hope.

"Buddy, you know that sometimes we have guests who stay here who are allergic to animals."

And I just killed the light in my own kid's eyes.

Mother of the freaking year, right here.

"Yes, ma'am."

"What kind of dog is it?" I ask wearily and hear Beau chuckle beside me, which earns him an elbow to the ribs.

"They're hounds," Rhys replies with a grin. "Short hair, mild-mannered, not chewers."

I narrow my eyes at him, as if to say, "Whose side are

you on?"

"Yeah, they're not chewers," Sam repeats triumphantly. "Like, not at all. And I'll clean up after it. And it can sleep with me, and we won't let it in the guest rooms so they won't be allergic, and I promise it'll be the best thing in the whole *world!*"

"Hmm. The whole world, huh?"

He nods and holds his breath, then takes my face in his sweet, sweaty little hands and leans his forehead to mine. "Please, Mama?"

"Will you teach it to play fetch?"

He nods.

"Will you teach it to go potty outside?"

More enthusiastic nods.

"Will you give me lots of hugs and kisses?"

He smiles, the hope in his giving way to elation and jumps into my arms, wraps his little arms around my neck and holds on tight before kissing my cheek.

Twice.

Without acting like he's going to catch cooties from it.

"A puppy is a lot of responsibility," I say sternly. "And a lot of work."

"I'm a hard worker, just like you," he says, knowing full-well he's buttering me up.

Beau smirks beside me, and I elbow his ribs again.

Just because it's fun.

"Okay, I'll call Miss Kate and tell her that you can have the puppy."

"Yes!" He jumps in the air and does his version of the happy dance, fist bumps Beau and Rhys and hugs me again. "You're the best mom in the history of moms."

"That's what you say to all the moms," I reply, but bury my nose in his hair and breathe him in, just for a minute.

My baby is getting big.

"Nope, just you."

"Okay, let's get ready for our guests this evening. I need to make dinner, too. Beau, are you joining us?"

"What are you making?" he asks.

"Pork chops, asparagus and red beans and rice."

"Mama's red beans and rice?"

"She's the one who taught me to make them," I reply and shake my head.

"I'm there," Beau says.

"Me too," Sam says, as if he has a choice. I raise a brow at Rhys. His face is sober, but his green eyes are still full of humor.

"And you, Mr. O'Shaughnessy?"

"I'm in."

"Well then, I'd better get started."

***

"Darling, this inn is just amazing." I smile at the sweet Mrs. Baker and fill her wine glass with more wine. "Ethel described it perfectly to me. I'm so happy that she convinced Carl and me to come here."

"It's a pleasure to have you, ma'am," I reply. This is my favorite time of day. The guests have returned to the inn from their adventures during the day. Some retire to their rooms to relax. Some sit outside and soak up the bayou. And some sit in the drawing room, sip wine, and chat.

Rhys, much to my surprise, decided to come down and chat with the guests. Despite being a guest himself, I couldn't talk him into leaving the dishes for me to do after dinner. He jumped in and helped as if it was the most natural thing in the world.

And now he's chatting baseball with Carl Baker. Sam is sitting at their feet, his eyes bouncing between them as they talk about innings and sliders and things that I really don't understand.

Because in my world, baseball is boring. But I will go to every game that Sam ever plays and I will love it.

Because I love him.

"Sam." I lean down and speak softly into his ear. "It's time for bed, buddy."

"But we're talking about baseball. Man to man."

"Yes, I see, and I'm sorry to interrupt, but it's time for one of these men to go to sleep. And you're the only one with a bedtime."

"Carl has a bedtime too," Mrs. Baker says with a giggle and sips more wine.

"Mom, this is important stuff."

"So is bed. I mean it. I won't say it again."

He sighs heavily and stands. "Don't say anymore important stuff without me."

"Deal." Rhys ruffles his hair. "Sleep well, kiddo."

"Good night."

Sam shuffles to the door that leads to our private quarters, then turns back.

"Mom! I forgot to tell you!"

"Tell me what?" I cross my arms and settle in for the battle of getting my kid to bed. He's fought bedtime since infancy.

The little monster.

"Um." He scrunches up his nose, thinking really hard. "Uncle Eli said to tell you hello today."

"Okay, now you've told me. Good night."

"'Night," Sam replies and leaves the room, then pops his head back through the doorway. "Mom?"

"Yes."

Rhys covers his smile with his hand and pretends to text on his phone.

"Did you call Miss Kate yet?"

"I'll call her tomorrow." He nods and leaves, but then his forehead and eyes reappear. "You're killing me, son."

"Will you tuck me in?" he asks with a small voice.

"Go get your jammies on, brush the hair off your teeth and climb in bed and I'll be there soon to tuck you in."

He nods and leaves for real this time with a sigh.

"He's a handful," I mutter. "There's a reason why they're born adorable and smelling good. Because otherwise they wouldn't make it past the toddler stage."

"He's just worried that he's going to miss something good," Mr. Baker says. "And I'm sure he's excited to have his favorite player staying here."

"True," I reply and check the scones and cookies before leaving the room to see to my boy, who is already in bed, in his jammies, but the teeth brushing is questionable. "Did you brush?"

"My toothbrush is wet."

I smirk. "That doesn't mean you brushed your teeth."

He smiles angelically, and I sit at his hip and tuck him under the covers. "I love you, my sweet baby boy."

"Love you too." His eyes are already heavy. He's like me, in that he runs and runs all day, and when he lays his head down, he falls asleep quickly. "Thank you for the puppy."

"You won't be thanking me when you're cleaning up his poop."

He giggles at the mention of *poop*, and I kiss his cheek, then his forehead.

"Good night."

His eyes are already closed when I leave the room, his door cracked, with the hall light shining the way he likes it.

Everyone has left the drawing room, retiring for the night. I can hear some footsteps upstairs, and low murmuring voices, but I'm alone for the rest of the night.

Thank goodness.

I wander into the kitchen and place a slice of the leftover peach pie on a plate and carry it out to the front porch, once again taking my favorite seat. I leave the lights off, comfortable in the dark of the bayou, and watch the lightning bugs as they flit through the trees.

"I thought I heard you come out here," Rhys says as he steps outside, holding two wine glasses.

"I'm sorry, I thought everyone had gone up. Did you need anything?"

He's shaking his head before I can stand up. "No, I'm fine. Thought you could use a glass of this."

He passes me a cold glass of my favorite wine. "How did you know I like this one?"

"Because it's in your fridge, and not in the one available for guests."

"And yet you got in it." I raise a brow and take a sip. The sweet wine complements the pie well.

Rhys simply shrugs and sips his own wine. "That pie is awesome."

"Yeah, I was following my heart and it led me to the fridge."

He laughs and I have to grip firmly onto my fork as chills run up my arm.

This man is potent. Sexy.

So damn sexy.

I finish my pie and set the plate on the ground, then settle back with my wine as Rhys leans his hips on the railing, facing me. I can barely see his face in the dark.

"What do you think of Louisiana so far?" I ask.

"It's beautiful. Hot."

"It is hot," I agree.

"This porch is nice and cool."

"It's the trees."

"May I?" he asks and points at the swing next to me.

"Sure."

"What do you mean, it's the trees?" he asks and leans his arm across the back, much like Beau did this afternoon. I'm acutely aware of Rhys's fingertips brushing my shoulder and sending zings down through my nipples.

Damn nipples.

"The trees were planted hundreds of years ago, before the house was even a thought," I reply, trying to maintain my professionalism. I can repeat this speech all day.

And often do.

"It's not clear if they were planted with the plan of a home being here at the end of them, but what we do know is that they form a wind tunnel. The Mississippi is right over that levy." I point straight ahead. "The wind flows right through these massive trees, and onto the property, providing the world's first air conditioning.

"So, my ancestors would open the doors and windows, and let the cool air through. But thankfully, we've since added the electric AC." I glance over at Rhys, able to see his face now, and feel the smile leave my face at the sight of his deep green eyes watching me.

"You're so damn beautiful, Gabby."

I frown and glance down but murmur, "Thank you."

"You don't believe me?"

"I'm not an idiot," I reply and turn my gaze back to him. "I come from beautiful people. Strong people."

He nods. "You're certainly that too. This place is impressive."

That makes me grin. "Thank you."

He picks a piece of my hair off my shoulder and lazily twirls it around his fingers.

"How long have you lived here?" he asks.

"All my life."

He raises a brow, prompting me to continue.

"We lived in the city during the school year, then came here in the summers. After Daddy died, and Mama wanted to stay in the city all year, it made sense for me to stay here and turn this into an inn. I've always seen it like this."

"Where is Sam's dad?" he asks. Not rudely, and not with any judgment in the question. If any of that were in his voice, I'd tell him to go to hell.

Instead, I answer with, "Gone."

"How long has he been gone?"

"Since the moment I told him I was pregnant." I take a deep breath and let it out. "And you know what?"

"What?"

"His loss."

"Fuck yes, it's his loss."

I whirl my head, surprised by the anger in his voice. He drops my hair, then buries his whole hand in it at the back of my neck and lets it sift through his fingers, and nothing has felt so good in… a *very* long time.

"He let you and Sam go. He's an idiot."

"We were young."

"He's an idiot." He repeats the motion, pulling my hair through his fingers, and I want to purr. "You have beautiful hair."

"Thank you."

"So let's finish our conversation from this morning."

I frown. "What conversation?"

He chuckles. "You're not stupid, Gabby. Let's talk about what was bothering you enough to beat the shit out of some innocent cinnamon rolls."

I bite my lip and turn my face away, but he catches my chin in his fingers and turns me back to him.

"I'm fine," I say firmly.

"Does anyone ever call you out on that bullshit?" He's not angry now; he's calm as can be, still pulling my hair lazily through his fingers, calling me a freaking liar.

"It's not bullshit. I *am* fine."

"You're more than fine. You're damn beautiful."

"That's not what I meant and you know it."

He grins, that sexy as hell half-smile that makes me squirm in my seat.

"Look, you don't know me. You just got here. You can't possibly know that I had anything on my mind this morning." I swallow hard as his hand rests on my neck and begins to gently massage my tired muscles.

"I don't know you," he agrees, "yet. But I can see when a person is worried or upset, and you were worried this morning."

"You know, I don't need a man to waltz in here and solve my problems."

"What *do* you need a man for?" he asks with mischief in those green eyes.

"I need a man who won't *become* a problem," I reply softly. Because that's the God's truth.

He swallows and watches his hand massage my neck. "I can understand that."

"Good."

"So are you going to talk about it?"

I simply laugh because this is ridiculous. I'm sitting out

here, in the dark, with the hottest man I've seen in... *ever*, and he won't take a simple no for an answer.

"Let's just say that sometimes the past comes back around to bite you in the ass."

"I'd like to bite your ass," he says casually. My eyes widen and my heartbeat speeds up, but before I can respond to his declaration, he continues. "And if anyone has done anything to hurt you, I'll kill them."

"No one has done anything." My voice sounds shaky to my own ears. Rhys pulls my face toward his again and pins me in his gaze.

"I mean it."

"So do I."

He nods. "Okay then."

"I should go to bed. I have an early morning tomorrow."

"You have an early morning every day," he replies, and if I'm not mistaken, there is concern in his voice.

"Not on Mondays. I don't keep guests Sunday nights, so I can catch up a bit around here, have dinner with the family, and sleep in on Monday. So, FYI, you'll have to fend for yourself Monday morning for breakfast."

"I can handle that. Why don't you hire more staff?"

"Because I don't need more staff. I have the girls who come clean for me every day. I can handle the rest myself."

"Yes, but you don't *have* to."

"It's my inn."

"Your family is beyond wealthy, Gabby. You could afford to have more staff so you don't have to work yourself and your son to the bone."

I blink rapidly, push his hand off my neck, and stand to face him.

"Yes, my family is wealthy, but this inn is *mine*. If and

when I need more help, I'll hire it, but I don't right now. And if you have a problem with how I'm raising my son—"

"Hey, calm down. I didn't say that I have a problem with how you're raising Sam. In fact, your kid is awesome."

Yeah, try to dig yourself out of your hole.

"Except I'm clearly abusing him by expecting him to have chores and pay for things he breaks."

"That kid is *not* abused by any stretch of the imagination, and teaching him a work ethic is a good thing."

"I'm pretty sure you insulted me back there."

"No, I'm worried about you."

And now I'm irritated all over again.

"I don't need you to worry about me. You're a guest. Just enjoy the inn and don't give me another thought."

"Impossible," he mutters and rubs his hand over his mouth. The rough sound of his skin on his whiskers is loud in the quiet of the evening, and my own hand itches to touch him there.

To touch him everywhere.

Which means I need to get the hell out of here.

"Is there anything else you need?"

He watches me for a beat, then shakes his head. "No, Gabby, there's nothing else I need."

I nod. "Good night."

CHAPTER THREE

~Gabby~

He's been here a week. You'd think I would be used to him by now, that the *shine* would have worn off, but no. No, I'm still perfectly aware of where he is, what he's doing, and dear God, I even know what he smells like: clean, spicy and like heaven.

And after he leaves a room, that smell lingers for what feels like forever, as if to remind me that he isn't far away.

Which, trust me, I'm not likely to forget. If he's not offering to help me with something, he's outside playing with my kid. Or my kid is telling me all about how great Rhys is.

As if I don't already know.

"Earth to Gabby," Charly says, snapping her fingers from across the table. "Where's your mind, baby doll?"

"Sorry," I murmur and turn back to my two sisters and Kate, my brother Eli's girlfriend. The girls came out to enjoy Saturday lunch at the inn. I have a beautiful gazebo in the back yard with a table that we often take advantage of. "How are things with Eli?" I ask Kate, purposefully deflecting the attention from me.

"Things are great." Kate wrinkles her freckle-covered nose and grins. "He's…" She shakes her head back and forth, as though she's trying to come up with the word.

"Stupid?" Savannah offers.

"Ridiculous?" Charly adds.

"A pain in the ass?" I say with a giggle.

"Sexy," Kate replies with a belly laugh.

"Ew," Savannah says with a shudder. "He's my big brother."

"Yes, he *is* big," Kate replies, still laughing, knowing that she's grossing us all out.

"Stop it right now," I demand, covering my ears with my hands. "I'm too young to know this."

"Right." Charly rolls her eyes. Charly is the eldest sister. She decided a long time ago that the family business of running Bayou Enterprises, a multi-billion dollar ship building enterprise, wasn't for her, and instead she owns an adorable shoe boutique in the Quarter called *Head Over Heels*. She's classy, put together, and smart as can be.

"I think we're all too young to know this," Savannah adds. Van is the middle sister, and Declan, our youngest brother's twin.

There are a lot of us.

"Why do you ask if you don't really want to know?" Kate asks and takes a sip of her sweet tea.

"Because Gabby was trying to get the attention off of her," Charly replies with a sweet grin, her hazel eyes pinned to me.

"You're not nearly as sweet as you'd like us all to believe," I inform her.

"Yes I am," she replies. We all carry the sound of Louisiana in our voices, but Charly's seems to be the thickest. It always makes me smile.

"Hi Mom!" Sam calls from the barn that he and Rhys just came out of. He's waving wildly until I wave back, then turns his attention back to the tall baseball player at this side.

Who happens to be grinning this way.

"I think the better question is, how are things going with Rhys?" Savannah's eyes are lighter than the rest of us, and they are lit with more humor now than I've seen from her since she left her husband a few months ago.

That abusive piece of shit.

"What do you mean?" I shift in my seat. *Do not look at him. He's just a man.*

"Oh stop," Charly replies and watches the baseball player unabashedly, licking her lips when he begins pushing some kind of heavy sled thing across the pasture. "He's a prime specimen of man. Surely you've noticed."

"Ew," Kate says with a frown.

"Turnabout is fair play." Van laughs and watches Rhys with calculating eyes while sipping her sweet tea through a straw.

"So spill it," Charly insists and leans forward in her seat. "Has he kissed you?"

"He's a guest!" I cover my face with my hands and lean back in my chair. "I'm running a business here."

"Oh, please," Kate says with a flick of the wrist. "I mean, yes you are, and it's awesome, but it's okay to have a private life too."

"I have a child."

"Who loves him," Charly says and gestures with her head for me to look.

Rhys has taken all the weight off the sled and is helping Sam push it, encouraging him with every step.

And my heart melts, just a little more.

"Yeah, he's good with Sam."

I've told Sam to leave him be, but every time Rhys

insists that he enjoys Sam's company and that when he needs a break, he'll tell Sam.

"Rhys loves kids," Kate says with a smile.

I keep my mouth shut for a moment, and then decide, *screw it.* These are my sisters. I trust them more than anyone in the world.

"I don't do the flirting thing well," I admit and fold a pink napkin into eighths.

"Why not?" Kate asks with a frown.

"Because," Van replies softly, her light eyes on mine, "she had a baby when she was very young and hasn't had the chance to flex her flirting muscles since she got pregnant."

I blink at her for a moment and then nod. "That about covers it."

"I say you practice on that tall drink of water over there," Charly says.

"Right." I snort and shake my head. "The first time I try, he'll laugh at me. He's a professional athlete, Charly. I don't want or need to be another notch in his belt."

"It's true that in his rookie days Rhys was a bit of a man-whore," Kate says.

"Kate! That's your cousin you're talking about." Van looks outraged, then giggles.

"Hey, he'll admit the same," Kate says reasonably. "But he hasn't been that way in a long time, Gabs. We joke about it, but he's been so focused on baseball, I couldn't tell you when the last time was that he had a girlfriend."

Interesting.

"Has he flirted with *you?*" Charly wants to know. I can't help but think of the night on the porch when he sifted his fingers through my hair. Or the occasions since then when he makes sure I don't carry anything heavy, or compliments my hair.

"He seems to like my hair," I reply softly.

"Flirt back," Van suggests and lays her hand on my arm with encouragement. "You never know what might happen."

"Mom!" Sam comes running into the gazebo. "Mr. Rhys let me push the sled! I pushed seventy-five pounds, all by myself!"

"That's amazing," I reply and ruffle his hair. "You're strong, that's for sure."

"I know."

"Say hello to your aunts." Sam takes turns hugging and chatting with each of his aunts, who kiss his cheeks, and he wipes the kisses off just to get more.

Although he'd deny that until the day he dies.

"Hello, ladies," Rhys says as he joins us. "Having fun?"

He stands to my side and rests his hand on my shoulder, perking my nipples right up.

Damn freaking nipples.

"Don't you know?" Charly replies with her eyes on his hand. "We always have fun."

Rhys grips a strand of my hair in his fingers and begins to twirl it absentmindedly. "I believe it," he replies with a wink. "Do you come out here for lunch often?"

"Not as often as we would like," Van says. "You look good, Rhys."

"Thanks, darling. You are beautiful, as always."

Van laughs, then sobers. "Thanks. How long are you here?"

I feel him shrug beside me, my hair still in his fingers, but then he starts to just comb my hair, sifting the strands through his fingers, and I want to purr.

And three sets of eyes, two hazel and one the same deep

green as her cousin's, are on me.

Challenging me.

Daring me.

Shit, what in the ever-loving hell am I supposed to do?

I bite my lip and clench my eyes closed for just a heartbeat, and when I open them, the girls are grinning.

He must have said something funny. I have no idea, because I've suddenly been struck deaf.

I hope it's not permanent.

All I can feel are Rhys's fingers in my hair and his body close to mine, so I decide to do what comes naturally. I lean into his touch, and rest my face on his side, as he continues to play with my hair.

He doesn't even miss a beat. He doesn't seem surprised, or taken aback. He just keeps running those fingers through my hair and talks to my sisters and Kate.

But Charly's eyes have widened, and Van has a proud tilt to her lips, and I'm proud with her. I did it. I flirted back.

And, oh dear sweet heaven above, does the hard wall that is his side feel good against my face. The man is pure muscle. I want to pull his T-shirt up and lick him, but I restrain myself.

Barely.

"We should go," Van says as she stands. "Kate and Eli have a date in a few hours."

"Let's help Gabby clean up first," Kate says as I pull away from Rhys's side, and he steps back. But when I look up at him, his green eyes are bright and warm and he's sporting that sexier than all get-out half-smile.

That smile holds promises.

And promises of what, I'm not sure yet, but I think I want to find out.

"No, you all go on." Rhys steps forward, authority in every line of his body.

Damn, if that isn't hot.

"The men will clean up while Gabby walks you out."

I frown and shake my head. "This isn't your job."

"Oh please," Kate replies before Rhys can. "Let the man earn his keep. Come with us."

I don't like it. He's a guest. He shouldn't be clearing a table. But I am swept away with the others to their cars.

"I'm so happy you came," I say and hug each of them. "We need to do this more often."

"Sounds good," Charly says as she hugs me. "Is Sam still going with Mama on her trip tomorrow?"

"Yes. Which reminds me, I need to get him packed."

"Enjoy your alone time with Hottie McHotterson." Charly wiggles her eyebrows, making me laugh. "I'm serious. Test out the flirting skills. There's no harm in it."

"She's right," Kate agrees. "And trust me when I say he likes you."

"Oh, sugar, you got that right," Van adds. "He couldn't keep his hand out of your hair."

"And when you laid your cheek on his side, I thought he was going to carry you off, caveman-style," Charly whispers.

"No way. He didn't even react," I insist.

"You couldn't see his eyes," Kate replies. "We could. We know. Flirt with him. And keep us posted."

"I think you're all nuts."

"You're nuts to ignore the two-hundred pounds of delicious man under your own roof."

***

"Maybe I shouldn't go," Sam says with a worried frown as I fold his clothes and organize them into piles on his bed.

"You go every summer, buddy." I march back to his dresser for more underwear and grab his swim trunks too. "It's only for a week."

"Eight days," he reminds me. "Did you know that an ostrich eye is bigger than its brain?"

"Wow. They must have small brains."

"Or big eyes," Sam replies with a grin. My smart boy. And then he sobers again. "Sinceriously."

"*Sinceriously* is not a word."

"It means I'm sincerely serious," he says and punches his fist into his baseball glove. "Won't you miss me?"

"I'll miss you every minute of the day," I reply, and mean every word. "But your cousins in Florida love to see you, and Nannan loves to have you with her. It would hurt her feelings if you backed out now."

Every summer we go through this, and every summer is the same. He's nervous about leaving me, until he's on the plane, and then it's just a big adventure and I practically have to bribe him to come home.

"What about Mr. Rhys?"

I stop folding clothes and glance at my son, who continues to punch his fist into his mitt. "What about him?"

"Will he be gone when I get back?"

Ah, there it is.

"No, sweetie, he'll still be here. He's going to be here for a while."

He lifts his big brown eyes to mine. "What if he doesn't like me anymore when I get home?"

I laugh and begin organizing his suitcase.

"Now you're just being silly. Of course he'll still like you. I still like you when you come home, don't I?"

"You have to like me. You're my mama."

I sit on the bed and pull him into my lap. When did he get so big?

"I love you, and Rhys likes you, and none of that will change when you get home."

He snuggles against me, and I bury my nose in his hair. "Promise?"

"Of course I promise."

"When do I get my dog?"

The change of subject makes me grin. "When it's old enough to come home. About a month, I guess."

"Okay."

He scrambles off my lap and tosses a baseball into his suitcase. "Last year, Lennie lost my ball, so I better take a spare."

"Good idea."

"What are we having for dinner?"

"Fried chicken with collard greens and grits."

"My favorite!"

"Of course. You're going to be gone for a whole week."

"Eight days."

***

I can hear the guests chatting and laughing in the drawing room. It's evening, and even on a Saturday night, they've returned to the inn rather than get wild and crazy in the city. I made sure there was plenty of wine, treats, and soft drinks to keep them happy before coming into the kitchen to deal with the dishes.

I don't mind washing dishes by hand. It gives me time to stop moving long enough to think. To make plans. To daydream.

"What are you doing?"

Apparently, I was daydreaming deep enough to not

hear Rhys come in the kitchen.

"I'm waxing the floor," I reply sweetly. His eyes narrow as he approaches and takes in all of the dishes I still have to wash.

"Why are you doing all of this by hand?"

"Because the dishwasher died on me this morning. I need to call someone to come out and fix it, but I don't want to pay weekend rates. Besides, the guests will be gone tomorrow." I shrug and plunge a dinner plate in the soapy water, scrubbing furiously.

Rhys joins me, standing entirely too close.

"What are you doing?" I ask him.

"Helping."

"No. You help out all the time. I draw the line at washing dishes by hand."

He smirks, grabs a towel and begins drying the dishes then putting them away. "You don't need to wait on me hand and foot, Gabby."

"Actually, I think that's exactly what you're paying me to do."

"No," he replies and brushes my hair behind my shoulder to avoid the water. "I'm paying to sleep in a room."

"I'm not going to argue about this."

"Good plan."

Don't argue, flirt!

Right. How do I do that, exactly?

"How was your day?" I ask, clearly failing at all things flirty.

"It was good. I had a call from a trainer that actually went well."

"You did?" I glance up in surprise. I had no idea.

"Yeah, they want to check in each week to see how my

workouts are going."

"If Sam is bothering you when you workout—"

He slaps my ass with the dishtowel, then resumes drying dishes. "I told you he doesn't bother me. He's good company. Smart as hell, that kid."

"I know." I nod proudly. "His homework is gonna scare me next year."

"He's a good baseball player too," Rhys adds. "He says you practice with him sometimes."

"I play catch with him. It seems to be the only thing that saves my windows." Rhys smirks, and that smile makes me clench my legs and my fists, and heat settles low and steady in my belly.

I want to freaking *climb* this man, and I've never had that urge a day in my life.

He brushes by me, braces his hand on my low back as he passes, again making me catch my breath, then returns to dry more dishes.

We fall into a quiet, comfortable silence, the sound of the water sloshing the only sound in the room, aside from the occasional laugh from the drawing room.

"Tell me about you and Kate," I murmur.

"Ah, 'tis a sad story," he begins with an Irish brogue, making me smile. "And that makes you smile. You have a beautiful smile." He drags the pad of his thumb down my cheek to my jawline, and every nerve in my body is suddenly on high alert. "You should never stop smiling."

"I liked your brogue," I whisper, watching his lips, which tip up.

"I'm sure you know we're Irish."

"The *O'Shaughnessy* sort of gave it away," I agree. "Plus, I know Kate."

"Have you heard this story?"

"Not from you," I reply and scrub the pan that I fried the chicken in.

"Fair enough." He nods and takes the pan from my hands, scrubbing it himself, just a bit harder than I can. When it's clean, he dries it and I resume washing. "So, Kate's da and my da were brothers. Kate's parents moved to the Denver area before she was born, for her da's work."

"Are you older than her?" I ask, interrupting him.

"Yes, but only by a couple years." I nod and he continues. "When I was four, my parents and I were in a car accident. They were both killed."

I still, my hands still in the water, and turn to watch him. His face hasn't changed. He's telling the story as if it happened to someone else.

And, I pray to God that he doesn't remember it, so that's how it feels to him.

"How did you survive?" I ask quietly.

"I'm not sure. I know that I was pulled from the car by the first responders, but my parents were killed on impact."

I dry my hands and wrap my arms around Rhys's middle, holding him close, my cheek pressed to his chest. I can't help it. That poor boy.

"Hey, I'm okay." But he wraps his arms around me and kisses my head, then takes a long, deep breath. "But if I'd known this was the way to get you into my arms, I would have told you this story *days* ago."

I laugh and pull away, then flick some clean water in his face, just for good measure. "Keep going."

"Will you hug me again?" He's playing. His mouth is smiling, but his green eyes have warmed again and he sighs as he waits for my answer.

"If you're good."

"Oh, sugar, I'm rarely good." The raspy tone of his

voice reignites that heat low in my belly. He leans in and whispers in my ear, "But I'm very, *very* good at being naughty."

I turn my face to his; our lips are inches apart, our noses almost touching.

"I believe you," I whisper, then take a deep breath when his eyes dilate and drop to my lips.

Which I lick.

Because hello, I just found my inner flirt.

And I like her. A lot.

"Keep going," I repeat.

He clears his throat and turns away, then picks up where he left off. "After my parents passed, Kate's parents came to Ireland and claimed me. They were my only family. So they brought me back to Denver and raised me."

"So you and Kate were really raised as siblings."

He nods thoughtfully. "And I was immediately enrolled in T-ball, and that was it. I was lost to the sport forever."

"Sam was the same," I offer with a grin. "It seems that he's had a glove on his hand since birth."

"He's a natural. And he loves you."

That makes me smile wide.

"Does that surprise you?"

"No. I know he loves me, but it makes me happy when it's obvious to others too. It's been just the two of us for a really long time."

"You have your family," he reminds me.

"Absolutely." I nod vigorously and pull the plug on the water, letting it drain now that all the dishes are washed. "And I don't think I could have done this without them. Especially when he was small and I was *so* damn young."

"You're amazing," Rhys says quietly, leaning against

the countertop.

"Why?"

"Your boy, this inn, who you are, are all something to admire about you. I saw you donate your day-old bread to the food bank."

"It shouldn't go bad," I insist. "Rhys, I'm flattered, but I'm not anything special. I'm a mom who loves her kid, and that should just be a given. I work hard. I give to the less fortunate. I'm just a woman." I shrug and start to turn away, but I'm suddenly pinned against the countertop, Rhys's big body caging me in. He's leaning on his hands, lowering himself to my eye level.

"You're wrong. You *are* special." His voice is raw and low. His thumb pulls the lower lip I didn't realize I was biting out of my teeth. "You're amazing, and I've barely scratched the surface with you."

"You sure push me outside my comfort zone," I whisper, not realizing until I hear the words that I'm speaking aloud.

"Nothing good ever came from comfort zones," he counters and leans further into me. "Are you afraid of me?"

"No." I smile and drag my fingertips down his cheek, and he turns his lips into my palm, closes his eyes and kisses me gently before returning his gaze to mine. "I'm just not very good at this."

"Good at what, Gabby?"

I swallow. Hard. My breath is coming fast. My heart is pounding. The lightning bugs in my belly are having one hell of a party.

He nudges my nose with his. "Good at what?"

"Flirting. *This*." I shake my head. "It's been a really long time."

"Good." He grins and rubs his nose against mine

again. His breath smells sweet from a scone he must have eaten before he came in here to find me. And just when I think he's going to kiss me, and I mean *really kiss me*, he kisses my forehead and then backs away.

"Where are you going?"

"To tell Sam more stories about last season. He told me about his trip tomorrow." He tosses me a mischievous smile. "I'm going to have you all to myself for a week."

"Eight days," I reply automatically, making his smile widen.

"Eight days. So, I'll give Sam some attention tonight, and then you're all mine for eight days."

I frown and prop my hands on my hips, but inside I'm squealing like a teenager.

"What is that supposed to mean?"

"You're going to exercise that flirty side, sugar."

And with that, he winks and leaves the kitchen, and I'm left standing in a puddle of *lust*.

Jesus, what did I just start?

CHAPTER FOUR

~Rhys~

She's a mess of gorgeous chaos.

And the kicker is, you'd never fucking know it. But the struggle is there, behind her smile, in her eyes. I've learned her face, and I've known her just over a week. She's beautiful, and I'd be lying if I said I wasn't attracted to that, but it's the whole package that has me tied in knots for the first time in… Jesus, I don't remember. She's funny, strong, kind. She's stern with Sam, but loving and affectionate, too, and it's obvious that the boy simply adores her.

But right now, she's sad. And it makes my stomach clench.

"Mom, it's going to be okay." Sam smiles up at his mom as he slips his baseball cap on his head. "All of the guests are gone, so you won't need me the rest of the day."

"Silly boy," she replies and crouches down next to him, her smile firmly in place. "I need you *every* day. Not just around here, but because I've grown attached to you." She smacks a kiss on his cheek, making him cringe and look my way, worried that his manliness might be in trouble.

I'd give just about anything to have her lips on me.

I smile at Sam and shrug, as if to say, "Women. What can you do?" Sam rolls his eyes and hugs his mom.

"Nannan will be here soon," Gabby says, but doesn't let him go quite yet. "And you're going to have so much fun."

"I know," he replies just as Gabby's mom pulls into the driveway. Sam and Gabby walk out to the car, and I follow more slowly, staying on the porch as they say goodbye.

"Hello, dawlin'," Mrs. Boudreaux says with a wide smile. "Are you ready for our adventure, Sam?"

"Yes, ma'am," Sam says with a grin then turns and waves at me. "Bye, Mr. Rhys!"

"Have fun," I reply with a wave and a smile. Goodbyes are said, hugs exchanged, and finally, Sam and his grandmother are pulling out of the driveway. Gabby doesn't move, watching them drive away, waving with a smile. When the car disappears around the corner, her hand falls at her side and her shoulders droop. She props her hands on her hips and looks to the ground.

Part of me is torn between letting her have her private moment and going to her, wrapping her in my arms, and holding on tight.

Then she kicks a rock, and she looks so damn sad I can't stand it. I walk down the steps and up behind her, wrap my arms around her shoulders and kiss her head, breathing in the sweet smell of her hair. She's such a small thing, fitting against me perfectly, tucked under my chin. She doesn't say anything, simply holds onto my arms and sighs, then tips her head way back so she can look into my eyes, upside down.

I automatically kiss her forehead. "Only be gone a

week."

"Eight days," she replies with a rough whisper.

"But who's counting?" I murmur and kiss her smooth skin once more before she turns in my arms and hugs me tightly around the middle, the way she did in her kitchen when she felt sorry for me last night. But rather than wanting to comfort, she needs to be comforted.

I'll gladly sign up for that job any day of the week.

"I feel guilty," she whispers after a long minute of us standing in the hot Louisiana sun.

"Guilty?" I frown and take her hand, leading her to the shade of the porch, and her favorite swing. But rather than letting her sit beside me, I pull her into my lap and hold her tight.

"I'm not sick, you know," she says with a smirk. But her eyes say thank you, and she leans against me, tucking herself under my chin.

"I know. Tell me why you feel guilty."

She sighs. "I struggle with it every summer. I'll miss him, of course. Every minute of every day. But at the same time, it's so nice to have a few days of alone time. To have a week—" She swallows. "Without him. And that makes me feel like a shitty mom."

"Everyone deserves a break, Gabby." And if the piece of shit that fathered Sam had bothered to do his job, she wouldn't be so overwhelmed with the task of parenting alone.

"I know."

"It doesn't make you a bad mom to enjoy that break."

She simply shrugs, not convinced. I tip her chin up so I can see her eyes and it kills me to see tears welled in them.

"You're an amazing mama," I say softly before laying my lips gently against hers, enjoying the way a shiver runs through her. "He knows you love him."

"I know that too."

"Good. So, what are you going to do with your reprieve?" I push my fingers through her hair, unable to resist. God, her hair is soft and smells amazing. The way she leans into my touch is sweet.

She's not touched often. She's like a love-starved kitten, and I can't wait to make her purr.

Because I'm going to have her in my bed, or hers, very soon.

"I have the inn," she replies and frowns up at me.

"So, the only difference between last week and this week is, you won't have Sam here?"

"Pretty much."

Oh, sweetheart, we can do so much better than that.

"You don't ever take a vacation?" I push her hair behind her ear and drag my fingertips down her cheek, loving the way her skin feels against mine.

She simply shakes her head, then sits up straight on my lap, bracing her hands on my shoulders so she can look at me.

"I have the inn, and I love it. I don't need a vacation from it."

Bullshit.

But I don't say anything; I simply watch her.

"You don't agree with me?"

"It doesn't matter if I agree or not." *No, I don't fucking agree.*

"But you don't."

"Gabby," I begin, then stop and frown. "Is your name short for Gabrielle?"

She blinks rapidly at the change of subject. "Yes, why?"

"Just curious. It doesn't matter if I agree. If I disagree,

will you take the week off?"

"I can't."

"Exactly."

Finally, she scoots off my lap and runs her hands down her pretty white blouse and denim shorts, as though she's smoothing wrinkles. "Thanks for the chat."

I stand next to her and cage her against the railing of the porch. "Look at me."

She raises her face to mine. Her eyes look almost gold today. They're still a little sad, and I'm going to do my damnedest to change that, as soon as possible.

She catches her lower lip between her teeth and braces her hands on my forearms, and there's that awareness, shooting between us again.

The chemistry is off the fucking charts.

I pluck her lip out of her teeth, and want with all of my soul to lean in and kiss her. My thumb brushes over the damp skin of her lip as I lean in and sweep my lips over her soft forehead.

"I have work," she whispers, but doesn't let go of me. "Sinceriously."

"Sinceriously?" I chuckle and comb my fingers through the hair at the back of her neck.

"It's a Sam word. He says it means he's sincerely serious."

"Ah." I kiss her forehead once more, acutely aware, with every seven-odd-billion nerves in my body, of her pressed against me. "Then I guess you should get to it."

She nods, her eyes closed, then snaps them open and ducks out of my arms. "Don't you have something to do?"

"I'm sure I can find something."

A cold shower might be a good place to start.

She nods and disappears inside, closing the door

behind her. I walk down the steps and between the ancient oak trees, take a deep breath to calm my freaking libido, and dial Kate's number.

"What's up, handsome?"

"Question."

"Answer."

I grin at her response. "How difficult would it be to have someone come cover at the inn for Gabby once or twice this week? During the evening, so I can take her out on a couple dates."

There's a long pause, and then I can hear the smile in Kate's voice as she says, "Are you sweet on Miss Gabby, cousin o' mine?"

"I am," I reply truthfully. There's no bullshitting anyone about this. I'm not ashamed of it. "So can you help me or not?"

"I can help. I'll make some calls. She has the rest of today off, you know. It's Sunday."

"I know, and I plan to do something fun with her, but she deserves a damn night off now and again."

"I completely agree. I'll make it happen. What nights do you want?"

"It doesn't matter," I reply. "Maybe one of the nights can be when Declan is playing."

"Wow," Kate says with a whistle. "You can be very sweet when you want to be."

"Don't let it get out," I growl. "I don't need batters thinking I won't crush them at the plate."

"Don't worry, your secret's safe with me."

***

It's late afternoon, and I've let Gabby be most of the day. It wasn't easy. I want to march in that house, scoop her up, and carry her off to bed.

And at some point, in the not too distant future, I'm going to do just that. I can't wait to watch her magnificent eyes go wide as I just reach down and lift her in my arms.

The thought of it brings a smile to my face.

Oh yeah, I'm gonna do that soon.

But for today, I think she needed some space. I could hear her music blaring in the house from the barn as I worked out and put my shoulder through a hell I wouldn't wish on anyone.

At one point, the music stopped and I could hear her laugh through the open windows in the back of the house. Her laugh makes my skin tingle.

Jesus, I have it bad.

The music is off now as well as I come out of my room, fresh from a shower and ready to have my eyes on her.

I find her in her office, her phone tucked between her ear and shoulder, filing papers.

"I'm so glad you're already having fun, buddy."

She sees me and offers me a sweet smile as I lean my shoulder against the doorjamb, cross my arms over my chest, and listen unabashedly.

"Okay, go jump back in the pool. I'll talk to you soon." She ends the call and sets the phone on her desk. "He's having fun."

"Good."

"What are you up to?"

I push away from the door and move to the desk, lean my hands on it, and stare her in the eyes, which widen. She bites that lip, and I'm suddenly on high alert, all over again.

"I want to take you somewhere," I whisper.

"Where?" Her voice is soft, and a little shaky.

"Anywhere. Let's just get in the car and drive, see where we end up."

Her face lights up, and I know in this moment, I'll keep doing anything she wants if I can keep that smile on her face.

"I haven't taken a drive in…forever."

"Let's do it then."

***

"Oh my God!" Gabby yells out with a laugh. "My hair is out of control!"

We are cruising down the highway, the top of my Camaro down, sending her hair flying all over the place. She reaches in her pocket and pulls out some kind of hair tie, then proceeds to twist those long, soft strands into a knot at the top of her head, bands it together, then grins at me. "Better."

"Where will this road take us?" I ask.

"All the way to Mississippi," she says, then flicks on the satellite radio, turns the station to current hits, and begins to sing along with Rihanna, about being the only girl in the world.

She's the only girl in *my* world, that's for damn sure.

She can't sing worth a damn, and her dance moves in the leather seat are questionable.

But she sings and moves like she just doesn't give a fuck, and that is the sexiest thing I've seen in a very long time.

We drive for miles, both of us singing along with the radio, Gabby dancing her ass off.

Laughing.

I glance over at her, and she looks *young*. Carefree.

Happy.

I take her hand in mine, kiss her knuckles, and rest them on the center console as she sings into the thumb of her free hand.

It's Maroon 5 now.

The sun is sinking to our left, bathing everything in a pink and orange glow. It's getting late.

"Oh! There's an awesome restaurant up ahead," Gabby says. "It's been owned by the same family for four generations. Best food in the South."

"Are you hungry?"

"I'm starving."

"Done."

I pull into the parking lot of a building that says *Mama's Place*. It looks like it should have been condemned fifty years ago.

"I know it doesn't look like much from the outside."

"Is it safe in there?"

Gabby laughs and jumps out of the car. "Don't be a wimp, O'Shaughnessy."

I narrow my eyes as I join her and take her small hand in mine. "If the roof is collapsed at all, we're leaving."

She simply shakes her head and laughs as we enter the dilapidated building, but once inside, my eyes widen in surprise. It's not only sound, it's amazing.

And the smells coming from the kitchen have my stomach weeping with joy.

"Best food ever," Gabby says with that sweet smile.

We're shown to a table, and I can't stop looking around long enough to glance at the menu. There are stuffed alligators on the walls, along with other animals, fishing poles, and signs that say, "Beware of Gators."

When the waitress arrives, Gabby orders for both of us. "Trust me," she says after the waitress gathers our menus and leaves.

"I do," I reply honestly. She tips her head to the side.

"I don't think you have trust issues." She sips her sweet

tea thoughtfully.

"Why is that?"

"Because I think that you just don't take shit from people. Plus, you're nice."

I cringe. "*Nice* is the kiss of death with women."

"Not this woman." She shakes her head and pushes her straw through the ice. "*Nice* is a good thing."

"How about you?"

"What about me?"

"Do you trust easily?"

She frowns, her eyes still on her drink. "I trust my family. And Sam, of course, although he always tries to tell me that it wasn't him who broke the window."

I smirk. "You know what I mean."

Gabby shrugs, not meeting my gaze.

"Look at me."

"Why do you always make me look at you?" She frowns as though she's irritated, and it only makes me smile wider.

"Because I love it when you look at me," I reply softly. "And I want to see your eyes when you talk."

"I don't trust men easily. Well, at all really."

"You can trust me."

She starts to say something, then stops herself and takes a drink of her tea.

"What were you going to say?"

She frowns again and shakes her head, but I take her hand in mine. "Look at me. What were you going to say?"

She meets my gaze, straightens her shoulders—*good girl*—and firms her lips. "I was going to say that in my experience, men haven't been exactly trustworthy."

"Well, what if I told you that your assessment was wrong?"

"Bullshit." She offers me a saccharine sweet smile, then sips her drink.

"I don't trust easily either, Gabrielle." Her eyes widen when I use her full name. "But I trust you. And you can trust me, too."

"I know," she whispers. "And it's weird."

"Weird?"

"Maybe *new* is a better word."

"Nothing wrong with new," I reply as our food is set before us. She stares at her plate for a long minute, then raises her gaze to mine.

"Don't make me regret trusting you."

I tilt my head, taking her in, her hair, her eyes, her mouth, neck, shoulders, then return my gaze to her eyes. "Never on purpose."

She nods and we're quiet as we eat our fried catfish. She only finishes half of her plate, so I eat what she can't, then pay the bill and escort her outside, where night has fallen.

"It's a bit cooler without the sun. Do you want me to put the top up?"

"No way." She smiles and sits in the car after I open the door for her. "You're quite chivalrous."

"They're called manners, sweetheart." I wink, walk around the car to join her and pull out of the parking lot, headed back toward the inn. "There was a sign for a scenic outlook up here that I'd like to check out."

"It's a pretty spot," she says and pats her flat belly. "I'm so full."

"You barely ate anything."

"I ate half my plate! And portions in the South aren't small."

"True." I take her hand in mine again, kiss her

knuckles, and this time rest our hands on my thigh.

"You have some pretty smooth moves, Mr. O'Shaughnessy."

"Who, me?"

Gabby simply giggles, and to my surprise, pulls her hand out, then links her fingers with mine, still resting on my thigh. Aside from the hug in her kitchen, this is the first time she's taken the initiative to touch me.

And I fucking love it.

I pull onto the road with the sign for the overlook, and we follow it for about a half a mile before coming to the top of a bluff that looks out over the Mississippi River. The sky is clear, with a full moon, and there is no light noise from the city, so the stars are stunning.

"Wow," I whisper and kill the engine. "Pretty doesn't really cover it."

"No," she agrees and leans her head on my shoulder, then pops back up. "Oops, that's your bad shoulder."

"Touch doesn't hurt," I reply and she returns to rest her head there, skims her fingertips up my hand and arm, and holds onto my bicep.

Since when does a woman touching my damn *arm* give me a hard-on?

Apparently, since now.

"So, this place has a history," Gabby says and tips her face up to mine, not taking her cheek from my shoulder.

"Do tell."

"Well, there's a legend that goes with this place that has been told for a couple of generations, probably longer. It seems there was a young woman, about nineteen, who came here from France with her well-to-do family." Gabby gently and absent-mindedly brushes her fingertips up and down the inside of my arm, sending goose bumps all over me as she tells her story. "She was lonely at first here, not knowing any English, and not having any friends. Her father had many slaves, as most of the plantation owners did. One of the slaves was a sweet boy about her age, and he helped her learn English. Of course, they had to meet in secret."

"Of course," I reply and kiss the top of her head, already knowing where this story is going.

"Well, of course they fell in love, but when her father found out, he was livid." Gabby shakes her head, as though she's talking about friends. "He sold the boy so his daughter couldn't see him anymore, and she went a little crazy. Story goes that she would run away from the plantation, trying to find him. And one stormy night, she came here to these cliffs, and in the dark, she fell to her death."

"That's a very sad story."

"Some say you can still hear her weeping."

"Of course they do. It's a tragic ghost story."

Gabby chuckles, then turns her face into my shoulder, and presses a kiss there. "Does it still hurt a lot?"

"Only when I exercise."

She kisses it again, then clears her throat. "There's another story about this place."

"Why do I think you're about to share it?" She pushes her finger into my side, and I yelp dramatically.

"Because I want to know just what makes you think I'm *that* kind of woman?"

"What kind?"

She smirks. "The kind you bring to make-out point."

I nudge her back so I can see her face and grin. "Is that what this is, sweetheart?"

She nods.

"Have you been here before?"

She shrugs one shoulder.

"Is that a yes?"

"In high school I came here once or twice. No one got past second base."

"Good girl."

CHAPTER FIVE

~Gabby~

Good girl.

Why do my insides quiver when he says that to me? Because seriously, those words come out of his sexier-than-should-be-legal lips, and my whole body does the happy dance.

Channel your inner flirt! She's fun.

I pull my index finger down the inside of his muscular bicep and draw circles on the thin, smooth skin inside of his elbow. His breath catches, drawing my gaze up to his.

His green eyes shine in the moonlight, as if they're on fire. His breathing has sped up. And I swear that through his shoulder I can feel his pulse speeding up too.

Talk about ego boost.

"Gabby," he whispers, his eyes pinned to my lips. "I'm going to kiss you."

"I hope so." Did those words come from me? His mouth tips up in that half-smile as he scoops me right up out of the seat, pulls me over the console onto his lap with my feet sitting in the passenger seat. He cups my cheek in his palm, his thumb circling over the apple of my cheek as he nuzzles my nose with his, just the way he did last night.

I can feel the warmth of his skin, not quite touching

me. His breath smells like the mint we ate after dinner.

And his eyes are dark, dark green and full of unadulterated lust.

His lips brush over mine in just a whisper of a kiss, once, then twice, before they settle at the side of my mouth and nibble, sending shivers through me.

His hand drifts down from my cheek to my neck, then over my blouse to cup my breast, and his lips settle over my mouth, firmly now.

Wet.

Needy.

Someone—me?—growls as the kiss deepens. He's a taker, that's for sure, but then he mixes it up, giving me more than I've ever had before.

And I'm no virgin. I'm a *mother,* for crying out loud!

But, oh, the way Rhys O'Shaughnessy makes me feel, it's like no one has ever touched me before.

Because they haven't. Not like this. Not like he's drowning and I'm his first breath of air. Not like the thought of *not* touching me is pure torture.

He grunts as I shimmy in his lap. I can feel his excitement pressed to my right hip.

And I want to feel it. *Right now.*

As if he's reading my mind, Rhys grips my hips and lifts me, helping me straddle him, and I press my center against him, making us both catch our breath.

"Jesus, you're the sweetest fucking thing," he growls against my lips. His hands are roaming up and down my back. I grip his face in my hands and kiss him. Deeply. Our tongues are stroking, lapping.

God, he tastes good.

He grips my ass in his hands and tugs me down more tightly against him, and I can't help but circle my hips, enjoying the way the ridge in his jeans rubs against my center.

Holy crap, can I come like this?

Surely not.

"Surely not what?" Rhys whispers against my lips.

"I didn't say anything."

"You said 'surely not.' Surely not what?"

I bite his lower lip as his hand takes a journey from my ass, up my side, to cup my breast. His thumb rubs over my tightened nipple, over and over again, making me squirm.

Everything this man does makes me squirm, and he's technically still at second base!

"You've kind of got me all worked up," I whisper.

"Back at you, baby."

He presses a button at the side of the seat, tilting his seat back just a few inches, then grips my sides and lifts me so he can nuzzle between my breasts, and down to my belly.

Which sets me on edge.

Please, God, don't lift my shirt and look at my disgusting stretch marks!

The scruff on his cheeks feels soft, yet prickly, on my skin.

"Why did you stiffen up?"

I shake my head and plunge my fingers in his hair, holding him close to me, loving the kisses he's pressing to my chest, and the way he brushes his nose over my nipple.

Holy fuck, I'm turned on.

The next thing I know, Rhys is lifting me back over the console into my seat and righting his own. He's breathing hard.

"What's wrong?"

"Nothing." He swallows, then takes a deep breath. "Absolutely nothing."

"Why did you stop?"

He turns to me now and kisses me, then pulls the seat belt over me and clicks it into place. "Because second base is as far as we can go here, and if I kept kissing you the way I was, you'd be naked and I'd be inside you right now."

I feel my eyes go wide and my pulse speed up even more, if that's even possible.

"Oh."

"Yeah. Oh." He kisses me once more, then starts the car. I can't help but cover my lips with my fingertips and giggle. "What's funny?"

"This."

His eyes narrow. "That's not exactly the reaction I was looking for."

"I can't believe I'm making out like a teenager here."

He smiles and brushes his knuckles down my cheek. I love how much he touches me. His touch is simply sinful.

Without another word, he pulls back out onto the highway and we drive the hour or so back to the inn in companionable silence. I'm tempted to lean over and give him a satisfying memory for later, but decide against it.

Hopefully, I can do that another time.

I'd love to taste him. To hear him, watch him, as I suck on him and work him over with my hands. I wonder how he likes it?

"What are you thinking over there?" he asks as he takes my hand and kisses my fingers.

"You don't want to know," I reply and turn my face to watch the darkness pass by.

"Oh, I definitely want to know."

"I—" I bite my lip, and feel my cheeks heat.

"You... Hey, look at me." I turn my face to see him smiling at me, in that special way he does, that I've learned is just for me. "What's going on in that gorgeous head of yours?"

"I was thinking about, um, going down on you." The last few words are said on a whisper, and I cover my eyes with my hand, completely mortified. Suddenly, the car stops.

Just stops.

He pulls my hand away from my face and grips my shoulders, turning me to face him.

"What did you just say?" His face registers shock, curiosity. Lust.

So much lust.

So I smile and reply, "I was thinking about going down on you. How you might like it."

He pulls me to him for a long, deep, wet kiss, and then, against my still-damp lips, whispers, "Any way you give it to me is how I like it, baby. Now, no more sexy talk about your lips wrapped around my cock, okay? I don't want to wreck this car."

I grin against his mouth. "Okay."

"Okay."

***

The house is dark when we drive up, aside from the porch lights and the light I always leave on in the foyer. The oak trees look like huge grey ghosts in the yard, framing the white plantation house perfectly.

It's a bit spooky at night, and I grew up here. I've felt things here. I've felt the sorrow of the slaves as I clean and stage the slave quarters so the guests can learn about that dark part of our history. I've felt joy in the rose gardens.

Doors have slammed when no one was there to slam them.

But this house is centuries old, and the Boudreaux

family is known for being a passionate one. It's no wonder that someone is still hanging out, just to keep an eye on things.

I often wonder if my father is one of those someones. I hope so.

Rhys stops the car and before he can even cut the engine, I climb out and onto the porch. Rhys follows me inside, his hands in his pockets, quiet as he watches me check the locks and the alarm system, then walks me quietly to my room.

My heart is heavy, knowing that Sam isn't here to fight bedtime with me. And I can't help but feel so fucking guilty that I enjoyed myself so much tonight with my son being gone.

I'm a hot mess.

"Hey," Rhys says quietly as he turns me to him and scoops me up into one of his hugs, rocking me back and forth. "Are you okay?"

I nod, soaking in the warmth of him. I want to invite him in, but I'm not sure that I'm ready to take what happened in the car further.

And yet, I don't want to be alone.

"Are you sure?"

"Yeah." I pull out of his arms and kiss his cheek. "I'm just a little sad that the house is so quiet without Sam, that's all."

His bight green eyes survey my face before nodding. He brushes his fingers down my cheek. "Okay. Good night."

"Good night."

He turns to walk away. I hold my breath for about two seconds, then burst out, "Rhys?"

"Yeah?" He turns back to me, concern on his

handsome face.

"Um, nothing." I shake my head and offer him a happy smile. "Never mind."

But rather than nod and walk away, he saunters back to me, his gaze pinned to mine. Wordlessly, he gently pulls my hair out of its knot and lets it fall around my shoulders, combing it with his fingers.

"Would you stay with me until I fall asleep?" I whisper. He just smiles softly, kisses my forehead, and gestures for me to lead the way into my room.

I've never had a man in my bedroom. Never shared my bed with anyone.

Ever. In my life.

The room is dark as I lead the man that puts me on hyper-drive to the edge of my bed. And to my surprise, Rhys calmly unfastens my shorts and lets them drop off my hips to the floor. Then, with his eyes pinned to mine, he pulls my top over my head. He reaches for the tank I sleep in that's laying at the end of my bed and tugs it over my head, pulls my hair through, and helps me into the bed. I watch with sleepy eyes as he pulls off his T-shirt, steps out of his jeans, and joins me, wearing nothing but snug black boxer-briefs.

And then, to my utter shock, he simply turns me away from him, curls up behind me, and whispers in my ear, "Go to sleep, sweetheart."

"You don't want to…?"

"For now, this is perfect. I'm just happy to share a pillow with you. Sleep." He kisses my neck, and his deep, even breathing eventually lulls me to sleep.

***

I wake to hands and lips and *heat*.

"You're still here." My voice is heavy with sleep.

"I fell asleep too." And his voice is just heavy with sexiness.

Dear sweet Jesus, how do people wake up like this every day? I'd never leave the bed!

Rhys is pressed up behind me, kissing my neck and shoulder. His hand is roaming down my side to my hip, then back up under my shirt over my skin, and every molecule in my body is now awake.

Wide awake.

"Mm, you feel so damn good," he growls in my ear, his voice still heavy with sleep, and nothing has ever turned me on so quickly. "Do you have any idea how fucking soft your skin is?"

"Mm," I moan, unable to form words.

Who in the name of all that's holy can form words when Rhys O'Shaughnessy's hands are all over them?

Not this girl.

I reach behind me and drag my fingernails up his thigh, over the fabric of his boxer-briefs, his thigh, to his belly, and he bites my earlobe.

"Careful, baby. I've been feeling your sexier-than-fuck body against me all night."

I grin and don't stop touching him. My panties are *soaked*. My nipples are hard nubs, rubbing roughly against the bra he didn't take off of me last night.

I turn onto my back. Rhys's face is still buried in my neck, kissing, licking, turning me the hell on.

Damn, this man is a master with his lips.

I love the way he feels. He's not super hairy, with smooth arms and abs, and just a light dusting of hair on his chest that feels amazing under my fingertips.

"You feel good yourself," I whisper and kiss his shoulder as my hand drifts farther south. I gently wrap my fingers around the length of his dick, over his underwear, then push my hand under the elastic waistband, cup him in my hand and brush my thumb over the tip, wiping away the moisture that's already gathered there.

"Oh God," he breathes against my shoulder, then kisses my jaw, my cheek, and finally my lips, cupping my face in his hand. I stroke him more firmly, but still slowly, watching his face as his breathing increases. Sweat forms on his brow. His eyes are closed.

"Look at me," I whisper against his lips, turning his words back on him. He pins me in his bright green gaze, and I have to clench my own thighs together, shocked at how much making him crazy makes *me* crazy.

"You're so fucking sexy," he says and kisses me, always watching me as he shifts his hips back and forth, working them down his hips and legs. "God, your hands are—"

He swallows hard, unable to continue. We're both breathing hard, him naked, me half-dressed and enjoying the way he feels, sounds, smells.

God, I don't think I'll ever get enough of him.

Suddenly, he grits his teeth, panting, and utters, "Fuck," as he comes into my hand. He closes his eyes and tips his forehead against my shoulder, his breath shuddering in and out.

Wow.

"Jesus, Gabrielle," he whispers. "I've haven't come in a woman's hand since I was a teenager." He plants wet, firm kisses on my shoulder, my neck. "What are you doing to me?"

I grin, very pleased with myself, thank you very much, and kiss his scruff-covered chin, then his lips. "Turning you on."

"You've been doing that for almost two weeks,

sweetheart." He pushes me onto my back, covering me with his impressive body, and kisses me long and deep. One hand is braced above my head, and the other takes a journey down my torso, over my breasts, to my belly, and he starts to pull my tank up. And I freeze.

"I'm not sure you want to do that."

He frowns down into my face. "I'm sure I do."

I bite my lip. "Maybe we can just leave my shirt on."

He frowns again, not in a mad way, but rather more confused, and then his face clears and he kisses me again. He braces himself on his elbows at either side of my head, his fingers plunge into my hair, and he rubs my scalp as he slowly, and thoroughly, kisses the ever-loving hell out of me.

"Gabby," he whispers against my lips. "You're beautiful."

"I've had a baby."

His green eyes don't leave mine as he pulls one hand down my side to my belly and simply rests it there. I'm a petite woman. Most of my body is slender, but my belly is full of stretch marks and flab that will never go away, no matter what I do.

Unless I get a tummy-tuck. Which I'm not above, by the way.

"You're a mom. You're a *real* woman. Your body is perfect, just the way it is."

I cringe.

"Stop it." He kisses me again and pushes his hand under my shirt. "Jesus, Gabby, you couldn't turn me on more than you do. I'd die."

The sincerity is in his eyes. He's not bullshitting me just so he can get in my pants. No one has ever looked at me the way he's looking at me right now.

"Trust me?" His face is sober as he asks, and when I nod, that slow, crooked smile tickles his lips. "Good girl."

I shiver.

"Are you cold?"

I shake my head no and he smiles wider.

"You just like it when I say *good girl*."

I nod reluctantly and he kisses my lips, my chin, and down my torso, following the path his hand took moments ago, as he pulls my shirt up and over my head. He reaches behind me and deftly unhooks my bra with one hand, then flings it to the floor with my shirt and continues to plant his lips down to my belly.

He nuzzles me there, his hands on my sides, just above my pelvis. He's spread my legs wide, and is on his belly between them, his chest pressed to my core as he kisses my belly. "So beautiful," he says, then kisses even lower. He shimmies further down the bed, glances up at me with a mischievous grin, then plants that mouth right over my panties, against the spot that turns my world upside down.

Sweet baby Jesus.

"God, you're wet," he says. "Your panties are soaked clean through."

His satisfied eyes find mine as he slips a finger in the elastic, pulls it aside, and returns his attention there, surging me up onto my elbows so I can watch. "Oh, my God."

"Like this?" he asks, lapping at me. "You taste amazing."

"Nobody's ever... I haven't..." I can't finish as he simply tears the panties off me and tosses them over his shoulder, all humor suddenly gone from his face.

"Are you saying I'm the first to do this?"

I nod, eyes wide.

"Lay back, baby."

"I wanna watch," I reply softly, then bite my lip. He smirks and doesn't argue as he lowers his lips to me, barely kissing me. His fingertips part my lips, then sink inside me.

Holy shit. I can't catch my breath. I lay back because I don't have the strength to stay on my elbows. All of my attention is centered on the bundle of nerves at my core, where Rhys is paying all of *his* attention.

And oh, my, is he good at paying attention.

His fingers sweep around and press against my inner walls and push up. He presses his tongue on my clit, and my legs begin to shake uncontrollably. My toes curl.

Even my hair follicles are standing on end.

"Rhys!"

"Mmm-hmmm," he mutters, but doesn't pull his mouth away. Everything seems to gather into a bright, tiny ball, and then that ball explodes, sending me into the most crazy orgasm I've ever had in my life.

I'm not even sure that you could call what I've had in the past an orgasm compared to this.

So *this* is what all the fuss is about!

Rhys kisses me some more, just on the outside of my very sensitive lips, my inner thighs, the crease where my thigh and center meet, then up my belly again.

And you know what? I don't give even *one* fuck that he's looking at my belly right now. Because clearly he doesn't have any fucks to give about it either.

Suddenly, he pulls me up into a sitting position and kisses my lips. I can taste myself, and damn if that isn't a turn-on in itself.

"Go have a shower, baby. Get ready for your day. I'm making breakfast."

And before I can argue, he jumps up, gracing me with an incredible view of his tight ass and sculpted back. His backside is almost as impressive as his front side. He grabs his clothes and leaves my bedroom, and me, sitting in my big, warm bed with the most ridiculous smile on my face.

Damn, he could make a girl fall in love with him.

CHAPTER SIX

~Rhys~

She's gotten under my skin. That's all there is to it.

I check the bacon and pull it out of the oven just before it burns. I hope Gabby likes it crispy.

Get your head in the game, O'Shaughnessy.

I'm scrambling eggs and dishing up fruit as Gabby walks into the kitchen, looking fresh from her shower.

And happy, with that knock-me-out smile on her face. Her eyes are bright and clear of any stress or worry.

I'm going to keep her this way.

"Hey," she says. "It smells amazing in here."

"I hope you like crispy bacon."

She nods as she walks around the island, stands on her tip-toes, and tips her face up to kiss me. I still have to bend down to oblige. Without looking, I take the eggs off the burner and pull her in for a long, deep kiss. Her hands cling to my sides, and when I pull back, her cheeks are flushed.

Matching mine, I'm sure.

"Are you hungry?" I ask.

"Mmm," she purrs and licks her bottom lip.

"For food, silly." I kiss her nose and turn back to the

task at hand, dishing up her plate, then mine.

"You made coffee." She pours us each a cup and sits next to me at the island. "You're a savior."

"Coffee addict?"

"Absolutely." She dives into her food, eating most of a slice of bacon, then holds the last bite up to my lips. "It's delicious."

I bite her fingertips on purpose, making her laugh. "Yes, it is."

She simply raises a brow and sticks a strawberry in her mouth, then clears our empty plates, a new little wiggle in her hips as she walks.

I love the new-found confidence she's discovered in the past twenty-four hours. I didn't lie to her; she *is* perfect, just as she is, and seeing her believe it is just magnificent.

"Music!" Gabby tethers her phone to a Bluetooth speaker system and grins as a Beyonce song comes on. "I like to dance as I clean up when guests aren't here."

"I guess I'm not a guest anymore?"

Her jaw drops and she blinks rapidly. "I'm sorry. Of course you are."

I catch her arm and pull her against me. "No, I'd say that crossing over into the intimate side of things means that I'm not a guest."

"I can't charge you for your room," she says fiercely. "But when Sam comes home, you can't sleep with me."

"Gabby, I didn't mean to start a panic attack." I brush her hair over her shoulders and massage her neck. She's biting that lower lip, worry creasing her brow. "I'll pay for my room, and continue sleeping in it when Sam comes home. And in the mean time, we'll take it one day at a time."

She relaxes and nods, then smiles. "Okay."

"Okay." She steps closer to me, pushing her hands up my chest to my shoulders. "You're muscular."

"It's part of the job."

Her eyes are happy as she watches her hands take a tour of my arms, and my own hands don't want to stay still. They fall down her slender back and around her sides, then back up again, and her eyes find mine.

I love the way her breathing changes when I touch her. The way her eyes glass over.

I reach down to her ass and lift her effortlessly, then set her on the island countertop so she's eye-level with me and I can easily touch her *everywhere.*

My lips brush over hers lightly, and she fists her hands in my T-shirt at the shoulders, as though she's holding on for dear life.

And I've barely touched her.

Jesus, I'll never get tired of her.

"Why are your hands on my sister?"

Our faces jerk to the back door, where Beau has just walked in, and neither of us heard him.

"Or, more importantly," he says with narrowed eyes, "why are your *lips* on my sister?"

"Beau, don't be an ass." Gabby rolls her eyes, looks up at me with an apologetic shrug, and jumps off the island. "It's none of your business."

"Bullshit."

His eyes, so much like his sister's, are pinned to mine, and he's on high alert. He's taller than me by maybe two inches, but I know that I match him in strength.

If my shoulder was at 100 percent.

Not that I'd ever fight Gabby's brother, or anyone else for that matter.

"I'm not a child, and I don't need you to defend my

virtue, Beau." Gabby squares off with her brother, who towers more than a foot above her, with her hands on her hips and fire shooting from her eyes.

Christ, she's stunning.

"You're not in the habit of fucking the guests, Gabby."

I fist my hands and narrow my eyes. Maybe I'll fight her brother anyway. "Don't talk to her like that."

"Beau!" She's outraged and hurt. "What is wrong with you?"

"Tell me I've got it wrong. Because it sure didn't look like it from here."

"You're a bully," Gabby replies, her voice shaking. "And you're a pain in my ass. You don't get to come into *my* home, *my* business, and call me a whore."

His face registers shock. "I didn't—"

"I don't want to hear it. I can't do this with you right now." She holds her hands up in surrender and flees the room. Not crying. Not in a dramatic huff.

She's just simply done.

Good girl.

"So, are you in the habit of making Gabby feel like shit, or is this just a special occasion?"

Beau's eyes narrow on me again. "You don't know dick about my sister."

"You're wrong. I know plenty, and I'm learning more."

"You've been here five minutes."

"You've been here for twenty-seven years, and you just tore her heart out." I lean my hips against the edge of the countertop and cross my arms over my chest. "And frankly, it pisses me off."

Beau sighs and rubs his hand over his face. "You don't know what we've been through with her. She's the baby, and she's been hurt as much as the rest of us."

"She's an adult, Beau. Hurt comes with the title." But my stomach clenches at the thought of anyone ever hurting her. "She's not a child."

"No, she *has* a child."

"I've met him," I reply steadily. "He's awesome."

"And he'll get attached to you. Have you thought of that? He already hero-worships you. So, you make them both fall for you, and then you leave?"

"Is this the *what are your intentions with my daughter* conversation?" I ask soberly, not moving. Beau is pacing the floor, agitation in every line of his body.

"I'm the closest thing she *has* to a father!"

"You're her *brother*." I shake my head. "And yes, you should protect her. But Jesus, man, you just spoke to her like she was sixteen. And you're lucky I didn't deck you for the 'fucking the guest' comment."

He frowns and paces away, then back again. "If you want to play games, she's not the one to play them with."

"Who said anything about playing games? She's amazing. And the fact that you'd think that a man would be with her simply because she's hot is a shot against you, and no one else." Now I *am* getting pissed.

"Are you saying you love her?"

I pause. "I'm learning her," I begin thoughtfully. "She just…devastates me. I'm saying I am going to keep learning her, making her laugh, making her happy."

"And Sam?"

"Sam's part of the package, and I wouldn't have it any other way," I reply evenly. "I'm assuming you know where his sperm donor is?" I refuse to call the man his father.

"I do." Beau's eyes narrow again. "Why?"

"Because I'd like to beat the shit out of him."

Beau grins now. "Eli and I did that a long time ago."

"Good, but I'd like my own crack at him." I shift my head from side to side. "Just for fun."

"He's far away, thank God." Beau firms his lips and watches me for a long minute. "If you fuck with her, I'll fuck with *you*, and it will hurt."

"Back at you."

CHAPTER SEVEN

~Gabby~

I would typically sit on the porch and enjoy being mad, but I'm so worked up, I need to walk. So I set off for the gardens, wandering through them. The flowers are full and heavy with bees flitting from bloom to bloom. Birds are singing in the trees above.

And I'm more pissed than I've been in a very, very long time.

"Gabby."

I ignore my stupid, pig-headed brother and continue walking.

"Gabby, I'm sorry."

"You should be!" I whirl on him and shove him in the chest, hard, but he doesn't even flinch or move.

Damn huge brothers.

"I'm not a baby, Beau."

"You're *the* baby, Gabs." He crosses his arms over his chest, looking all tall and steady.

"But I'm not *a* baby. I'm a grown woman, who runs a business and single parents her child. You don't have to protect me from anything."

He frowns and looks ready to argue. "Look, I'm sorry I made you mad—"

"You humiliated me," I reply passionately. "You embarrassed me in front of a man that I happen to *like*. And do you have any idea how long it's been since I liked anyone, Beau? Since Colby."

"No way," he replies with shock.

"Way. I've done nothing but what I'm supposed to. I am a damn good mom, and I'm damn good at running this inn, and damn it, if I want to kiss a man, I'll damn well do it!" I'm pacing back and forth now, punctuating each *damn* with a finger in the air, pointed at my idiot brother.

"Okay."

"I mean, it's not like Rhys is a damn serial killer, for crying out loud! He's practically Kate's *brother*. He's a good guy. And for some incredible reason, he likes me."

"I know."

"And I would never do anything to hurt Sam, so don't stand there and look at me like I'm whoring around in front of my son."

"I would never think that, and I'm sorry if I implied it."

Finally, I come to a stop and stare at Beau. "You're agreeing with me."

"I am." He nods and offers me that smile that makes it so I can't be mad at him for long.

"Why?"

He shrugs and pulls me into a hug. "I don't like making you mad, or upsetting you. I never could stand to see you off-kilter, even as a baby."

"I'm not a damn baby." My voice is calmer now, resigned. "Why are you agreeing with me?"

"Rhys put me in my place." He chuckles and backs away from me. "I think he might be good for you."

"Meaning?"

"Just that." He tugs on a strand of my hair, and I realize that he's not in work attire.

"Why are you home? It's Monday."

"I took a personal day."

I blink and frown. "I'm not sure I understand."

"A *personal day*, Gabby. As in, a day off that isn't a weekend."

More blinking and frowning. "I don't even know who you are right now."

"I'm your idiot brother who should have turned around and backed away when he found some guy sucking my sister's face into his mouth." He shudders dramatically, making me laugh.

"Oh, I know you, then." I hug him to me once more. "What am I going to do with you?"

"Feed me?"

"Dude, you missed that train. But I'm sure I can find you some scraps. Rhys will be around."

"I'll be nice."

"Yeah, and alligators might fly out of my ass."

"Ouch."

***

I think I'm going to die from sexual frustration. I wonder if anyone has actually died from being too horny? I should Google it.

I smirk and pull a sheet of fresh cookies out of the oven.

It's been two days since Rhys gave me the best orgasm of my life.

Like, *of my freaking life.*

And I figured for sure that he'd be in my bed Monday night to seal the deal.

And he was in my bed. But all he did was hold me all

night. Oh, there was kissing and heavy petting, and it was very, very nice to be held and shown affection.

But there was no sex.

And then yesterday went to hell in a handbasket.

If it could go wrong, it did. The newly repaired dishwasher leaked water all over my kitchen. Two sets of guests showed up on the same day, but one of them was supposed to come on Tuesday of *next* week. They messed up the dates, but that meant that I had to call around and find them a bed for the night because I'm booked solid.

Because I'm stubborn and refuse to put anyone in Rhys's room.

And lost business for next week.

Then, at the evening wine time, a guest ate a cookie that had coconut in it and had a violent allergic reaction, needing a call to 911, and a trip to the hospital because he forgot to bring his EpiPen with him, not to mention he forgot to inform me of any special dietary needs.

So by the time I fell into bed with Rhys last night, I was so exhausted that I was asleep before my head hit the pillow, and had to get up before him this morning.

"I'm never getting laid again," I grumble to myself and push a fresh pan of cookies into the oven.

"We're here to make sure that isn't true."

I whirl to find Van, Charly and Kate grinning from ear to ear, standing just inside my kitchen.

"How long have you been there?"

"Long enough to hear you bitch about coconut and not getting laid."

I nod. "That about covers it."

"Well," Charly says with a smile and lifts a bag from her shop. "We are here to make sure that sad travesty doesn't happen."

"What do you mean?"

"Rhys called me, and he wanted to surprise you," Kate says and claps her hands.

"So we are going to help you get ready, and then the three of us are going to man the fort for the next twenty-four hours." Savannah pulls the cookies out of the oven, turns it off, and takes my hand to lead me upstairs.

"But I have to work."

"We're working for you," Charly says.

"But you guys have to work."

"Jesus, is she slow?" Kate shakes her head. "We took the rest of today and tomorrow off so you can too, and so you can go have fun."

"Fun." I follow my sisters into my bedroom, sit on the bed where directed, and frown at the three women. "I don't have time for fun."

"Yes, you do." Savannah takes the bag from Charly and pulls the contents out. "Now, Charly brought you some *gorgeous* new wedges. I'm totally jealous over these shoes."

"You're welcome," Charly adds as she emerges from my closet with my smallest suitcase and about seven outfits draped over her arm.

The shoes are seriously pretty; black patent-leather with a peep-toe.

It's too bad I haven't had time to paint my toenails.

"So, we're not allowed to tell you where you're going," Kate begins as she and Charly sort through my tops. "But we can say that you're going out for dinner tonight, so you should wear something flirty and pretty."

I'm getting better at flirty.

"And tomorrow is more casual." Van grins as she finds some black lacy underwear in my drawer. With the tags still on them. "Who are you saving these for?"

I shrug. "I don't know. They probably don't even fit anymore."

"Yes they do," Charly says and passes them to me. "Go put them on while we pick out your outfit."

"You guys got really bossy." I march into the bathroom, leave the door open, and strip down to try the underwear on.

"Come on, let us have fun." Van calls from the other room "We never got to help you get ready for special dates before."

"You were at college, or married and off having lives of your own," I call out calmly as I shimmy into the pretty underwear, then smile when it fits perfectly.

"Oh, those are divine," Kate says with a sigh as I walk out of the bathroom. "I have a weakness for pretty underwear."

"Rhys will love it," Charly agrees with a nod. "But I think the wedges are better suited for tomorrow. For tonight, you need fuck-me heels."

"Do I own fuck-me heels?"

Charly looks stricken as she dives back in my closet, then reemerges a few moments later with a sexy pair of black heels that I forgot I even owned.

"These are awesome," Charly says with a satisfied grin. "And perfect for tonight. And I might borrow them later this week."

"Your feet are bigger than mine," I remind her.

"Have I taught you nothing?" Charly asks with her hands on her hips. "Beauty is pain, Gabby."

"So, why do you think you're never getting laid again?" Van asks as she approves a black dress that hits me mid-thigh, with white chevron stripes. "Rhys obviously likes you."

"Because I don't think he wants it." I wrinkle my nose and all three girls stop what they're doing to stare at me.

"Do we have to have *the talk?*" Van asks, then turns to Charly. "I told you we should have given her the talk."

"Well, she got pregnant and had a baby, and I just assumed she already knew the basics." Charly shakes her head in disbelief. "Of course he wants it, sweetie. He's a man."

"Well, we've kissed, and touched, and..."

"Has he buried his face *downtown?*" Charly asks with raised brows.

"Uh, yeah."

"He wants it," she replies. "Guys don't go downtown for nothing, trust me."

"Well, with Sam gone, he's been sleeping in here with me," I begin, then bump Kate's fist when she offers it. "And I just figured we'd have actually had sex by now, but yesterday was a cluster and I was so exhausted last night, I was practically already asleep by the time I crawled in bed."

"Well, you won't have that issue tonight," Kate says with an encouraging smile. "Nothing at all to worry about. We have this covered, and you can just take the night off and have a good time."

"And by have a good time, she means get laid," Van says helpfully. "You know, in case you didn't know."

"Thanks," I reply as I pull the dress over my head and step into my shoes. Charly zips me up from behind.

"Oh, this looks fantastic!" she says with a happy smile. "Now, your hair and makeup."

"It's just dinner. It's not the prom or anything." But I turn a circle, pleased with my reflection. How long has it been since I wore anything other than jeans or shorts? I don't even remember.

"Oh, here, put this in your purse." Charly hands me a silver packet.

"Just one?" Van asks with a frown, and I let the whole string of condoms fall in a long line, dangling from my fingers. "Oh, good."

"Well, whether he wants to do it or not," I say with a giggle, "we'll be safe."

"He wants it," Charly says with confidence and kisses my cheek. "Have fun. Be safe."

"And please, get laid," Van adds.

***

Dinner was amazing, at my favorite restaurant in the Quarter, Café Amalie. Kate must have told Rhys to take me there.

The food was delicious, Joe the waiter was kind and flirty, and my date was attentive, sexy and funny.

I've come to learn that effort is attractive. Rhys is here with me because he wants to be, and he put a lot of effort into getting me here.

Totally sexy.

And if that wasn't enough, he took me to the club that my brother, Declan, is playing in tonight. We have front row seats, so Rhys must have given Declan the heads up that we were coming.

I don't remember the last time I got to watch Dec perform. It's been years. And there is nothing in the world like watching my handsome brother croon, sing, play the instruments like he was born to it, and flirt with the audience.

He's always reminded me of Harry Connick Jr., another New Orleans native musician. Like Harry, Declan is funny, and so damn talented.

He's singing a bluesy number I don't know, his long fingers dancing over the keys of the piano, and he glances over at me and winks.

I'm swaying in my seat, holding Rhys's hand in my lap, soaking in the music and the strong, captivating man sitting next to me.

Rhys leans over and kisses the crown of my head, then murmurs, "Are you having fun?"

"So much fun," I reply immediately. "I don't remember the last time I heard Dec play."

"He's good," Rhys says, his eyes on Declan.

"He's the best." I nudge Rhys with my shoulder playfully. "And I didn't get even a drop of the musical talent that Dec has."

"You have other talents," he replies softly, his green eyes suddenly hot.

"Like you'd know," I mutter low, but suddenly Rhys's arm is wrapped around my shoulders and his lips are against my ear.

"Trust me, baby, I want you, and I'll have you. But I'm enjoying this easy evening out with you."

I smile up at him as Declan finishes the song. He stands from the piano and sits on a stool with his guitar. "Ladies and gentlemen, I have a special guest here tonight."

He smiles down at me and I pray with all my might that he doesn't pull me up on stage. I'm terrified of people.

But he just gives me a tiny shake of the head and keeps talking.

Because he knows.

"My baby sister, Gabby, hasn't heard me perform in about three years, and I'm pleased that she's here tonight, with a special friend."

I raise a brow, but he keeps talking.

"Gabby is one of the most special people in my life, friends." His eyes soften on me. "She's the best. And this is a song that our father sang to her, and that she now sings to her little one. I'd like to sing it for her tonight."

I hold my breath, and reach out for Rhys's hand as Declan begins to sing the Johnny Cash version of You Are My Sunshine, and just like that, tears fill my eyes as I watch my big brother sing the song that's more familiar to me than just about anything else.

The guitar sounds...well, *stringy* is the only way I can describe it because I don't play the instrument myself. It's a slow, gritty version of the song, and I love every note.

When he's done, he comes off the stage to me, hugs me close, and whispers in my ear, "Love you, sunshine."

"Love you." He returns to the stage, and I glance up at Rhys. "Thank you."

***

This evening has been nothing short of a fantasy. After the show, Rhys walked me back down Royal Street to a bed and breakfast and led me up the stairs, where our luggage was already waiting in our room.

The room is beautifully decorated with antique furniture, lovely, bold colored linens and a huge bathroom is attached.

"This is charming," I murmur and turn to see Rhys's eyes on me.

"I watch you move and I can't think straight," he says as he slowly walks toward me. "Do you have any idea how beautiful you are in this dress and heels?"

"Charly says they're fuck-me heels." I swallow and watch his lips as they tip up in that half-smile that always does me in.

"She's right," he says on a sigh. "I think we'll leave

them on for a few minutes."

"Okay. She also gave me condoms." *Jesus, shut up, Gabby!*

"Well, she's a planner. We're going to take this dress off."

I swallow again. "Okay."

He slowly turns me away from him and pushes my hair over my shoulder, out of his way, and then lowers the zipper of my dress and pushes it down my arms, and lets it simply fall in a heap around my feet.

"Holy fuck," he hisses between his teeth. His fingertips trace the straps of my bra, then the elastic of my panties around my waist and my whole body is on fire. Just the lightest touch sends goose bumps all over me.

His lips graze my shoulder, then up my neck to my ear. "You take my breath away, Gabrielle."

I turn to face him and slide my palms up his torso, on either side of the buttons of his black button-down. When I reach the top, I unbutton the shirt, then push it down his arms and off, admiring the smooth, tanned skin that covers his muscled body. His abs are ridiculous. It should be illegal to look like this in slacks. I stick my fingertip in the waist of his pants, right over the zipper, and can feel the tip of his already-hard cock.

"Gabby—"

"You make me crazy too," I whisper and lean in to kiss his chest, right over his heart. "You've kept me crazy for days."

"You were so tired last night, baby."

"I know." I smile softly and look up into his deep green eyes. "But I'm not so tired now."

He cocks a brow before lifting me into his arms and laying me back on the bed that's already been turned down.

Hmm…maybe I should offer turn-down service at the inn. I bet guests would appreciate it, for moments like this.

"No thinking about work."

I glance up in surprise. "How did you know?"

"You get a crease between your eyebrows." He rubs the spot with the pad of his thumb, then gently brushes it down the bridge of my nose and settles beside me.

"When did you take your pants off?" I glance around. "And grab condoms?"

"While you were daydreaming about work." He smirks and kisses my shoulder again, then drags the tip of his tongue up my neck and turns my face to meet his. "If, at any time, you need or want me to stop, all you have to do is say so."

I nod, fully trusting him.

"How long has it been?"

He wants to talk about this now?

He simply raises a brow when I hesitate.

"Since I got pregnant," I whisper. His eyes widen, and then narrow with pure male possessiveness. "How long has it been for you?"

And then he frowns.

"Hey, I get to know too."

"More than a year. Maybe close to two."

"Right." I roll my eyes, but he pins me beneath him, my hands in his, pressed to the bed above my head, and he kisses me deeply, until I am gasping for breath, then pulls back.

"I don't lie, Gabby. No one has interested me in a very long time. And I no longer waste my time with anything that doesn't interest me."

I bite my lip and nod. "Okay."

"And I'm not going to take this fast." He plants those

full lips at the side of my mouth and nibbles, then drags his nose down my jaw to my ear. "I'm going to take my time. Your body will burn."

He tugs on my earlobe with his teeth.

"You'll be drenched."

"I already am," I reply and wiggle under him, earning a deep chuckle.

"You *will* beg for me."

"I don't beg for anything." But my voice doesn't sound as sure as I'd like it to.

"Oh, baby," he whispers as he releases one of my hands and pulls his fingertips down my arm to my breast, still covered in the sexy underwear the girls talked me into. "Challenge accepted."

I think I'm in trouble.

Or I'm in for the best experience of my life.

His mouth wanders down my torso, leaving a wet trail. He sucks my nipples through the lace, then tugs it down and licks them some more, teasing them into tight nubs. Finally, he rips the last of my underwear off and tosses them over his shoulder.

"The shoes stay."

It's not a request.

And damn if it isn't sexy as hell.

He nuzzles my belly on his way *downtown*, but rather than kiss me there, he flips me over onto my belly and continues the assault on the backs of my legs, alternating wet kisses and light touches over the delicate skin behind my knees and inner thighs. Finally, he grips my ass in both hands, spreads me apart and laps at my core, from my clit to my anus and back down again.

"Oh my God!"

"Jesus, you're wet."

"It's not my fault," I reply breathlessly. "You're sexy."

He chuckles and bites my ass cheek, then the other to match, and nibbles up my spine to my neck and speaks into my ear again.

"Your body was made to make a man weep with joy. I want to fuck you, and spank you, and pamper you, all at the same time."

Jesus, he can't say shit like that to me.

"You like that?"

I shrug, unable to move much from this angle, but God, I can't talk either. I'm a big, tight ball of lust.

"I think you do," he whispers and bites the lobe again before kissing his way back down. "I think you like it when I talk dirty to you."

I moan in agreement and tip my ass up, hoping for more attention, and he readily obliges, rubbing two fingers through my folds.

"Your lips are swollen," he says as he kisses down my back. "And your clit is coming out to play."

His thumb draws circles around the center of my universe, making me cry out.

"Oh my God!"

"That's right, baby." He repeats the motion, and slowly sticks two fingers inside me. "God, you're tight."

I whimper, my hips moving in circles. Damn, if only he'd touch me a little harder, a little faster—

And suddenly I'm on my back again and Rhys is kneeling between my legs.

Finally!

But he doesn't push inside me. He just smiles and kisses back down my torso, over my belly, to my core, and pulls my clit between his lips, tugging just hard enough to send me over the edge.

"Fuck!" I jackknife off the bed, but Rhys pins me down with his hand firmly between my breasts as he has his way with me.

And it's amazing. Like, the kind of shit you write home about.

But it's not exactly what I want.

"Rhys."

He shakes his head, and that makes my eyes cross.

"Rhys, I'm serious."

"Do you want me to stop?"

"I want you inside me!"

He grins against my core. "That's not stop or no," he replies and drags that tongue through my lips and inside me, then back up to my clit.

"You're trying to kill me."

He chuckles. "You're not ready."

"Sweetheart, I don't think I could be any more ready." I grip the covers at my hips and hold my breath as he kisses the inside of my thighs, my pubis, and finally kisses up my body.

"Do you want me?" he whispers against my lips. The sound of a foil packet tearing open is the only sound as he hovers over me. I can smell and taste myself, and rather than answer, I pull his mouth down to mine, kissing him deeply, loving that our scents are mingling around me, and I reach between us, grip him firmly in my fist, and guide him to my entrance.

"I need the words," he growls.

"I don't just want you, Rhys, I *need* you."

He pauses, his eyes on mine, his hands framing my face, breathing hard. And finally, *finally*, he pushes lightly, just burying the tip in my wetness.

"Fuck," he whispers. "God, Gabby."

He watches my face as he slides in farther, until he's seated balls-deep, and then he stops again.

"Don't move," he says, kissing me softly.

"Are you okay?" My fingernails are dragging lazily down his sides to his ass, then up again.

"So much more than okay," he replies and kisses me more firmly as he pulls out, then pushes in again. "I don't want to hurt you."

"It doesn't hurt," I reply truthfully. "God, it feels so good."

"So good," he repeats and moves again. "I have to move, baby."

"Good, 'cause you're killing me."

He chuckles, then sighs as he pushes up on his hands and begins to move even faster, a little harder, watching my face all the while to make sure that I'm okay.

And boy, am I okay.

I clench around him, loving the way the ridge of his head drags against my walls, shooting little electrical sparks down my spine. I have to reach above me and push on the headboard, tipping my hips up to meet him, as our tempo grows. He's sweating, breathing so damn hard, and I'm going to lose it.

"Rhys."

"Yes, baby, go over."

I rest my feet on his calves and clench down as his pubis hits my clit, and I go blind with ecstasy, my body gripping him with everything I have.

"Fuck," he whispers and follows me, coming hard, his whole body shuddering. As the shivers slow, he leans his forehead against the headboard, working to catch his breath, and I've never seen anything like him in my life.

Crap, I'm in love.

CHAPTER EIGHT

~Gabby~

I can hear him moving about the room quietly. He thinks he's letting me sleep in, I'm sure, and while it's very sweet of him to try, a woman doesn't wake up at five in the morning six days a week and sleep past seven on her day off.

But I lie here and listen to him, imagining him naked, or maybe wrapped in a towel from the shower I heard him take a little while ago. He moves back into the bathroom and closes the door, and I can hear him murmuring into the phone.

I stretch and roll over to my other side, smiling in pure contentment at the pull of sore muscles from a long night of lovemaking. I mean, seriously, *six times?*

The man is a machine.

Did last night seriously happen? Because…wow. He did things to me that I thought were only urban myths. Things women talk about, but haven't ever actually *done.*

Like the whole pushing my legs up around my ears, hands pressed to the back of my thighs and making me see stars.

Or the way he can wrap those strong arms around me and just *move* me where he wants me. As if I don't weigh anything at all.

And the dirty talk! Holy hell, the things that come out of Rhys's mouth are probably illegal in some states, but I hope he never stops talking that way. It makes me feel sexy and fun.

Desired.

Wanted.

And that hasn't happened in a *very* long time.

The sink turns on in the bathroom, and for several minutes I debate about getting up and joining him. It could be fun to play in the shower. Sure, he already took one, but I'm pretty sure I can talk him into another.

But then there's a knock on our door, and he quickly comes out of the bathroom. My eyes are open now, and he flashes me a smile, wrapped in one of the robes offered by the B&B, and opens the door.

He returns to the room with a silver tray. There is only one covered plate on it, along with a single red rose.

"Breakfast," he says with a wink. "Did I wake you?"

"No." I shake my head and sit up in the bed, tucking the sheet under my arms. "I rarely sleep past seven."

"Have I told you before how beautiful you are in the morning?"

I chuckle. "No."

"Well, you are."

He leans over the bed and kisses me back into the pillows, covers me with his lean body, and simply continues to kiss me.

He makes me dizzy.

He makes me forget my own name, for God sake.

"So beautiful," he whispers against my lips, then sits up, uncovers the plate, and with his fingers picks up a strawberry and holds it up to my lips. I bite it and his fingers, then laugh as he scowls. "And a biter."

"Hey, you're the one who held food up to my lips."

"Let's see if you can be nicer about it." He grips a piece of pineapple in his fingers and offers it to me. I lean in, smiling, and gently take the fruit from him, chewing happily, slurping the juice.

"Better."

"My turn." I choose a slice of apple and hold it up for Rhys to take from my fingers. "No biting."

"I seem to remember you enjoying my teeth on your skin last night."

I feel my face flush as I remember the way he skimmed those teeth over the ball of my shoulder, my ear, my neck.

My pussy.

"Yeah," he whispers and bites the apple, then leans in and bites my lower lip. "You like it."

I lick my lip where he just bit it and taste the apple there.

"The fruit is delicious."

"You're delicious." He's finished with the fruit now, nibbling down my neck to my shoulder, making my eyes cross. "How do you keep your skin so soft?"

"Genetics," I reply hoarsely. "And I try to stay out of the sun."

"It's working," he replies and kisses my chin. "Are you still hungry?"

"We ate three bites of fruit," I remind him. "Aren't you still hungry?"

His green eyes smile into mine as he reaches over and plucks the rose from its vase on the tray. "I'm hungry for you."

I snort. "Charmer."

"You're not an easy charm, Gabby." He lightly drags

the soft petals of the rose down my nose. "But just because you don't need the pretty words, doesn't mean that I don't mean every single one of them. You *are* beautiful. You *are* amazing. And—" He pulls the petals down between my breasts, over my belly, and down my hip, making me gasp. It tickles. "I'm hungry for every inch of you."

Suddenly, he flips me over onto my stomach, brushes my hair off my back and away from my face, and returns to skimming the rose down my spine to my ass, barely over the crack, then in a circle over each of my butt cheeks.

"I enjoy your skin," he murmurs and kisses between my shoulder blades.

"I enjoy you enjoying my skin," I reply with a grin. "I feel pampered."

He pauses. "You should feel pampered every day."

I snort. "Who are you?" The rose skims down my inner thighs, making me moan. "Who says stuff like that?"

I hear him toss the rose away, and suddenly his naked—he must have lost the robe—body is covering mine and his mouth is next to my ear.

"I'm the man about to be deep inside you." His voice is rough, his breathing already different. Hard. "I'm the man that can't get enough of you." He spreads my legs with his own. I hear him rip open a condom, and with me flat on my tummy, he pushes inside me, all the way inside, making me bite my lip.

"Oh, my God."

He kisses my neck, pulls out most of the way, then slams into me, harder than he has before, and I gasp, shocked at how fucking good it feels.

"Too much?" he asks.

"No." I shake my head and try to tilt my hips up to meet him, but he holds me down, his hands on my ass, pushing me into the mattress.

"I'm the man who's about to fuck you into this mattress, Gabrielle."

Holy hell.

And he does. Hard and steady. I can't wait to see his fingerprints on my ass later.

"Rhys."

"That's right. That's who I am."

I freaking know who he is!

"Damn, I'm gonna come." I bury my face in the bed, but suddenly he pulls out and flips me back around.

"Look at me." He props one leg on his shoulder and kisses my calf as he wraps the other leg around his waist and slips back inside me. "I want to see you while you fall apart."

I can't look away from his face. He's intense, but his eyes are happy as he watches me. I know that most men are visual creatures, but Rhys *loves* to watch me. We kept the lights on all night long.

His eyes never leave me.

And it makes me feel just what he says. Amazing. Beautiful.

I reach between us and circle my clit with my fingertips, sending little zings through my limbs and spine, and Rhys's jaw clenches.

"Oh, fuck yes, touch yourself."

I reach farther down and press against his cock as he pulls in and out of me, and for the first time, his eyes close.

Well, look at that.

I file that away for later.

"Tell me you're about to come," he growls. I can feel him swell even more inside me and I know he's so close.

And so am I.

I cup his face in my hands and rise up to kiss him, tightening my core and pussy, clenching around him even harder, and we both fall over the edge into ecstasy.

We're panting, a little sweaty, as I fall back onto the bed and Rhys follows me, careful not to crush me, but his head is on my chest and his arms are gripping my sides. I summon up enough strength to push my fingers through his hair as we regain our senses.

"You're good at that," I say finally, staring at the ceiling. "Now I know what all the fuss is about."

I feel him smile against me. "Oh baby, we've just gotten started."

***

"This is Jackson Square." I point to the park surrounded by wrought iron fencing in the heart of the French Quarter. "And behind it is St. Louis Cathedral. We can go inside, if you like, to look around."

Rhys shrugs. "If you want to. I'm just enjoying the walk with a beautiful woman."

He's holding my hand, and when we have to push our way through a crowd, he simply rests his hand on the small of my back, or my ass, to let me know he's right behind me.

The man is forever touching me.

And I freaking *love* it.

Instead of leading him to the cathedral, I lead him down Royal Street, away from the heart of the Quarter. There are so many amazing art galleries and shops on this street. It's one of my favorites.

One boutique in particular catches my eye, and I pause to stare in the window.

"I have a soft spot for pretty things," I say softly.

"What do you see that you like?" Rhys asks. I shrug my shoulder, then point at a simple silver chain with an amethyst pendant.

"That's pretty."

And then I begin to walk away, ready to look into the next window, and feel Rhys behind me. We pause to watch some street performers, who secretly give me the willies. I mean, it's weird that some guy is dressed like a transformer, driving on the street, then stands up.

How does someone fall into that line of work?

"I'll be right back. I need a bathroom." Rhys kisses my cheek.

"I'll be here," I reply and toss him a smile over my shoulder as he walks away. Afraid that Mr. Transformer is going to decide to drive right up to me and freak me out, I return to the sidewalk and admire the art in the window there. The colors are bright, too bright for my home, but it's interesting.

"Art lover?" Rhys asks as he joins me.

"I appreciate art," I reply, still thoughtfully staring at the piece in the window. "I would never buy this, though."

"Me neither," he replies with a smile.

"Wow, are you Rhys O'Shaughnessy?" Two teenage boys have approached us. They're obviously brothers, with their matching red hair and blue eyes. The older one is wearing a Cubs T-shirt.

"Baseball fans," Rhys replies with a grin. "I am, yes."

"Wow, I'm your biggest fan," the older boy says and offers his hand for Rhys to shake. "You're awesome. Why aren't you playing this season?"

"I'm getting my shoulder back in shape, man. I'll be back in the spring."

"Awesome!"

"Maybe you just play for the wrong team," the younger brother says. "I'm a Cardinals fan."

"Nah," Rhys replies with a good-natured laugh. "I think you just root for the wrong team."

"No way!"

"Hey," the older one says as he pulls his phone out of his pocket. "Can we get a picture? My friends won't believe this!"

"Sure."

"I'll take it," I offer, reaching for the phone. Rhys stands between the boys, one hand on each of their shoulders, and smiles widely for the picture.

"Thanks so much!"

"Yeah," the younger brother adds, "you're pretty cool. For a Cub."

"You're welcome."

I'm quiet as we walk away. I'm so impressed with him! This is exactly why Sam and all of his fans love him so much. He's approachable. He's friendly.

"You're quiet," he murmurs beside me. "Talk to me."

"I'm so proud of you," I reply honestly. "You were great with those kids."

He looks surprised for a moment, and then chuckles. "You surprise me."

"Why?"

"I thought you'd decided that it was weird, and you were trying to figure out a way to tell me to get lost."

"Nah, there would be other reasons to tell you to get lost. Being loved by teenage boys everywhere isn't one of them."

"Good to know." He steers me around a group of people standing on the corner, talking and laughing. "I seriously love my job, Gabby."

"I can tell. What do you love about it? I'm really interested.."

"It's an honor. And I don't mean that to sound as trite as it does. I'm a part of the all-American sport. There's nothing more American than apple pie and baseball."

"Do you like apple pie?" I ask.

"Doesn't everyone?"

"Point taken."

He takes my hand in his, links our fingers, and kisses my knuckles before continuing.

"I can't describe what it feels like to stand on that mound, with sixty thousand fans in the stands, whether they're rooting for our team, or the opposing team, to hear them cheer. It's humbling. It's amazing."

"You've done it a long time. Not many people can say they've played professional baseball."

"True." He nods. "I think it's why I'm so stubborn about this shoulder injury. I know that at thirty, I only have a few years left in me. Most pitchers don't play past my age. It's a physically demanding sport. But I'll be damned if this shoulder is the reason I can't play anymore. I want to end my career on *my* terms. I'm not an idiot. I'm not going to play until I'm crippled. But I want to say when it's over. Does that make sense?"

"It does." I kiss his bicep and then rub it with my free hand. "It makes perfect sense."

"Do you like baseball?"

"Meh." I purse my lips and shrug. "It's okay. I really love MMA fighting."

"MMA fighting?" He stares down at me like I'm crazy. "Why?"

"Are you kidding? Hot men, scantily clad, rolling around on the floor together. I mean, it's really a no-brainer." I chuckle inside, and give my inner flirt a high-five. I'm getting so good at this.

Suddenly, he's pinned me against a brick wall, caging me in the way he does that makes my toes instantly curl, and he's hunched over so his face is level with mine.

"You like looking at half-naked men, baby? I can get half-naked for you."

"You *are* pretty remarkable half-naked," I say thoughtfully. "Okay, you'll do."

He laughs and kisses my forehead, then takes my hand and leads me down the sidewalk. "What am I going to do with you?"

"I don't know. What are you going to do with me?"

He winks down at me. "I'm not telling."

***

"I had a wonderful time." We're standing at the trunk of the car as Rhys pulls our bags out and drops them on the ground before tugging me into his arms and planting his lips on mine, kissing me for all he's worth.

And he's worth a lot.

A lot.

"How do you feel?" he whispers as he pulls away.

"Happy."

"Perfect."

"You're home!" Savannah waves from the porch. "Stop kissing and get in here. Not you, Rhys."

"She's not obvious at all," I say as I wave at my sister and roll my eyes.

Rhys also waves and carries our bags around the back of the house. "I'll take these in, then I'm going to work out in the barn for a while. Just yell if you need me."

I nod and join Van, who takes my hand and quickly leads me inside the house. She glances around, as if someone could be listening in, despite the fact that guests haven't started arriving yet for this evening, then begins the inquisition.

"How was it? How many condoms did you use? Was he sweet? Did he hurt you? Do I need to have the boys kick his ass?"

"Stop." I hold my hand over Van's mouth to shut her up.

"Mmmp mmmp brachd."

"What?" I pull my hand away.

"Tell me everything."

"No." I smile as I set my purse on the desk I use to check guests in. "It's all mine."

"Come *oooonnnnn*." She pouts. She knows I can't resist the pout. "I want to know details!"

"Where are Kate and Charly?"

"They both went in to work. I stayed and handled things here. Now, spill."

I sigh and push my hair behind my ear. "It was fun."

Her face falls. "That's it?"

"Fun is good."

"You have *fun* at the movies, Gabby."

"Okay, it was…nice."

"*Nice?*" She shakes her head sadly. "We had such high hopes for him."

"We did?"

"Sure. He's hot. He's nice."

I nod. "Yeah. And he gave me the best night I've had since Sam was born."

A slow smile slides over Van's face. "That's promising."

I lean in and lower my voice. "It was amazing. He's just…wow."

"This is so much better than *nice*. So give me details."

I shake my head. "No, those really are just mine. But

you can sleep well tonight, knowing that he took very good care of me."

"Good." She hugs me close, clinging more tightly than she normally does, which makes me a little sad.

"Are you okay?" I ask softly.

"Yes."

"Something isn't right."

She pulls back and her eyes are sad now. "Lance called."

"That fucker isn't supposed to call you!" The rage is hard and instant. Van's ex-husband abused her, emotionally, physically and sexually. "Tell me you called the police!"

"I did," she assures me. "And I told Beau and Eli too."

"Good." I nod. "You wouldn't have done that before. Did you call Ben?"

She looks down. "No."

"Why not?"

"He's not my brother."

No, he's just been in love with you forever and a day.

But I don't say that because she won't believe it, and she doesn't want to hear it.

"No, but he cares about you too. You know that."

"One of the boys will tell him, I'm sure."

"Van."

She shakes her head adamantly. "Drop it, Gabs."

"Okay, what did Lance say?"

She chews the inside of her lip, then simply drops her head into her hands with a resigned sigh.

"The usual. I'm a pain in the ass. All of his troubles are my fault. Blah blah blah."

"I'm going to kick his ass."

Van bursts out with a laugh. "You're half his size."

"I don't give a shit. I'll kill the fucker."

She sobers, her eyes, the same color as mine, holding my gaze. "I know you would. But he's not worth it, Gabs."

"Ben got to beat him up," I reply with a pout.

"Ben could have gotten hurt," Van says.

"Have you met Ben?" I shake my head and laugh at the lunacy of her statement. "*No one* hurts Ben."

Except you, Van.

"If you have this handled, I'll head home."

"I have this." I hug my sister close. "And I have your back, too, if you ever need me."

"I know. I love you."

"I love you more."

CHAPTER NINE

~Rhys~

My shoulder is improving every day. Kate was right to suggest that I come here to recover. I don't know if it's the quiet, the calm of this particular place, or if it's that there is no pressure from coaches and trainers constantly breathing down my neck, watching my every move, always asking, "How do you feel *now?*"

Having Sam around to ask questions and be the fun, silly kid that he is has been awesome, and I admit that I miss him.

It's probably a combination of all of the above.

I'm in the barn, working out on Friday afternoon. There is barely a hitch in my shoulder as I execute one hundred push-ups. I'm ready for more weight. Maybe I'll have Gabby come out and sit on my shoulders.

I know that being with Gabby has been awesome. Easy, and yet one of the most complicated relationships I've had, which doesn't even make sense to me. It's easy to be with her. To talk to her, make her smile, listen to her laugh.

Make love to her. Let's be honest, lose myself in her. She's pushed everything around me out of focus, even baseball, and *no one* has ever done that for me before.

It scares me and exhilarates me at the same time.

Baseball can't shift out of focus for me. It is my life, and it'll continue to be my life after I leave this place.

This isn't permanent.

I need to remember that.

I'm a sweaty mess as I brush my hands off and walk toward the house. Maybe I'll talk Gabby into a shower with me.

Probably not. She'll be in work mode, and she's fierce when she's in work mode, which just makes her all the more sexy to me. Her work ethic is incredible, and whether that's in spite of, or because of, her privileged upbringing, I don't know.

All I know is, I admire the fuck out of her.

As I walk in the back door and into the kitchen, I can hear her voice coming from the desk where she greets guests. The voices are just murmurs, and then she laughs, and I can't help but smile and feel a little jealous of whoever made her laugh in the first place, because they get to see her eyes shine and the way she wrinkles her nose, just a little, when her smile is wide.

Jesus, I have it bad.

I pull a bottle of water from the fridge, twist off the cap and guzzle two-thirds of it before walking down the hall toward the sound of the voices. I stop dead in my tracks when I see my teammate, Neil Miller, leaning on the desk and smiling at Gabby as she gestures with her hands, telling him something that I can't hear over the roaring in my ears.

Neil leans in and brushes Gabby's hair behind her ear and that's it. I'll be fucking damned if another man will put his hands on her while I'm still in the picture.

Hell no.

"You might want to drop that hand before I remove it from your body," I say, surprised to hear the words come out calmly, as I approach the desk.

"Just the man I'm looking for!" Neil says as he saunters to me, but my eyes are still pinned to Gabby, who's now frowning at me. Her cheeks are pink with anger or embarrassment, I'm not sure, and I don't give a fuck which it is, honestly.

"What's up, Neil?"

He glances between me and the woman he was flirting with, then tips his head back and laughs. "Was I poaching, bro?"

"I'm not your bro," I reply and turn my gaze to my young teammate, taking in his tired eyes and rumpled clothes. "Did you say you came here looking for me?"

The humor leaves his face and he nods as he looks at the floor. "Can you take a minute?"

I nod and gesture toward the kitchen, but before following him, I pull Gabby against me, kiss her hard and murmur against her lips, "Reserve thirty minutes for me this afternoon."

I turn and leave before she can respond, following Neil through the kitchen where I pull more water bottles out of the fridge. Then I push ahead and lead him outside, back toward the barn where I know we can talk without any guests listening that may be milling about.

We push inside the surprisingly cool barn, thanks to thick oak trees overhead. I straddle the weight bench that arrived the other day, drink water, and watch Neil as he paces back and forth, agitated.

Exhausted.

"What's going on?" I finally ask. "Does Coach know you're here?"

He shrugs, then stops, shoves his hands in his pockets, and stares at his feet. Neil is in his mid-twenties, tall and built, and a favorite among the female fans. He joined us last year, coming up from the minor leagues, and he's a gifted player, but it's no secret that he's been struggling.

"I think I'm fucking this up," he finally admits and reaches for one of the water bottles, tears the cap off and throws it across the room before drinking half of it in two gulps.

"Okay."

"Coach doesn't know I'm here, but he made me take the week off."

I cock a brow, surprised. "Which means that you're either about to get arrested, or kicked out of the League if you don't get your shit together."

He rubs the back of his hand over his mouth, and then just sits down on the floor, right where he was standing, and rests his elbows on his raised knees.

"Pretty much."

"What have you been doing since I left?"

"Are you coming back?" he asks, his eyes on mine now, looking hopeful.

"That's the plan."

He nods. "I love baseball."

"I know. You play it like you love it." He blinks rapidly, clearly surprised by the compliment. "You're my catcher, Neil. I watch you, all game, every game."

"My knees hurt," he admits. "I'm twenty-five fucking years old, and my knees are killing me all the time."

"Are you hooked on pain pills?" I ask bluntly.

"No." He shakes his head and sucks down more water. "The minors were very different," he begins softly. "I mean, there were parties after games, and there was some stupid shit that went down, but that was *nothing* compared to this. There's drugs and women and money being flung at me from every direction."

"Are you in trouble?" I ask again.

"No. Coach told me to take a week to get my head on straight before I get arrested or kicked off the team." He pushes his hands through his hair, scrubbing his scalp. "So I got in my car and drove straight here. You're the one I've always been able to talk to."

I miss this. Talking with the younger guys, giving them advice. I realize that when baseball is all over in a few years, this will be what I miss the most.

My teammates.

"So you've acquired a taste for hot women and money? Because if you tell me you're doing drugs, I'll take you down so fast you won't wake up in time to go back next week." I calmly drink my water, watching his face.

"I'm not doing drugs," he replies fiercely. "That's not me."

"Good."

"The women and money, I like."

"Nothing wrong with that."

He shrugs his shoulders, and won't meet my gaze.

"I have two separate women claiming they're pregnant with my kid," he says softly. "And I don't even remember fucking either of them."

Ouch.

"Are you sure you did?"

He shakes his head. "Dude, I get so fucked up after a game, especially a win, I can't be sure of anything."

"Idiot."

He winces and nods. "I know."

"Obviously, there are lawyers for this, Neil. It happens in professional sports all the time."

"Has it ever happened to you?"

"Hell no."

He smirks. "Of course not. You're fucking perfect."

I shake my head and sigh. "Not even close. Do you think I wasn't dazzled by tits and ass when I was young? Of course. I'm a red-blooded man, for fuck sake."

"So you fucked around too."

"For a minute, in the beginning. But I wanted baseball more. It's not about the money or the women or the fame for me. It's about the game. I've never been willing to give it up, and I'm not going into a relationship with anyone unless I can give it everything it deserves. And I don't think I can do that while I'm still playing baseball."

"If you try to tell me you've been a fucking monk for ten years, I call bullshit."

"No." I grin and shake my head. "But the women I choose are discreet and they know the score."

"What about the honey inside?" he asks, and the way he calls Gabby a *honey* sets my teeth on edge.

"None of your motherfucking business."

"Hey." He leans back, hands up in the resigned position. "No offense."

I shake my head again. "She's spoken for."

"Does she know the score?" he asks with a raised brow.

"Touch her and I'll end you," I reply with steel in my voice. "I'm not fucking with you over her. She's off limits, and that's the end of the story."

"I get it." Neil nods, then smiles. "I hope it works out for you guys."

I stand, ignoring the statement, because I don't even know what I want where Gabby is concerned.

Except, I know I want her naked and beneath me, right now.

"What do you need from me, Neil?"

"This." He stands and holds his hand out for me to shake. "I needed to talk it through with someone I respect and trust."

I nod, understanding. "Just call me if you need me. No need to drive for days for a conversation. Come on, let's go in."

"If I look at her, will you take my head off?"

"Probably. Don't look at her."

***

"Neil is staying in my room tonight," I inform Gabby as I walk into the kitchen and find her arranging flowers from the garden in a large vase.

"Are you two typically snuggle buddies?" she asks with a sarcastic smile.

"Funny." I walk up behind her and wrap my arms around her middle, just under her breasts because she's so short, and bury my nose in her hair, breathing her in. "Do you mind?"

She smells better than the flowers.

"It makes sense," she says as she pushes a sunflower in the vase. "You've been staying with me anyway, and Sam doesn't get home until Monday."

"Mmm," I agree. When the flowers are done, I turn her in my arms and cage her in between me and the kitchen island. "We need to talk."

"So talk." She raises her chin, meets my gaze head-on, and can't hide the little touch of fear in her amazing eyes.

And it's the fear in her eyes that calms the fear in me, because it tells me that we're on the same damn page.

"I don't like seeing you flirt with other men."

She raises a brow. "So?"

I tilt my head and lean in to press my lips to her ear. "It makes me crazy to see another man look at you the way that I do. To know that he wants you, naked, panting, moaning, wrapped around him, the way you were with me just this morning."

She swallows hard and grips onto my arms, her nails barely digging into my skin. I know she's turned on. I'm right there with her. Jesus, I can't get within twenty feet of her without an erection. The pull she has on me is completely new to me.

"I didn't mean to flirt with him." Her voice is a rough whisper.

"I'm not saying you did anything wrong. It was innocent enough. But you need to know that even something that innocent makes me crazy, rational or not." I slide my hand down her back to her ass, then around to the front and push inside her shorts, over her panties, down to her center. I can feel the heat coming off of her.

Fuck, I can *smell* how turned on she is.

"This is *mine.*" I kiss her neck and drag my nose down her jawline. "Your body, your skin, your scent, drive me wild. I crave you. And I don't want anyone else even thinking about you."

"That's awfully selfish," she replies, trying to be sassy, but she's panting now. I push my hand farther into her pants and press my fingertips against her firmly.

"I'm a selfish bastard. I never claimed otherwise." She's so close to the edge. Her eyes are glassy, her lips shiny and plump from biting them. I know how delicious they are.

So I lean in, pull her bottom lip between my teeth and nibble.

Her hands clench my arms as she holds her breath to keep from crying out as she comes in my hand.

Fuck, I want to carry her up to her bedroom and sink inside her right now.

"Excuse me, Miss Boudreaux."

She stills. I block the view of the intruder with my body, discretely pull my hand out of her shorts and smile down at her with a wink. She clears her throat.

"Yes, ma'am?"

"I'm sorry to interrupt. Would it be possible to get extra towels in our room?"

"Of course. I'll bring them up in just a few moments."

"Thank you."

The guest leaves and Gabby expels a long, deep breath. "What's up with this kitchen?"

"I'm going to fuck you in it on Sunday when we're alone. Just out of principle alone."

"Stop saying stuff like that," she says with an exasperated frown. "I'm working!"

I cup her face in my hands and just take her in. "You're beautiful."

"Still working."

My thumb brushes her bottom lip. "I didn't like what I walked into this afternoon."

"I get it," she replies and lifts her hand to press her palm against my cheek. "It was nothing. You're the one I'm sharing my bed with. You're the one that can make my body explode on command, and I'm not entirely sure how you do that, by the way."

A slow smile works its way over my face. "Damn right."

"Laughing at something funny isn't a big deal."

"Walking into a room and seeing a man with his hand on my woman is a big deal." Her eyes widen. "If there was any confusion, let's clear it up right now. For as long as there is a physical relationship between us, no one else touches you."

"That goes both ways."

"Of course." I kiss her forehead and back away. "Now, get to work. You're incredibly lazy today, with all the kitchen shenanigans and stuff."

"You're nuts," she says with a laugh.

"Nuts about you."

***

"This is delicious," Neil says as he inhales the fried chicken Gabby made for dinner. "There is nothing like southern fried chicken."

"Thanks," she replies with a smile. "It's Sam's favorite."

"Sam?" Neil asks.

"My son," she says. "He's seven. He's with my mom this week on vacation. He texted a little while ago. It seems that he and his cousins exhausted my mom and her sister at Disney World today."

"Good. I'm glad he's having fun." I push my finished plate away and rest my arm on the backrest of Gabby's chair, lift a lock of her hair between my fingers, and begin to mindlessly twirl the soft strands.

I can't stop touching her damn hair.

Neil's eyes are watching my hand as he continues to talk to Gabby.

"Sam's a big Cubs fan," I add.

"I have some things in my car. A few balls, and I'm pretty sure I have a jersey he can have too. I'll be sure to give them to you before I leave."

"Wow, thanks. He'll be thrilled."

Neil grins, and when Gabby stands to begin clearing the table, he joins us, insisting that he should earn his keep.

The cleanup goes quickly with the three of us pitching in.

"Do you have a girlfriend, Neil?" Gabby asks.

"No, ma'am," he replies and then laughs. "I should steer clear of women for a while. I seem to be getting into trouble with them."

"Why?" she asks as she folds a hand towel and hangs it in the oven door handle.

"Because I'm an idiot."

"Well, some people are." She nods thoughtfully.

"I thought you were going to say that some *men* are." Neil crosses his arms over his chest and leans back on the counter, genuinely interested in what Gabby has to say.

And so am I.

"No, *people* can be idiots. Not just men." She shrugs. "Especially when it comes to love."

"No one said anything about love."

"Maybe that's the problem," she says with a smile. "Sex and love together, that's a powerful thing." She seems to shake herself and offers Neil a shy smile. "Or I've been told."

"I'm not ready for love."

"You're what, in your mid-twenties?" she asks.

"Yes."

"So, grow up." Both Neil and I raise our brows, him in surprise, and me in pride. "You have an amazing job that many people would kill for. You don't have to fall in love today, but you don't have to be a jackass either."

"I think I did just fall in love."

I growl, but both of them ignore me.

"Trust me when I say," she continues, "screwing anything with boobs isn't attractive. It doesn't make you a hot baseball star. It makes you a pathetic athlete with less than questionable morals. And later, when you are lonely and you want to fall in love, it won't be easy. Do your thing.

Play baseball. But don't be a jackass."

"You're smart," Neil says, looking shell-shocked.

"I've had my share of jackasses," she replies simply. "My brothers sometimes have jackass qualities, but we yank them back to reality quickly. My dad was no jackass. And I'm certainly not raising one. If you act respectably and respectfully, the right girl will come along."

"You should add counseling services to your menu here," Neil says with a laugh. "But I hear you. And I don't disagree with you."

"Of course you don't disagree. I'm right."

I can't stand it anymore; I have to touch her. I pull her in front of me, against me, and wrap my arms around her shoulders, holding her close. Neil smiles at her thoughtfully, then raises his gaze to mine.

"I've never seen you like this, man, but now I know why. You've never met anyone like her."

"Not even close," I agree.

"I'm going to bed." Neil nods at both of us and turns to leave the room. "Do you mind if I stay tomorrow night too? I'd like to see a bit of New Orleans."

"No problem," Gabby replies. When he leaves the room, she tilts her head back, looking up at me upside down. "Did I say too much?"

I kiss her forehead softly and rest my lips there. "No, sweetheart. I think you said exactly what he needed to hear. He's having a rough time."

"I could tell." She sighs and closes her eyes, still resting her head back against my chest. "Your lips feel good."

I grin against her skin. "Let's go put them to use in other places."

CHAPTER TEN

~Gabby~

"Here, give these to Sam." I glance up as Neil climbs the steps of the porch with a Cubs tote bag in his hands. "I signed a couple balls. You can have Rhys sign them too. And there's a jersey in there."

"You really didn't have to do that," I say with a smile and accept the bag. Sam is going to be so excited! "But he will love it. He'll be sad that he missed you."

"Maybe I'll meet him another time," Neil says. "Gabby, thanks again for what you said the other night."

"Look, I'm sorry if I crossed a line—"

"No. You didn't." He shakes his head. "I needed to hear it, and you were right. It's time to grow up and enjoy this career. Who knows how much longer I'll be able to play? Professional athletes have an expiration date, especially catchers. My knees won't last forever."

"Well, if you ever need advice, you know where to find me. You know, southern women aren't exactly known for keeping their mouths shut."

"I'll remember that." He grins and turns to walk away, but stops and looks back at me. "Rhys is a good man."

"But?"

"No but. He's a good man. Just thought I'd let you

know, for what it's worth."

I smile, touched by the sweet baseball player. "It's worth a lot."

He nods, gets in his car, and pulls away, leaving just me and Rhys at the inn. The rest of the guests left earlier this morning, and given that it's Sunday, I'm officially off duty.

I find Rhys in the kitchen, finishing a phone call. "Everyone is gone."

"Good." He grins and folds me into a hug. "Do you want to go somewhere today?"

"Nope." I press my ear to his chest, enjoying the sound of his heartbeat. "I want to show you around my home."

"I've been here for a few weeks, baby." He chuckles against my hair. "I've seen it."

"Not the slave quarters, or some of the other fun spots. I have stories to tell and everything."

"I'm getting the official tour?" he asks with surprise.

"Absolutely." I take his hand in mine and lead him outside, toward the slave quarters first. "We renovated these along with the house when I decided to move forward with the inn," I inform him and he smiles indulgently. "What?"

"Your tour guide voice just came on."

"Well, I am guiding."

"It's sexy." He's smiling in that way he does that's reserved just for me, and there go the lightning bugs in my belly again.

"I'm glad you approve. As I was saying, I wanted the guests to see what the slaves lived in, and how they lived, here at the plantation back in the day." The doors and windows of the small buildings are Plexiglas, so you can see in, and the elements don't disturb the displays inside. "These are original slave homes that I had moved closer to the house. There is writing on the walls inside. See?"

"I didn't think slaves were allowed to know how to read or write." He's not just humoring me now, he's really interested, and it makes me proud to share this with him. "It looks like dates and names."

"Most weren't allowed to learn. It depended on the owner. As far as we know, my ancestors allowed the slaves to have an education, and some came here already knowing how to read and write."

"Interesting." He backs away and leads me to the next cabin. "What made you decide to do all of this?"

"Well, because although this isn't a piece of our history that we're proud of, it is a part of the plantation, and I want the guests to learn about it all. And the rest is a long story."

"I happen to have you all to myself today," he reminds me as he rests his hand on my neck, rubbing gently. "So, talk away, beautiful."

"I had Sam very young. You know that." He nods, patiently listening. "When I told my daddy that I was pregnant, well…I was so scared." I swallow hard, thinking back on that day. "He found me over in the gardens, crying, the day I told Sam's biological father that I was pregnant, and he told me to get rid of it.

"Dad scooped me up, sat me in his lap the way he did when I was little, and asked me what was wrong. I couldn't make the words come. I was scared and ashamed. *So ashamed.*"

"Why were you ashamed? You didn't do it alone." Rhys takes my hand in his, links our fingers, and leads me to the gardens.

"No, but I was old enough to know better. But, I told him that I was pregnant, and that the boy wanted me to abort it. And he said, 'What do you want, baby-doll?'"

Rhys kisses the back of my hand. "What did you want?"

"I wanted to keep the baby." I sigh and sit on the bench next to Rhys. "I didn't want to get rid of it. So, Daddy said what he always did when times got rough. *You can't control the wind, but you can adjust your sails. So we're just going to adjust our sails and get on with it.*" I smile sadly, wishing for the hundredth time since Dad passed that I could hear his voice say those words to me again.

"And you did."

I nod. "We did. My family rallied around me. Sam is loved fiercely and we were very well taken care of, of course. I didn't go to college. I'm lucky, Rhys. I come from a very influential family. A wealthy family. I'd told Dad on a few occasions that I wanted to turn the plantation into an inn. He liked the idea, and was helping me with plans. He was funding the renovations and the startup costs.

"And then he died." The tears come the way they always do when I think about this part. "So, he didn't get to see it when it was finished."

"He sees it," Rhys murmurs as he lifts me into his lap and holds me close, stroking my back and kissing my forehead. "And I'm sure he's very proud."

"I hope so. Everything I did to this place, I did with him in the front of my mind. I constantly asked myself, 'Would this make him happy? What would he think about this?' I had Beau and Eli here a lot. Beau ended up staying, living in the old caretaker's house that we remodeled as well, as you know. They were amazing, never balking at the cost of things, because we all wanted it to be top of the line, and restored perfectly. Daddy wouldn't have spared any expense. This place has been in our family for six generations."

"That's amazing," Rhys says softly.

"Not many people can say that," I reply. "And I'm proud of it. I always have been. This has always been where I'm happiest. So working on it, watching guests enjoy it, is such a pleasure and a privilege."

"I'm glad that you do something that makes you so happy." His arms tighten around me in a firm hug. "You deserve happiness, Gabrielle."

"So do you," I reply. "Are you happy?" He doesn't answer me for a long minute. I finally lean back and look up into his deep green eyes. "Are you?"

"I will be, when I get your sexy ass into the house where I can spend the rest of the twenty hours we have left to ourselves lost in you." He stands, easily carrying me toward the house. "I'm going to make you scream, baby."

"I'm not a screamer." And it didn't escape me that he didn't answer my question.

"You're about to be."

I press my face into his neck, smiling like a loon, clinging to him as he walks to the house. He's not even breathing hard. I've always said that strength is sexy, and I just wasn't referring to physical strength. But holy shit, that's sexy too.

Like, really sexy.

Rhys sets me on the countertop of the kitchen and stands between my legs, lifting my maxi skirt to my waist, his green eyes on fire as he stares down at me.

"We're not going up to the bedroom?"

"We'll get there." His lips tip up in a half-smile as his hands roam from my sides to my thighs, and then his thumbs work up my inner thighs to my center and make my eyes cross. "You're not wearing underwear."

I shake my head and lift the hem of his T-shirt,

needing to get my hands on his smooth skin. The muscles twitch at my touch, making me smile, but then he groans and leans into me as my hands travel over his torso, reveling in how *hard* he is.

God, he feels spectacular.

Suddenly, Rhys squats before me and pushes my thighs farther apart. I have to lean back on my hands to keep from falling. He glances up at me with mischief all over his handsome face before he leans in and that mouth of his goes to work.

God, how can he do this to me, every single time? He makes my body *sing*.

He's just barely brushing his tongue back and forth over my lips, gently touching me, teasing me. I plunge one hand into his hair and urge him to lick harder, suck harder, but he reaches up and takes my hand away and sets it on the countertop.

So much for being helpful.

"Rhys."

"Patience," he murmurs against me, then licks up to my clit, making my hips jerk, but licks back down again.

"Killing me."

I feel him grin against me. His hands travel down my calves to my feet, and he rubs them—*rubs them!*—as he continues to lick me. Jesus, it's sensory overload. My breath is heaving. Sparks of electricity are shooting through every nerve in my body.

"I want you, Rhys."

"Right here," he says.

"In me."

Suddenly, he stands and boosts me off the countertop. "Not yet."

"That was just mean."

He chuckles and leads me to the hallway. *Finally!* He's taking me to the bedroom. Thank God, because I was about to beg.

And that just won't do.

But suddenly, I'm caged against the wall, and he's leaning into me. I can smell myself on his mouth so I stand on tip-toe and lick him, right across his lips.

My inner flirt is *very* pleased.

Rhys groans and leads me to the stairs, but I stop short. He glances down at me with a raised brow. "Problem?"

"No, I just can't wait to do this." I unfasten his jeans, pull his pants and shorts off, tossing them to the side. "Sit."

"Sit? On the steps?"

I nod and kneel as he complies. His cock is already at full attention. Rhys watches with wide eyes as I take him in my hand firmly and brush my thumb over the tip before licking him from his scrotum, up the underside to the head and take him in my mouth, against my tongue.

"Fucking hell, Gabby."

I can't believe I've never done this to him before. He never gives me the chance. He just takes over, and that's fine, but I love making him crazy too.

Rhys leans back on the steps and alternates between dropping his head back and staring down at me as I work him over. His breath is choppy. His fingers are in my hair, gathering it into a ponytail to hold it out of my way as I lick, suck, and just barely skim the edge of my teeth over him.

"Jesus Christ, you're good at that."

I smile up at him, damn proud of myself. I don't have a lot of practice in this area, or any area when it comes to sex really, so the fact that he's enjoying it is a huge boost to my sexual ego.

I'm massaging his balls, which tighten, and I can tell he's about to come.

"Stop."

I shake my head, wanting to make him explode, but he stands suddenly and pulls me to my feet, leading me up the stairs.

"Damn it, I wasn't done!"

"Gabby, we're just getting started."

I'm pouty as he leads me to the bed, but when I see the heat in his gaze as he strips my clothes from my body, I lick my lips in anticipation of what's going to happen next.

Because knowing Rhys as well as I do now, it's going to be fantastic.

He scoops me up and lays me on the bed, but instead of covering me with his body, he begins to massage me.

I appreciate the gesture, but I'm on fire here!

"Rhys."

"I love your skin."

"Seriously, I need you inside me." He glances up at me, but continues to massage my legs.

"You have the best legs I've ever seen."

"They're short."

"They're perfect."

I snort, and he narrows his eyes on me. "Are you calling me a liar?"

"Nope." I shake my head, resigned to the massage rather than mind-blowing sex.

"Spread your legs wider."

Now we're getting somewhere.

I comply, but he still doesn't move up my body to push inside me. Instead, his hands massage higher on my thighs, then he shoves his hands under my ass and lifts me to his mouth, as if I'm simply a piece of fruit.

Holy hell.

I brace my feet on his shoulders as he lowers his face to me and takes his time licking me, lightly again. Frustratingly lightly.

What's the female version of blue balls? 'Cause that's what I have right now.

But then he licks my clit, just a bit harder, pulls it between his lips, and sends me right off into space.

I cry out, gripping the bedding in my fists. Rhys lowers me to the bed, then flips me to my tummy, tugs my ass up into the air, and slaps it good and hard on the right cheek.

"Do you trust me?"

"Of course," I reply immediately.

"Good girl. Grab onto the headboard," he instructs me, his voice harsh. I have to stretch out, flat on the bed, to reach the railings and grip them in my fists. "Don't let go." He rubs his palm over my bottom in slow, hypnotizing circles, then drops his fingers into my folds, sending my hips back against him, and finally I hear the tear of a foil packet and he guides himself inside me.

Oh. My. God.

He covers me completely with his long, lean body and presses his lips to my neck, then beside my ear.

"Your body makes me fucking crazy," he whispers. "I always want to take it slow, and then I can't."

"Next time," I whisper. "Just fuck me, Rhys."

He growls and picks up the pace, pushing harder, just a little faster. His hands cover mine, holding on tightly to the bed. Suddenly, he pulls out of me, gently guides my hands away from the iron rungs, and turns me over. He's sweating, panting, and the sexiest fucking thing I've ever seen.

Rather than lie back and let him have his way, I take

him in my mouth, tasting him *and* me.

"Holy fuck," he growls. "Gabrielle." His hands are immediately in my hair, as if he's torn between making me stop and encouraging me to continue.

So, I just keep going until every drop of me is licked off of him.

"I thought I should clean you off," I say with a sassy smile as I lie back on the bed and open my legs, then crook my finger at him, inviting him to join me.

"You surprise the shit out of me," he says as he kisses my belly, and then each of my breasts, teasing the nipples with his nose and tongue. The change in pace is fun, going from wild and urgent to lazy and playful.

He slips back inside me and covers me once more, his arms braced on either side of my head, hands in my hair, mouth just inches from my own.

"Every time I slip inside you is like the first time," he murmurs. "It's so fucking amazing."

"Mmm," I agree and close my eyes as he moves in long, slow strokes. "You fit me perfectly."

He kisses me softly. "I can taste you on your lips."

I grin.

"It's damn sexy."

"That was fun. I've never done that before."

His eyes flair. "I want you to have lots of firsts with me, baby."

"There have already been quite a few."

My hands trail down his back to his ass. God, I love his ass. I pull him even closer to me and we both gasp. "You have a great ass."

"Ass girl, are you?"

"I'm pretty much a fan of every part of your body."

He pauses and kisses the corner of my mouth. "I can't

get enough of you."

"I'm right here." I clench down on him and watch his eyes dilate. "Like that, do you?"

"God, you're going to kill me."

"I'm going to take that as a compliment."

"I'm concerned that you can string sentences together," he says matter-of-factly. "I think that means that I'm not doing my job."

"Oh, you're doing it." I catch my breath and bite my lip when he slips a hand between us and presses his thumb to my clit. "Oh yeah, definitely doing it."

He nibbles down my jaw to my neck while still pressing to my clit, moving just a little faster in and out of me, and now I can't even remember my name.

God, he makes me come undone.

Every. Time.

"Lost your words?"

"Fuck."

"That's a good one." He chuckles and grinds into me, pushing his pubis against his thumb and that's all it takes. I fall right over into oblivion.

He follows me over, then collapses on the bed next to me, breath heaving, sweating.

Sexy as ever.

"Why is this so easy with you?" I ask, staring at the ceiling, waiting for my heart to return to normal.

"Maybe I just know what I'm doing?" he replies sarcastically.

"Well, you do, yes." I chuckle and turn on my side, facing him. "But I'm comfortable with you. It's amazing, but it's also just...*easy*."

"Because we trust each other," he replies and gently runs his fingertip down the bridge of my nose. "I feel like

I've known you a long time. This might sound silly, but I feel like your heart and my heart are very old friends."

I blink at him as my heart swoons. But he's exactly right. I trust him. I feel like I've known him forever.

This feels like…*home.*

CHAPTER ELEVEN

~Gabby~

"Mom! Mom!" Sam jumps out of my mom's car and runs right for me, smiling and happy to be home. His face is a little darker from all the sunshine he's been soaking up in Florida.

And nothing ever looked so good in my life.

"Hey, sweet boy." I swoop him up in a big hug, holding him extra close, kissing his head and breathing him in. "Oh my goodness, I missed you."

"I was only gone for eight days," he says with a giggle, but he doesn't pull away quite yet.

"It was a long eight days. Entirely too quiet. And you're my baby. I missed you."

"I'm not a baby," he whispers. "But if it makes you feel better to hug me a really long time, I guess it's okay."

"Thank you so much," I say sarcastically, then pull back and take a look at him. "You had fun?"

He nods enthusiastically. "It was a lot of fun! But I think Nannan is ready for me to be home." He leans in and whispers in my ear. "I'm a handful."

I kiss his cheek, laughing, as I stand and smile at my mom. "Yes, you are. Hi, Mama."

"Hello, dawlin'." I pull Sam's suitcase out of the trunk and hug my petite mother. "Sam is the apple of my eye, and I couldn't love him more."

"But I'm a handful," Sam announces proudly. He's leaning against my side, his arm around my waist. He'll be extra clingy tonight at bedtime, and this is one time that I don't mind in the least.

"That you are, sweetheart," I reply. "Was he okay?"

"Oh, he's an angel," she says and I scoff. "He really is very good. Those kids just have so much energy! I need a nap." She hugs Sam and then me. "You look beautiful, sweet girl."

"Thank you, Mama."

"Thank you for taking me, Nannan," Sam says with a smile.

"You're welcome, child. I need to rest up for next year." She waves and drives away.

"I have something for you," I tell Sam as we walk up the steps of the front porch.

"You do? Where?" He starts searching my pockets, but I hold his hands away, laughing.

"Not on me. Here." I pass the bag that Neil left for him and watch him dig in, then look up at me with wide eyes.

"Wow! All this stuff is signed!"

"Yep. Neil came down to visit Rhys, and he left this stuff for you."

"Oh, man! I miss all the good stuff!" His shoulders slump and he pouts for just a moment, but then he pulls the jersey over his head and grins. It hangs down to his knees, but he doesn't care in the least.

"Lookin' good."

"Where's Rhys?"

"Right here." The man in question walks up the porch stairs and pats Sam's back as my son hugs Rhys around the waist. "Hey, buddy."

"I'm so happy that you're still here!"

Suddenly, my phone rings in my pocket. The caller ID says Unknown Number, but I answer anyway. "Hello?"

Nothing.

"Hello?" I say again with a frown, but the line clicks and the call ends. Huh. Must have been a wrong number.

"No one there?" Rhys asks.

"Nope. Probably a telemarketer." I shrug and pocket the phone.

"Mom, can I go play catch with Mr. Rhys?"

"Why don't you join us?" Rhys adds with a grin.

"Moms don't play catch," Sam says with a frown. "She's a girl."

"Hey, now." I prop my hands on my hips and narrow my eyes on my son. "Girls can definitely play catch. I do it with you all the time."

Sam grins. "Prove it."

"And the gauntlet has been thrown!" Rhys claps his hands. "Do you have another mitt, Sam?"

"Sure!" He runs inside to gather the mitts and balls.

"He loves you so much," Rhys says, surprising me.

"I love him back," I reply.

"I know."

"I found them!" Sam comes running back outside, down the steps, and into the front yard. "Come on!"

We each put a mitt on, and Sam starts by tossing the ball to Rhys, who then throws the ball to me. I easily catch it.

"Wow, Mom, good catch!" Sam laughs and spins in a circle.

"Pay attention. It's coming for you." I throw the ball to Sam, and he catches it.

"Nice arm," Rhys says.

"Don't sound so surprised. I had three older brothers, you know."

Sam throws the ball back to me.

"Show me what you've got," Rhys says and backs farther away from me, then holds his hand up, ready to catch what I throw him.

So I do.

I throw it just like Beau showed me when I was kid, and the ball lands in Rhys's glove. I hold my glove up. "Don't be easy on me."

"I will hurt you, sugar. I've been clocked at one hundred miles an hour."

"Don't throw me a fast ball," I reply with a roll of my eyes. "I'm not Neil. But I'm not a wimp."

I punch my fist into my mitt and spread my legs, ready for whatever he throws at me.

He watches me for a minute, his eyes full of humor, and not a little bit of lust, and finally he smiles at me in that way that makes my stomach clench. He winds up, as if he's at the mound, and throws the ball right into my mitt.

It stings the hell out of my hand, but I'll be damned if I'll say so.

"Nice catch."

"Nice throw."

Rhys smirks at my compliment as Sam jumps up and down.

"Throw it to me!" I oblige Sam just as two cars pull into the driveway.

"Okay guys, looks like it's time for me to work. You play."

"Hold on." Rhys holds a finger up for Sam to wait a second to throw the ball and jogs over to me. He leans in to whisper in my ear. "You throwing that ball the way you just did was hot."

"I have all kinds of hidden talents you don't know about yet."

He smiles widely and kisses my cheek, then backs away. "So noted."

***

All of the guests have checked in, settled their things, and have set off again on adventures. Food is prepared for both tonight's wine hour and breakfast for tomorrow.

I'm officially caught up.

So I set off in search of the boys. I saw them walk around the house earlier toward the barn.

As I approach the barn, I can hear music playing and my son giggling.

"Twenty-nine! Thirty! Thirty-one!" Sam is counting loudly, almost gleefully. I step inside and stop short when I see Rhys executing perfect push-ups with my son sitting on his shoulders, smiling as if he were on a ride at Disney. "Hi, Mom! Mr. Rhys needed more weight!"

"I see."

"Oh good, you're here." Rhys stops and smiles up at me. "Hey, Sam, hop off. I need more weight than you. Let's give your mom a turn."

"It's really fun, Mom." He climbs off and waits expectedly for me to climb on.

"You're serious."

"Yep." Rhys grins. "Climb on."

I raise a brow, my mind immediately taking a dive into

the gutter, and Rhys's smile widens, clearly reading my thoughts.

"You want me to sit on your shoulders?"

"Yes."

"Why?"

"Because I need more weight."

I look between both of these handsome men, then shrug and sit Indian-style on Rhys's shoulders. He pushes up, surprising me, making me yelp.

"How's your balance?" he asks, as if he's not lifting a whole separate person as he does push-ups.

"Off," I reply with a giggle and hold my hand out for Sam, who immediately takes it and walks around to stand at Rhys's head. "That's better. My boy saved me."

Sam smiles widely, missing half of his teeth. I decide to make this a game. Each time Rhys pushes up, I kiss Sam's cheek, making him giggle.

"How many kisses can I give Sam, Rhys?"

"How many do you want to give him?"

Smack.

"Lots and lots." I kiss Sam's other cheek, making him giggle. He doesn't often let me kiss him anymore, but this is a fun game.

I'm going to take advantage of it.

"How many is that?" Rhys asks as I kiss Sam loudly.

"Ten!" Sam exclaims.

"Oh, we can do better than that," Rhys says. After twenty-five kisses, Rhys collapses, finally breathing heavily.

"Are we done?" I ask.

"For now."

I climb off and Rhys stands, but before I can turn and walk out, he takes my hand and leads me to a bench, making me straddle it on one end.

"Sam, I have a question," Rhys begins, holding my gaze in his.

"Okay," Sam says.

"Would you mind if I kissed your mom?"

I feel my eyes grow wide and I start to shake my head, but Sam makes a gagging noise.

"Why?"

"Because," Rhys replies with a chuckle, "I think she's pretty, and I want to play another exercise game."

"Oh." Sam seems to think it over, and then shrugs. "Okay. If you want to."

"Gee, thanks." My tone is dry, but I'm smiling at both of them. Rhys straddles the bench, facing me. God, he's beautiful. He's only wearing a black tank and shorts. He's sweaty. A little dirty.

And I want to strip him bare and climb him.

Instead, I wait for him to give me instructions.

"I'm going to do sit-ups," he says and gently glides his knuckles down my cheek, making me soften and go all gooey inside.

Sweet baseball player.

"Every time I come up, I get a kiss."

"How many sit-ups do you plan to do?" Sam asks curiously.

"About a hundred."

"Ew. I'm gonna go throw my ball at the tree." He runs out, clearly disgusted at the thought of Rhys kissing me one hundred times.

I'm not disgusted by it in the least.

But instead of lying back to begin, he leans forward and touches his lips to mine. "You look happy."

"I am happy. Sam's home. I know he can be a lot of work, but he's the best part of my life, and I missed him."

"I missed him too," he admits softly. "And I don't think he's a lot to handle. I think he's a kid who has a lot of energy and he's intelligent, so he has a lot to say. There's nothing wrong with that."

"Yeah, he gets the talking a lot from me."

"He has so much of you in him. He's amazing."

I blink at him, stunned. I know that Sam is lovable. I'm proud to be raising such a great kid. But to hear Rhys say such kind things about my son touches me in a whole new way.

Because Sam *is* my world. If someone wants to be with me, I'm a package deal.

"I'm glad you like him. He likes you, very much."

Rhys kisses me again, then lies back on the bench, ready to get down to business. "Okay, enough slacking."

He begins to easily execute the sit-ups, kissing me with each one.

"This is the best workout I've ever participated in," I tell him as I watch his body flex. Good God, he makes me crazy. I even like the stubble on his face. "I'm getting all kinds of affection today."

"Why do I get the feeling," he says, but pauses to kiss me, "that you don't get nearly enough affection in your life?"

Because I don't.

"I'm not complaining," I reply.

"I didn't say you were." *Kiss.* "But you should—" *Kiss.*"—get kisses all the time."

"My seven-year-old isn't very hip on kisses these days." He sits up, kiss me, and rests, panting just a bit. "How do you exercise so hard, and you're barely out of breath?"

He shrugs and takes a sip of the water bottle that was sitting by his feet. "I've been doing it a long time."

"I'd want to die by now."

"No you wouldn't. You're a tiny thing."

"I'm petite, but that doesn't mean I'm in shape, it just means my mom passed on good genetics."

"True enough." He lies back and begins another long set of sit-ups, kissing me with each one. I really should go inside in case any of the guests come back and need something, but this is so…*fun.* "Okay. One more round of push-ups."

He assumes the position on the mat on the floor.

"Instead of sitting on my shoulders, you can lie on me. It'll be easier for your balance."

"I think you just want me to lie on you."

He flashes me a smile. "Guilty."

I climb on him, face down, and wrap my arms around his torso, cross my ankles so my feet don't get in his way, and lay my cheek between his shoulder blades, enjoying the ride as he effortlessly and quickly executes fifty push-ups.

I'm actually disappointed when it's time to climb off of him.

"I almost fell asleep."

"I'm glad one of us did," he says, breathing heavily. "I'm done for the day."

"How is your shoulder feeling?"

"Good." He rolls his shoulder, rubbing it with his opposite hand. "There's no more ache."

"That's great."

Does that mean you'll leave soon?

I should ask the question, but I don't want to know the answer. Not yet.

"You okay?" He tips my chin up gently and searches my face.

"I'm great." I offer him a smile and turn my face into

his hand, kiss his palm, and then pull away. "I should just go in and get a little work done."

"Need any help?"

The best part about this man? Aside from the smoking hot body and the sex? He's sincere. He's a millionaire, but helping me with menial household tasks is a no-brainer for him, just like it is for my family, and that is very, *very* attractive to me.

Maybe too attractive, because I could get used to it. And that's not good.

"I've got it handled. I also need to take a trip to the grocery to pick up a couple things. Do you mind keeping an eye on Sam?"

"We could all go."

I shake my head. *No, I need a break from all the testosterone flying around here.*

"It'll be really quick. I just need a couple things."

He tips his head to the side, watching me carefully, but then he just kisses my forehead and nods. "No problem."

***

"Mom, I'm bored."

I roll my eyes and continue chopping celery for the tuna salad. "Baseball camp starts on Monday."

"That's, like, *four days* away. What am I supposed to do for four days?"

"Read? Ride your bike? Clean that pit you call a bedroom?"

"None of that is fun." He lowers his head to his arms, sulking at the breakfast bar.

"I don't think that's true. Besides, Uncle Beau will be around over the weekend and you can pester him, I'm sure."

"Yeah. Maybe we can build a birdhouse or

something."

"That would be cool."

"Maybe Mr. Rhys can help."

"I'm sure he'd enjoy that."

Sam nods. "But that's still *days* away."

"Two days." I load the bread up with tuna salad and pass Sam his lunch. "And guess what?"

"What?"

"Your puppy is coming home on Tuesday, after baseball camp is over."

"Really?" He squeals, all smiles. "He's coming home?"

"He is." I nod and ruffle his hair. "So, you'll have plenty to keep you busy in just a couple of days."

"We need to get him food bowls and blankets and toys."

"And a bed."

"No, he's going to sleep with me."

"He can sleep in your room, but he'll have his own bed." Sam frowns at me, and it's like looking in a mirror when I'm being stubborn.

It takes everything in me not to laugh.

"I mean it."

"Yes, ma'am."

"Why do you look like someone just took your birthday away?" Rhys asks as he saunters into the room. He eyes the tuna salad, then me, as if he'd like to devour both of us.

He must be hungry.

I immediately make a sandwich and set it before him.

"Mom won't let the puppy sleep in my bed with me. She's going to make him sleep way down on the *floor!*"

"Dogs are supposed to sleep on the floor," Rhys says reasonably and bites into his sandwich. "They aren't people."

"But he's a baby. He might get scared."

"We'll cross that bridge when we get there," I say sternly, giving Sam the look that says that this conversation is over.

"Yes, ma'am."

"I just got a call from Chicago," Rhys says, watching my face, and my stomach clenches.

This is it. He's leaving.

God, I don't want him to go.

"The team wants me to come up for a checkup with their doctor and therapist, and I need to have a meeting with the coaching staff. I'm flying out on Tuesday."

"Are you leaving forever?" Sam asks with wide eyes, voicing exactly what I'm thinking, and it breaks my heart that he's clearly become just as attached to Rhys as I have.

And I don't know what to do about it.

"No, buddy, just overnight."

"Oh, good!" Sam goes back to his lunch.

Oh, good.

"You should come with me." Rhys's eyes are still pinned to mine, watching me closely. "I'd love to show you Chicago."

"I can't." I shake my head and turn away, cleaning the kitchen.

"Think about it."

"Let's go, Mom!"

"I can't," I repeat. "I have a business to run, Rhys. I can't leave on such short notice. And Sam starts baseball camp that day." He looks disappointed, so I soften my tone and reach over to cover his hand with mine. "Thank you for inviting us. Really. But I can't get away."

He turns his hand over and grips mine tightly. "I

know. I just thought it would be fun."

"It would be fun," Sam grumbles.

"You're grouchy today," I say to him and spoon some fruit onto his plate.

"You're mean today," he replies. I take a deep breath and let it out slowly.

"Samuel Beauregard Boudreaux, I love you, but you are on my very last nerve today. Please adjust your sails."

He sulks some more. "Can I just go read in my room?"

"I would be thrilled if you did that."

He skulks away to his bedroom.

"What's wrong?" Rhys asks.

"He's bored."

"No, what's wrong with you?"

I frown and keep my gaze pinned to the countertop as I wipe it down. *You're leaving soon, and I'm falling in love with you, and my child loves you, and I need to work harder at keeping a distance from you.*

"Nothing."

"Bullshit." He circles the island and cups my face in his hands, searching my gaze.

God, his eyes are potent.

Dumb eyes.

"You've never lied to me before."

"Or so you think."

His nostrils flare in annoyance. I think this is the first time he's been angry with me.

And I don't like it.

"Nothing's wrong, Rhys. My mood is probably reflecting Sam's. Maybe I just need to adjust my own sails."

He pulls me into a tight hug, tucking my face against his chest, right over his heart, and the sound of his heartbeat makes me want to cry.

And why that is, I have no idea.

Except *he's leaving*. And even if it is just for one night, there will come a day in the not-too-distant future that he'll be leaving for good.

And that hurts.

CHAPTER TWELVE

~Gabby~

It's a gorgeous Monday morning. There are still a few hours before the guests will start to arrive, and Sam is at his first day of baseball camp. His friend Henry's mom picked him up and will drop him back off when it's over.

Tomorrow I have car-pool duty.

The ceiling fans are whirling above on the front porch, combining with the breeze coming off the river to make us cool. Rhys is sitting next to me, his computer in his lap, typing away. Every once in a while, he'll murmur to himself, scratch his head, then get back to it.

I actually have a little time to read, so I'm indulging in the newest Laurelin Paige novel, full of lust and sex and lots of romance.

Romance novels are my biggest guilty pleasure.

And this woman can *write*.

I glance up as a car pulls into the driveway, surprised to see my longtime friend Cindy. I haven't seen her in a couple of months. I usually don't hear much from her when she's with a new guy, and last I heard, she had found some rich guy to dig her claws into.

Cindy climbs out of her car and waves, a smile on her pretty face. She's much taller than me, with long, platinum blonde hair and a pretty face, but she's always dressed way too skimpy for my taste, and she makes no apologies for the fact that she enjoys men.

More specifically, she enjoys sex and what those men can do for her.

I didn't say she was a *good* friend.

"That's Cindy," I say before Rhys can ask. He looks up from his computer, seemingly unaware that Cindy even showed up.

I wonder what he's working on.

"Hey, girl!" Cindy climbs the stairs of the porch and gives me one of those side-hugs, where you barely touch the other person.

"Hi there. What's up?"

"I couldn't just come by to say hi?"

I roll my eyes and shake my head. "You never do that."

"I know. Sorry." She so doesn't look sorry. "I was wondering if I could borrow that black dress you wore out a few months ago? The off-the-shoulder one? It's super cute, and I have a date on Friday."

"It's short on me." I frown, glancing down at Cindy's long legs. "It'll be super short on you."

"Exactly." She smiles, showing off a dimple in her left cheek, and winks at me.

"Sure. I'll go get it."

I hear Cindy introduce herself to Rhys as I climb the stairs to my room. While I'm rummaging through my closet, the screen door slams shut, and when I'm on my way back down the stairs, I can hear voices in the kitchen. I check the front porch just to be sure, and just as I thought, it's empty.

"Oh, come on," Cindy says, stopping me from walking into the room, listening. "I'm one helluva lay. You must be bored to tears out here all by yourself with the stick-in-the-mud Gabby and her bratty kid."

"Not interested," Rhys says simply.

I bite my lip. My hands are in fists, gripping the material of my favorite black dress.

"Are you telling me you're not interested in these tits? I paid a lot of money for them."

No, someone else paid a lot of money for them, Cindy.

"I can make you really happy, handsome," she continues. Her voice makes me sick. I've never heard her talk like that before. My blood is boiling, and I should march in there and rip her a new one, but I'm dying to hear what Rhys's response is.

He doesn't disappoint me.

"I'm only going to tell you this one time," he says with a cool, hard voice. "I'm not interested in anything you have to offer. Ever. You're not sexy. You're not attractive. And I want you to stop trying to hit on me."

"You're seriously passing this up?"

"Give it a damn rest, Cindy," I say as I barge into the kitchen. She narrows her eyes on me, and Rhys simply crosses his arms over his chest and leans his hip against the countertop. Cindy is standing closer than I'm comfortable with to Rhys, and she moves closer to him, making him scowl.

"Rhys was just flirting with me."

My jaw drops and Rhys tips his head back and laughs long and loud.

"You know Cindy, I always knew you were a slut, but I didn't think you were stupid enough to come into my home and try to have sex with my guests."

"Oh grow up," she spits out and then cackles. "I've fucked every man in your life, going way back."

She shakes her head and stares at me like she feels sorry for me, and my whole body stills.

"I fucked that high school guy you liked. What was his name? Scott?" She smirks. "And then there was Colby. He was fucking me the whole summer that you two were together."

Bile rises in the back of my throat, but I simply raise a brow and act like I could give a shit.

And really, it's not that I care *now* that she slept with Colby; it's that she clearly has no respect for me. She doesn't even *like* me very much, and while I've always known that Cindy is selfish, I didn't realize how much she flat-out hated me.

"I even fucked your brother, for Christsakes."

"Yuck," I mutter, still clueless as to what Eli was thinking when he made *that* mistake.

He must have been drunk.

"So what you're saying is," I begin and chew my lip. "Is that you're nothing but a dirty whore who uses me to find guys who are willing to throw you a pity fuck."

She blinks furiously, her cheeks redden with pure rage and she fists her hands.

"You *bitch!*"

"Watch your goddamn mouth," I growl at her and toss the dress on a stool while advancing on her. "You will not speak to me, or anyone, like that in *my* home. I don't care if you decide to screw every man in the state of Louisiana—"

"Except me," Rhys adds.

"But you won't come in here and try to get laid. As far as our friendship, it's over as of five minutes ago, as is the extra money you used to make off of me. *I'm done.* I've stuck up for you for *years,* Cindy. I gave you a job in my inn. That's all over."

I glance over at Rhys, to find him watching me, his green eyes warm and smiling. Hot. His mouth isn't tipped up, but I can see the pride in his eyes as I give Cindy the tongue lashing she deserves.

She's lucky I don't cut a switch and take it to her backside.

"Look, I'm sorry that I hit on the guy you're fucking, although why he'd waste his time on you, I have no idea."

"That's it," Rhys says calmly, almost *too* calmly. "Get the hell out of here."

Cindy's gaze whips to mine and I simply tip my head to the side. "Are you deaf *and* dumb?"

Her lips are pursed, she's panting with anger, her blue eyes are flashing as she stomps out of the kitchen, and a few seconds later the front door slams shut.

I sigh deeply and shake my head.

"I'm sorry about that."

"What in the hell are you sorry for?" Rhys asks.

"Well, that was...unpleasant."

"That was a shit-show," he replies and then chuckles. "And you took care of it."

"Well, you are hard to resist," I inform him, smiling now. "I mean, I understand why she hit on you. You're all tall and muscly and stuff."

"Muscly and stuff?"

"Mmm."

"Well, you were fucking hot with your big hazel eyes flashing, telling her what the score is. How did you ever end up with a friend like that anyway?"

"I've known her since the first grade." I shrug. "I guess it was just habit. I don't think I even particularly liked her. I just never got rid of her."

He nods. "Women are weird like that."

"Yeah."

"Come on." He holds his hand out for mine and leads me to the porch again. "I have more emails to send, and you still have time before people start showing up."

"I should work."

"I'm leaving in the morning, and I want every minute with you I can get." He grins back at me. "And yes, I plan to sneak into bed with you after Sam goes to sleep."

Thank God.

***

"I wish you'd come with me," Rhys murmurs against my lips early the next morning. We're standing next to his rental car. He's holding me close to him, kissing me as if he's never going to see me again.

Is this what it'll look like when he finally does leave for good?

"Be safe," I say, gripping onto his arms. "I'll see you tomorrow, you know."

He sighs and leans his forehead against mine. "Why does it feel like you won't miss me?"

"Are you going to miss me?"

He tips those lips up at the corner, giving me that sexy half-smile. "More than I'm comfortable with, Gabrielle."

Well, okay.

"I might miss you a little."

He slaps my ass, then lowers his long body into the driver's seat and slams the door.

"See you tomorrow," he says when he lowers the window.

"See you." I wave as he pulls away, and then return to the inn to make sure that all of the guests have had breakfast, and the ones leaving today are checked out. My cleaning crew is already here, working hard on the rooms. I have just enough time to take Sam to camp for a couple hours, then come home and get to work.

It'll be a busy day, but that's good. It'll keep my mind occupied on things that aren't the fact that Rhys isn't here.

Because that's just silly.

"Are you ready, buddy?" I ask Sam as I bustle through the kitchen, tuck a box of Cheerios back into the pantry and set Sam's bowl in the sink.

"Yep! We get the puppy today!"

"I know." I smile and take his hand in mine, leading him to my car. "It was nice of Rhys to take us out yesterday to buy all of the things we'll need."

"The puppy is going to like the plastic baseball the best," he informs me.

"How do you know?"

"Because he's *my* puppy."

"Oh, right. Of course."

Baseball camp is fun for the kids. They spend a few hours learning all of the basics, then play a short three-inning game. There are the usual falls and tiffs, and inevitably one of the boys bursts out in tears, but for the most part, it's just fun.

When they're done, Sam and I drive just a few miles away to a parking lot where we're meeting the lady with the puppy.

"Oh, Mom, look!" Sam jumps out of the car and goes running to the smiling woman with the puppy in her arms. The dog is squirming, trying to break free and join Sam, but she holds him strong.

"Hi there," I say when I join them.

"Hi. Well, Sam, what do you think?"

"I think he's awesome!" Sam is rubbing the pup's ears

gently. "He likes me."

"I think so too." She passes the dog to my son, who laughs as he gets his face kissed, which really just makes my stomach turn.

I'm pretty sure I know where that tongue has been.

"That's it, unless you have questions. But you have my number, so feel free to call if you need anything."

"Thanks." I get the boy and his dog settled in the back seat and set off for home.

In the short ten-minute drive, the dog has been in the front seat, the back seat, and returned to the front seat seventeen times.

Seventeen.

I'm relieved that we live on enough land that I'm not worried about Sam and the puppy playing in the yard. We also don't live near a busy road, so Sam should be able to play with him without the leash.

And that puppy definitely needs to burn off some steam.

"What are you naming him?" I ask Sam.

"Derek."

I choke, sputtering and laughing at the same time.

"Derek? Why that?"

"Because Derek Jeter retired, and I know I'm not a Yankees fan, but it's all about respect, Mom."

"Ah," I reply seriously. "What if you called him Jeter?"

"Jeter is a *last* name." He rolls his eyes like I just don't get it, making me smile more. "Derek is a first name."

"Okay, it's your dog." I hold my hands up in surrender, then lift the puppy into my arms, cuddling and nuzzling the sweet little guy. He really is adorable. He's red in color, and his ears are almost as big as the rest of him. And oh, that sweet puppy smell. I might be a little in love with him myself. "Make sure he goes pee, then you can take him in and show him your room and the kitchen."

"Okay! Come on, Derek."

Derek.

My kiddo is hilarious.

I walk to my desk to fetch my iPad so I can open my scheduling program for the inn to double-check the guest list, who is staying where, and to see if anyone has booked online since yesterday afternoon.

But it's not on my desk. I check the kitchen, my bedroom, and even my car.

Nothing.

Where in the hell did I leave it? I'm crippled without it. I hate flying blind, not knowing which guests I've assigned to which room, and I definitely can't take phone reservations without my scheduling program.

My phone suddenly rings, and glancing down at it, it's the same *unknown caller* again.

"Hello?"

There's a long pause, and then the call ends.

God, I hate that.

Okay, Gabby, adjust your sails. You can't find the iPad. What now?

My computer. I can log into the program on my computer and use it there until I find the damn iPad.

I hope.

I try to log in, but it says my password is wrong. Did I forget it? I always use the same one: SAMSMOM.

Nope, won't let me sign in.

What the freaking hell?

I don't have time to deal with this, so I call Beau.

"Can I borrow your iPad? I can't find mine."

"Sure, but I brought it to work with me."

"Great." I hang my head in my hands. I'm going to have to fly blind as it is, at least until Beau gets home. "Will you please bring it to me when you get home?"

"Sure."

"Thanks." I hang up and suddenly hear a commotion coming from the kitchen.

"Mom! Hurry!"

I jump up, running for the kitchen and my phone rings again.

"Hello?"

Silence and then the call ends. This is getting incredibly annoying.

I hurry to the kitchen and then stop dead in my tracks at the scene before me.

Derek is splashing in two inches of water on my kitchen floor, getting both him and Sam wet. My dishwasher is moaning and making the craziest noise I've ever heard.

Why didn't I just replace it, rather than have it repaired? It's not like I can't afford it. What the hell is wrong with me?

"Is that dog poop on my kitchen floor?" I yell, pointing to the pile just outside the edge of the water line.

"Sorry," Sam says, then giggles when Derek splashes him. "He didn't mean it."

"Get him outside. Now." I scrub my fingers through my scalp, and then reach for a mop and sanitary wipes to clean up the mess.

And then my phone rings. Again. I wouldn't answer the *unknown number*, but it could be a guest.

"Hello."

Now my patience is wearing very, very thin. "Hello, damn it!"

Click.

"You know what?" I rant and pace over to the fridge, open it, and set the phone inside. "I'm done with this. I need to put it out of sight out of mind for a bit. I have poop—*poop, for God's sake*—to clean up, a lake to sop up, and I can't find my goddamn iPad!"

I take care of the stinky mess made by the formerly cutest puppy ever, and get busy mopping up water, working quickly because guests should be arriving soon.

And just when I think the last of the water is gone, I hear a very familiar, horrifying crash upstairs.

"Oh, crap!" I hear Sam yell outside. Yep, he's broken another window. "Mom, Derek threw the ball through the window!"

I bend over the countertop, bury my face in my arms, and pray for a martini and about four more of me.

This is the day from hell.

***

"I can't believe Sam broke another window, on top of everything else," Beau says with a chuckle, earning a glare from me. "Not that it's funny."

"It's not funny," I reply, but then can't help but let out a tiny giggle. "Okay, it's kind of funny now."

"We'll replace the dishwasher," he says.

"Don't tell her how to run her business," Van says as she bustles into the kitchen with an empty plate from the wine hour in the sitting room. "She has this handled."

"Clearly, I don't."

"Today was just a crappy day, sugar," Van says and pulls me in for a big hug that feels *so good.* I didn't even realize how badly I needed it until right now. "Go to bed. I'll finish up with this. There's only an hour left anyway. You could use the rest."

"Are you sure?"

"Wow, she is tired if she's barely putting up a fight," Beau says. "Yes, go. Oh, here's my iPad."

I frown at it. "Just leave it on my desk. I'll deal with it in the morning."

Beau nods just as Sam sticks his head around the doorjamb. "Derek doesn't want to go to sleep."

"And here we go," I mutter.

"I can deal with this," Van says, but I shake my head.

"No, I'll put them to bed, then go that way myself. Thank you for this."

"Good night."

"Come on." I take Sam's tiny hand in mine and lead him to his bedroom, where Derek is dead asleep, under the covers, with his head on Sam's pillow. "Scared, huh?"

Sam nods solemnly.

I glance at the chair in the corner of the room that I used to rock Sam in, and rather than over think it, I lift the sleeping puppy and give him to Sam, then lift Sam and settle in the chair with my boy and his pup in my arms.

"What are we doing?" Sam whispers.

"We're going to rock for a little while. Want me to sing?"

He yawns and nods, petting Derek, who isn't even aware that he's been moved. Infants and puppies sleep like the dead.

You are my sunshine, my only sunshine...

I begin to rock slowly and softly sing the song that my daddy sang to me when I was a little girl. I've sang this song for Sam since the day he was born. It soothes us both.

And for some reason, I need soothing.

It's not because it was a craptastic day. I've had plenty of those.

I miss Rhys.

And he's been gone for twelve hours.

Sam nuzzles against me and breathes deeply, falling asleep, and I just rock and hum for a long while, enjoying the way my sweet baby feels in my arms. The demon puppy is cute too, curled up on Sam's chest, snoring softly.

This. This, right here, is the most important part of my life, and I'll do good to remember that.

Finally, I stand and lay Sam in his bed. I leave Derek with him, resigned that I'll lose the *no puppies in beds* rule.

After all, what's the harm?

Once in my own room, I change into pajamas, brush my hair, and search for my phone on my way to the bed. God, I'm so damn tired, but I would like to hear Rhys's voice before I fall asleep, and I haven't spoken to him all day.

But I have no idea where I left my phone, and honestly, I'm just too tired to go hunt for it.

So I fall into bed, curl into a ball, and simply crash into sleep.

CHAPTER THIRTEEN

~Rhys~

"You're doing great, Rhys," Doc says as he sits at the conference table with me, Coach, and the trainers for the team. "The PT you've been doing is working. The muscle is healing nicely."

"I feel one hundred percent," I reply honestly. "I'm not achy or sore anymore."

"Ever?" he asks with a raised brow.

"If I push myself too hard, I feel it," I admit. There's no need to lie. This isn't going to put me out of the game forever.

Thank Christ.

"That's to be expected," Doc replies with a nod. "I'm going to keep you out for the rest of this season, but keep doing what you're doing, and you'll be ready for spring training."

"This is great news," Coach says with a sigh. I know that he and everyone else were worried that I wouldn't come back from this.

It terrified the fuck out of me.

"What can I expect when I return?" I ask.

"Good question," Doc says. "There are a number of possibilities. You could lose or gain velocity on your fastball. You could tire more quickly, and you'd need to be replaced early in a game."

"Fuck that," I mutter.

"But you could also come back stronger than ever, and never have another problem. We won't really know until it happens."

"What, exactly, have you been doing?" A young female trainer named Julie asks. "Can you walk us through your routine? The exercises you're doing? How it feels in your shoulder when you do them?"

I comply, describing the hours and hours of hard work, pushing and pulling weights, executing pushups with Gabby or Sam on my back, and the dozens of other small range-of-motion exercises I put my shoulders through every day.

"In the beginning, it hurt like a sonofabitch," I say with a rueful smile. "And now I'm able to flow from one exercise to the next. If I push too hard, it aches. It doesn't feel like it's going to tear again; it simply feels tired. But I ice it and rest it for a day, and I'm fine."

"When can we start advertising that Rhys is returning?" Melanie Sloan, my publicist, asks.

"Whenever you like," Doc replies. "He'll be back in the spring."

"Thank you," I reply. "I'm ready to get back to work."

"Enjoy a few more months off," Coach says as we all stand to leave. "I'm going to work your ass off before long."

He isn't lying.

Coach Adams is the most demanding, hard-ass coach I've ever worked for.

And I admire and respect him like no other.

He demands a work ethic from each of his players that is unparalleled. He expects a lot from us, but that's what gets the job done.

I just smile and follow him out of the room.

"Don't forget," Melanie says in her stern voice as she follows behind us. "You have to film the commercial for the Children's Hospital in about five weeks."

"I'll be back for it," I reply. "Don't worry."

"You're not the one I have to worry about," she says. "But it doesn't hurt to remind you."

One of the trainers catches Coach's attention, giving me a second to check my phone. No messages from Gabby. I haven't heard from her all day. I've sent several texts, and even tried to call once, but she isn't answering.

I'm getting worried.

I quickly type out another message.

How's your day going?

There are handshakes and man-hugs exchanged as the trainers and Melanie leave, and now it's just Coach and me.

"I heard what you did for Neil," he begins, following me to my rental car. I lean my ass on the driver's window, facing the man who's almost as tall as me, and at fifty-five, almost as fit as me too.

"I was surprised that he drove all the way to New Orleans," I reply.

"I'm not. I was hoping he would when I told him he needed a week off to get his shit straight."

"How's he doing?"

"Better." Coach sighs and drops his hands into his pockets. "And how are you? Really?"

"I told you, I'm—"

"I know what you told the doctor to get cleared to play.

And I'm fucking relieved as fuck that you'll be back in the spring. But how are *you*?"

How am I? I brush my hand over my mouth, thinking of Gabby and Sam and the inn. Despite being out for the season, I'm content.

I'm *happy*.

"I'm doing really well."

"Who is she?" Coach asks with a twitch to his lips. He's always been an arrogant know-it-all ass.

Of course, he's always right.

"Gabby," I reply softly and stare at the mostly empty parking lot.

"And she lives in New Orleans?"

"About thirty minutes outside of the city, yes. She runs the inn that I've been staying at."

"An innkeeper." He raises a shaggy grey brow. "Hard worker."

He's always right.

"Fucking hard worker," I agree with a nod. "She's beautiful. Smart. So much smarter than me." I smile and shake my head, rubbing the back of my neck anxiously.

Why am I anxious?

"She has a little boy. He's seven, and probably the biggest Cubs fan there is."

"I bet he's enjoying having you around," Coach says with a smile.

"I enjoy having him around too. He's as smart as his mom, and the things he says are funny."

"You're in love with them."

I sigh and nod and then I just stare at this man that I trust as much as I trust anyone in my life.

"I don't know what the fuck to do about it."

He laughs. "Keep loving them."

"Is it that simple?" I ask and pace a few feet away, then back again. "How can I make it work? I have a demanding career that keeps me on the road more than half of the year. I'm based out of *Chicago*, for fuck sake. She has a thriving family business in New Orleans."

"Last time I checked, you make a shit-ton of money."

I smirk. "Sam's in school."

"The majority of our season is during the summer," he replies. "Look, a lot of players manage to have happy families and a baseball career. It can be a juggling act during the season, but it's doable. Bring them with you. You can afford it. Live in New Orleans in the off season."

He makes a lot of sense. Maybe I can talk Gabby into hiring some help and she and Sam can join me during most of the season.

Because the thought of living without them leaves an ache in me that the thought of losing baseball never did.

"You've never been one to shy away from hard work, Rhys."

I scowl. "Fuck no. You know hard work doesn't scare me."

"Good because if you thought baseball was hard, just wait until you start working on a relationship. Is she worth it?"

A slow smile spreads over my face as I think of Gabby, with her long dark hair and hazel eyes. How she makes me laugh, and simply makes me feel damn good.

"Yeah, she's worth it."

"I look forward to meeting her and her son." Coach grins and claps me on my uninjured shoulder. "Maybe I'll bring the missus down there after the season is over to check out her inn. My wife is insanely patient during the season. She deserves a trip."

"You should. It's great."

"You know, if you ever have questions about bringing a family along for this ride, or if Gabby ever needs anything, you can call my wife, or any of the other married players. We stick together, and no one wants you to fail."

"Thank you." I nod, feeling even more comfortable, *relieved,* and convinced that this is going to work. "I may take you up on it."

"Wouldn't offer if I didn't expect you to." He claps my shoulder again and then backs away toward his own car. "Safe travels back, son."

I wave and settle in the car, but before I drive toward the hotel, I check my phone again.

Nothing.

It's late evening now. I spent all day in tests and meetings, consultations and hours and hours with my publicist, discussing all of the endorsement opportunities that she has lined up for me.

I'll be damned if I'll plug athletes' foot cream. Fuck that.

I also spent part of the day in meetings with lawyers going over contracts, financial advisors.

The whole gamut.

I check my phone and frown when there is no response from Gabby. I try to call her again, but it goes to voice mail.

Where the fuck is she? What if something happened to her?

I chew on my lip and tap my fingers on the steering wheel. I'm supposed to head back down there tomorrow morning, but I can't reach Gabby.

Fuck it.

I dial Melanie's number.

"Did we forget something?" she asks with a smile in

her voice.

"I want to go back to New Orleans tonight instead of tomorrow."

There's a pause. "I can try to switch your flight, but at this hour, there probably isn't anything until morning anyway."

"Charter a flight."

Another pause. "Are you okay, Rhys?"

"I'm fine. I need to get to New Orleans *tonight*. I can afford the damn plane, Mel."

"Okay. Consider it done. I'll call you when I have the details."

"Thanks."

I click off and head for the hotel to get my bag and check out. I'm sure she's fine. I'm sure I'm overreacting, but damn it, I need to see her.

I need her.

***

It's late when I arrive at the inn. Or, early I guess, since it's about four o'clock in the morning. The inn is dark, aside from the foyer light that Gabby always leaves on, and I'm thankful that I still have my room key so I can get inside without having to wake her.

It's quiet, and yet, it already feels more like home than the house in Denver that Kate and I shared ever did.

I walk back to Gabby and Sam's private quarters. It's simple back here, just two bedrooms, a bathroom and a little sitting area with a TV and comfortable couch for Sam to play and watch his shows.

I check on Sam first. He's sleeping hard with his puppy curled up beside him. Neither of them even flutter an eyelash when I kiss Sam's forehead and rub the pup's ears.

I close the door the way Sam likes, leaving it cracked

so the hall light shines in just a bit, then quietly let myself into Gabby's room. It's dark, and just as quiet as the rest of the house, and when my eyes adjust, I can see that she's curled up in the center of the bed.

She's so fucking tiny. I can lift her like she's nothing. But fuck me, what she lacks in size she makes up for in spirit.

The woman has a big personality. I love it.

I undress and slip between the sheets, pulling Gabby gently into my arms. She startles and gasps.

"Rhys?"

"I'd better be the only one crawling in bed with you, baby."

"What are you doing here?" She checks the time and sees how early it is. "Is something wrong?"

"Yes. I couldn't reach you." I cup her face in my hand and look into her eyes, thanks to the glow of the full moon coming through her wide window. "I tried to call and text all day, and I couldn't get you to respond."

"I'm not sure where I put my phone," she replies softly, and I realize she's on the verge of tears. "I had a really shitty day."

I drag my fingertips down her cheek, then brush her hair back over her shoulder. Fuck, it feels so damn good to have her here in my arms. To know that she's okay.

"What happened?"

"I lost my iPad, which means that I can't schedule bookings, or even see which rooms are supposed to have which guests. It completely threw me off for the day. The dishwasher broke again, flooding my kitchen."

"That thing needs to be replaced," I murmur and kiss her forehead.

"The puppy pooped on my kitchen floor, before he

jumped in the water, getting himself and Sam completely drenched," she continues and burrows closer to me, burying her face in my chest and wrapping her arms around me for dear life. God, has anything ever felt like this in my life? If it did, I don't remember it. "And then, to cap it all off, Sam broke another damn window."

Her voice catches, and then she sniffs and begins to cry. "Beau and Van came and let me go to bed early while they finished up the nighttime chores for the inn."

She's so fucking exhausted. That's what the tears are for, because any of those events by themselves wouldn't have phased her. But all of it in one day is a lot to handle, and I wasn't here to help her.

Fuck.

I just hold her, caressing her, rubbing her, crooning to her, and let her cry it all out. And when she's finally done, when the sniffles slow down, I feel my lips twitch.

"The puppy was splashing in the water?"

She nods.

"And there was poop on the floor?"

She nods again and then grumbles, "Thankfully, he didn't poop in the water."

I chuckle, and then bite my lip, because it's not funny. It made her cry.

"And then Sam went outside and broke a window?"

"I told him to take the demon puppy outside so I could clean up the huge mess in the kitchen, and then *crash*. Broke the window in your room."

"This is my room," I reply without thinking. And then I can't help it. The laughter just comes.

"It's not funny," she says and leans back to scowl at me.

"Sorry." I clear my throat and try to sober my face, but

it's no use. A slow, shy, sleepy smile spreads over her beautiful face.

"Okay, it's kind of funny."

And then here, in the cool darkness of this bedroom, we laugh in each other's arms, until finally we just lie here, smiling, staring into each other's eyes.

"Fuck me, you're beautiful."

She tries to look shyly down, but I catch her chin in my finger. "No, don't look away from me. You are the most beautiful woman I've ever seen. There are seven billion smiles in this world, and yours is my favorite."

Her smile widens. "Thank you. That makes me feel...*special*."

"You are special." I kiss her forehead, then her nose. "You are beautiful."

"You are charming."

I smile against her skin. Always back to this. She has to get up in about an hour, and although I thought I was exhausted when I got here, I suddenly have some extra energy to expel.

Of course, I can't stop fucking touching her. I'm drawn to her in ways I never saw coming.

I push her onto her back and kiss her neck slowly. Gently. I'm going to take this very slow.

"Want you," she whispers in my ear.

"On the same page," I reply and drag my lips up her jawline to her lips, then spend time thoroughly kissing her, biting that plump lower lip, nibbling at the corner. She shifts, pushing closer to me, and I happily pull her more tightly against me, slipping her tank top off, reveling in how warm and sweet she is. Skin to skin.

My fingers drift down her torso, lightly glide over her nipples, her stomach, then over to her ribs. I know she's self-conscious of her post-baby belly, but I couldn't care any less about a few stretch marks and some extra skin. She's amazing just as she is.

Fuck me, I can't stop touching her. Looking at her. I could stare at her all damn day.

She pushes her fingers into my hair and grips a handful, making me growl against her neck as I kiss my way down to her chest. Her tits are fantastic. I pull one nub between my lips and tug, just a little, making her arch her back and sigh.

The sounds that come out of her sexy mouth make my already hard cock twitch. Her legs are restless, moving back and forth, clearly trying to ease the ache between them.

I'll be happy to do that for her.

But not quite yet. We're taking this slow.

"Rhys," she whispers.

"Your skin is so soft." One hand drifts down her belly and under the elastic of her panties, my fingertips lightly grazing over her smooth pubis, making those hips shift. "I love the way you sound. Move. *Smell.*"

"Smell?" She chuckles softly and shifts her hips so I can guide her panties down her legs. "How do I smell?"

"Like you want me inside you." Her eyes flare. "Like you want me to move in and out of you, and make you come like crazy."

"The smell is right." Her eyes are wide, watching me, wondering what I might do next. But I don't want to make this wild and crazy. I want to keep it slow and lazy. Sleepy.

Loving.

Because for the first time in my life, I feel like I'm *making love* to a woman. I'm not fucking her. I'm not having sex.

This is way more intimate than that.

"You're so much more, Gabby."

"More?" She sighs as my fingers slide lower into her folds, massaging them lightly. "More than what?"

"More than anything." I tug her nipple back in my mouth and press one finger into her sopping wet center and grin happily when those hips come up off the bed and she grips onto my shoulder.

"I'm gonna come."

And that's my cue to slow down. "Not yet."

"Party pooper," she pouts, sticking her bottom lip out.

She's fucking adorable.

I bite that lip and smile down at her. Why does my face feel different when I smile at her compared to when I smile at anyone else?

It's the damndest thing.

Finally I slide my body over hers, brace my elbows on either side of her head, careful not to crush her. She's less than half the size I am. I settle between her thighs, rest my pulsing cock against her sopping wet pussy and just rest here, smiling down into her happy face.

"I love this with you," I whisper against her lips.

I love you.

God, I'm such a pussy when it comes to words. But surely she can feel it. Surely she *knows*. I've never been in love before, but it's so *big*, there's no way in hell that she doesn't see it.

"You feel amazing." Her hands are drifting up and down my back, her fingertips on my spine, making my eyes cross.

"You're good with your hands."

She smiles sweetly and hitches her legs up higher on my hips, shifting me enough for a little friction and I growl, "Fuck."

"Yes, let's."

"No." I brush her hair off her face, pull my knuckles down her soft cheek. "We're not fucking right now, Gabrielle."

"No, we're not." She turns her face into my palm and kisses me there. "But I'm going to need you inside me, please."

I tilt my hips back, and when I'm aligned with her opening, I slide in, pushing slowly, making us both moan. God, she's so fucking tight. She hugs my cock, and my spine immediately tingles.

"God, Rhys, it feels amazing every damn time."

"It's like the first time every damn time," I reply softly and hold still inside her, reveling in how good she feels.

And realize that I don't have a fucking condom on.

Shit.

She clenches down and I have to bite her neck to keep from coming. "If you keep doing that, this won't last nearly as long as I want it to."

"I don't think I can stop," she says. Her hands are gripping my ass, she's circling her hips and her snug pussy keeps rippling around me.

She's going to come spectacularly.

So I start to move again, in short pulses, tapping her G-spot with the tip of my dick. I shove my hands under her ass to tilt her up more, making the angle even more incredible, and her legs begin to shake the way they do when she's about to lose it.

And I'm not going to last much longer than she does.

"Give in to it, Gabby," I whisper against her lips. "Go ahead."

She tilts her head back and whimpers as she shudders around me. There is no shouting, or crying out, but it's no less intense.

It's *everything.*

I come with her, quickly pulling out and spilling onto her stomach, panting. But I can't take my eyes off of her gorgeous face.

"So much more," I whisper.

CHAPTER FOURTEEN

~Gabby~

I'm running late. And to be perfectly honest, I don't even care, one little bit. Because I just spent the two most amazing hours of my life in bed with Rhys where he freaking *worshipped* my body for every single minute of those two hours.

Worshipped. There is no other way to describe it. The way he touched me, looked at me, spoke to me. Yes, some of it was still dirty, thank God, but he was also gentle and thorough—so damn thorough—and loving.

Tender.

It was maybe the best moment of my life. I can't believe that he came here early just because he couldn't reach me.

And speaking of that, where in the hell is my phone?

I hurry into the kitchen to get breakfast ready for the guests, and there on the countertop is my phone, along with a note from Van.

Gabs,

Found this in the fridge. Was the phone spoiling? Were

you worried about mold? Rhys tried to call.

Love,

Van

"In the fridge?" Rhys asks, reading over my shoulder.

"Yeah. I put it in there because I kept getting annoying calls from the unknown number. And I was irritated with the whole poop/water thing, so I stuffed it in the fridge and forgot about it."

"Talk to me about this unknown number."

"There's nothing to tell. They hang up."

"So don't answer."

"It could be a guest calling. I have to answer."

He pours us each a cup of coffee, then leans his hips against the countertop and crosses his arms over his chest. He's shirtless, wearing just a pair of loose-fitting workout pants, and dear sweet God, my body just went into hyper-alert mode.

Seriously, his muscles are ridiculous.

"See something you like?" he asks with that half-smile on his lips.

"Meh." I hide my smile behind my mug as I take a sip of coffee, and Rhys's eyes narrow.

"What was that?"

"Maybe." Now I smile innocently and arrange cinnamon rolls in a pan. "I mean, you'll do."

"I'll do." His voice is dry, but his green eyes are full of humor as he watches me bustle around the kitchen.

"Shouldn't you be in bed? You haven't slept in two days."

"I'm fine for now. Where's Sam?"

"He just got picked up for baseball camp."

He nods. "So, I'll do."

"Wow, do you really need me to stroke your ego?" I

shake my head and turn toward the oven, but I'm suddenly caught up in Rhys's arms and he's kissing the hell out of me. His hands are *everywhere*, his mouth firm and sure on mine, as he simply takes what he wants.

And what he wants is *me*.

"I don't need you to stroke my ego, baby," he whispers against my lips. "That's not what this is about. There are no egos here. It's just you and me, and I have no problem admitting that I'm hot for you. I have a permanent hard-on when I just *think* of you. I haven't been this turned on by a woman since I was a kid. I would hope it's reciprocated just a little bit, or I'll feel like a fool."

"I always want you," I reply and swallow hard. "Your body is insane, Rhys. In. Sane. But more than that, I want the way you make me feel."

"How do I make you feel?"

"Safe. Beautiful. Sexy."

"Yes." He grins and kisses me once more. "You are those things."

I lick my lips, tasting him there, and watch as he resumes his place against the counter.

"Can I bring something up without you biting my head off?" he asks, staring down into his coffee.

"Maybe. Not if it's about my hair. Girls are touchy about their hair."

He shakes his head. "No, I love your hair. I think you should hire help."

I bite my lip and wince. "I can do this, Rhys."

"I know. I'm not saying you can't. That's not the point. You *can*, but you shouldn't have to do it all alone. I would think that the past twenty-four hours would have shown you that an extra pair of hands around here would help you out considerably. Maybe just bring someone on to handle breakfast and check-outs. Or even just breakfast."

He shrugs, and I can't help but think that he could be right. It would be nice to be able to take Sam to school, or sleep a little later, or just have my hands freed up to do other things. And the inn is busy enough now that an employee is completely affordable.

"I'll look into it," I finally reply, and Rhys's eyes widen in surprise.

"You will?"

"Yes. You're right, it would be nice to have some flexibility in the morning."

"Wow. That was easier than I thought it would be."

I laugh and kiss his arm as I pass by him. "I'm not unreasonable; I'm just stubborn."

"You? No. I had no idea."

"And you're a smart ass."

"Better than being a dumb ass," he says with a wink and then frowns when he watches me pull drawers out, search through them, then push them back in. "What are you doing?"

"I'm trying to find my iPad."

"Did you think you might have stored it with the freezer bags?"

"No, but I can't find it. Anywhere. I mean, my phone was in the fridge, so you just never know."

"Good point. Don't you have that app that you can use to help you find it if it's stolen or lost?"

"Oh, I think I do!" I reach for my phone and activate the app, then touch my way through the screens, until it shows me where my iPad is.

"It's not in the house," Rhys says grimly, again looking over my shoulder.

I make the map bigger and try to figure out how I

know that address. "I've been there before. How do I know it?"

"I don't know."

"Oh my God!" I spin and stare at Rhys in horror. "I know where this is."

"Okay, where?"

"It's Cindy's condo in the city. She must have taken it the other day when she was here. Why would she do that?"

"To make your life hell," he replies grimly. "You know, I don't condone violence against women, but I'd really love to wring her little neck."

"I wonder if she changed my password to the program too," I mumble, trying to figure out what to do.

"What do you mean?"

"I need the program on there for all of the inn scheduling. It's my Bible. I can log into it from the computer too, and when I tried, the password wouldn't work. I always use the same password, Rhys. The only explanation is that she changed it."

"You need to report it stolen and file a police report."

"What?" I shake my head incredulously. "That's crazy."

"No. She stole it, Gabby. Obviously with the intention of hurting you. She didn't accidentally slip away with it. She's not your friend. Let the cops get it back for you."

"I can afford to replace it."

"That's not the point." His jaw is firm. "She took something that isn't hers."

He's right.

"Okay. But to do that, I have to go into the city."

"We'll go right after breakfast."

"Guests—"

"Won't arrive until late afternoon, and the ones who

are staying over will have keys to get in if they come back before us. We'll be gone a few hours."

I really need to hire help.

And stop choosing thieving friends.

"Okay." I nod and pull the rolls out of the oven. "Hungry?"

"Yes." I turn to see his green eyes on my ass.

"For food?"

"Sure, if that's all you're offering."

***

"So, we filed a police report," I say while nibbling on chips and salsa. Rhys and I met up with Kate and Eli for lunch. Eli is currently glaring at Rhys because Rhys has his arm around my shoulders.

God save me from overprotective brothers.

"I can't believe she stole it right under your nose," Kate says, shaking her head, also munching on chips and salsa. "What in the hell is her problem?"

"I wouldn't sleep with her," Rhys replies. "And Gabby stood up to her, told her off, and kicked her out of her house."

"Actually," I say, looking up into Rhys's face, "I think it was *you* who finally kicked her out."

"Either way, she got kicked out."

"Good, but you should have called me," Eli says, then sighs when Rhys kisses my hand. "Are you going to continue to touch my sister for all of us to see?"

"Yes," Rhys replies simply, making Kate grin.

"I'm not sure how I feel about this," Eli says.

"You don't have to feel any way about it," I reply in frustration. "I'm a grown-ass woman."

"It's my job to protect you," Eli says, as if I'm being difficult.

"But it's not your job to be an ass," Kate says, but softens the blow by kissing his cheek. "It's Rhys. You know him. And they're cute together."

"Hurt her, and—"

"Seriously," I interrupt, not wanting to hear the *hurt her and I'll kill you* speech. "We're fine."

"I get it," Rhys says to Eli. "I feel the same about Kate; you know that. We've had that conversation. I almost decked you when you showed up in Denver."

Eli sits back in his chair, and his eyes calm a bit, but he looks no less foreboding.

"Don't make me regret trusting you," Eli says calmly, just as our meals are delivered.

"Back at you," Rhys replies with a cold smile. Kate catches my eye, and we both sigh, and shrug as if to say, *what can you do?* They love us. They're worried about us.

Damn it, sometimes they're idiots.

But lunch is delicious.

"Beau said this morning that you need a new dishwasher," Eli says.

"I do. I'll find time to pick one out in the next few days."

"Just come to the office with me after lunch and sign off on one, and I'll have it delivered. It's your inn, but damn it, we can help with that shit. You're busy enough."

"Too busy," Kate agrees.

"I think I'm going to hire some help," I reply. "Rhys might have talked me into it."

Eli's eyebrow shoots up in surprise. "We've been trying to talk you into it for over a year."

"I didn't need it a year ago." I shrug and twirl a long string of cheese around my fork. "But I'm much busier now, and Sam is getting more involved in things, so it's time to have some help."

"I'll take care of it," Eli says, as if there is no room for argument, and I simply laugh at him.

"No, you won't."

"Gabby, I have a whole HR staff that can easily find someone qualified to help you."

"I'm perfectly capable of finding someone to help me," I reply. "You run your business, and I'll run mine, big brother."

He sits back in his hair and tilts his handsome head, watching me. "Okay. You handle it."

"I will." I nod once and sip my Coke. "I wonder if I should specify in the ad that felons aren't welcome to apply."

"Gabby, let me handle this!" Eli exclaims, and I can't help but dissolve in a fit of giggles.

"I'm teasing. It sure is fun to get you all riled up."

"Most wouldn't dare," Kate says good-naturedly. "I wonder what people would say if they knew that he's nothing but a big softie."

"I will take you over my knee, Kate," he murmurs to her, and Rhys tenses up beside me, but Kate just laughs and leans her head on Eli's shoulder.

"Right. Except you have this thing against spanking me, so I don't think that'll happen."

Eli's lips twitch as he buries them in Kate's hair and kisses her head.

"I don't mind being spanked," I add and eat a chip loaded with cheese and beans, just as Eli's eyes go cold again, pinned on Rhys, who simply laughs beside me.

"I don't need to know this," Eli growls.

"It's not like he leaves marks. Well, they don't stay for long."

Kate is laughing like a loon into her hand, Rhys is smiling widely, and Eli looks like he's about to spit nails.

Or spank me himself.

God, this is fun.

"Gabby," he says, always in control, "you're my baby sister. I don't ever want to hear about any sexual encounter you ever have. In my head, you're a virgin."

Rhys snorts, earning a glare from Eli.

"She has a child, Eli. She's clearly not a virgin."

"And you should know," I remind him with an evil smile.

"For the love of fuck," Eli mutters, scrubbing his hand down his face.

"I'm full," I report and sit back to pat my belly. "Let's go handle the dishwasher at the office."

"Good idea," Eli says with a sigh. "Before I go to jail for murder."

***

"I don't have space for an industrial sized dishwasher," I say and roll my eyes at my controlling brother. "And I don't need it. I like the one I picked out."

"Fine," Eli replies and shoves his hands in his pockets, the way he always does when he's agitated. Dad used to do the same thing.

Eli reminds me a lot of Dad.

"Do *not* send me that huge dishwasher that I don't want." I point my finger at my brother, looking up more than a foot. His lips twitch, and then he pulls me in for a big hug.

"Yes, ma'am."

"Love you," I whisper to him.

"Love you more," he says. Rhys is with Kate in her office, so I leave Eli and go in search of him.

"Well, hello, gorgeous."

I glance up at the deep, sexy voice, and smile widely when I see Rich, an old friend from high school.

"What are you doing here?" I ask as he scoops me up into his arms and hugs me, turning a circle before he puts me back down on my feet. "I haven't seen you in forever."

"I'm Kate's assistant," he replies, gesturing to Kate's office, which is only a few feet away. Her door is wide open. "And you look amazing."

"Thanks. You're looking good yourself. You haven't changed a bit."

And it's not an empty compliment. Rich looks the same that he did in high school, aside from filling out a bit into his manhood. He always had a killer smile.

"So when are you going to take me up on my offer to take you out to dinner?" he asks with that charming smile of his firmly in place.

"I don't remember you asking me," I reply.

"I'm asking now."

Movement in Kate's doorway catches my eye. Rhys is leaning against the doorjamb, his arms crossed, listening unapologetically, his eyes hard.

There's no humor in his face now.

"What do you say?" Rich asks, unaware that Rhys is behind him.

"You *do* look great, Rich, but I'm going to have to pass."

"Married?" His face falls, which actually makes me laugh.

"No."

"Oh." His face brightens again, and he looks like he's about to try again when Rhys steps forward.

"She's not available," he informs Rich as he slings his

arm around my shoulders and pulls me against him.

"I see." Rich offers us a fake smile. "It was good to see you again, Gabby."

"You too, Rich."

He leaves and I frown up at Rhys. "Was that necessary?"

"Yes. Are you ready?"

I nod and he leads me out of the building and to his car, all in silence. What in the hell is his issue? I didn't say yes to Rich. I mean, I didn't really have time to say no either, but I would have if Rhys hadn't interrupted.

The ride home is full of thick, irritated silence. I don't know who's more irritated, me or him.

I think it could be me.

I've had men slinging testosterone around me my whole life. And this particular man seems to have more than most.

And it's usually pretty hot.

He pulls into the driveway of the inn, throws the car in park and walks around to my side to help me out, then takes my hand and leads me inside, through the house, to my room.

I kick the door shut behind us and cross my arms over my chest.

"What in the hell was that all about?"

"Do you think that I don't know what the other day with Cindy was all about?" he asks rather than answer me, and I'm instantly confused. "When she was coming on to me like a dog in heat, I knew you were just outside the room and could hear us. I was sure to tell her, in no uncertain terms, that I wasn't interested, out of respect for you, and because that's how I honestly felt."

He's advancing on me, moving slowly, but toward me,

until my back is against the door and he's caging me in. His eyes are on fire. His jaw tight.

In fact, every muscle in his body is pulled tight.

"I would have expected the same from you today." His voice is hard.

"You didn't give me the chance to. You interrupted before I could say anything." His fingers are inching my shirt up over my head, then he throws it on the ground and nimbly unfastens my shorts, letting them fall around my ankles.

"You said he looked good—"

"And he did." Now my panties are gone.

"When what you should have said was *no thank you.*"

"I was getting there."

"Not fucking fast enough." He unzips his pants and rolls a condom over his cock, lifts me effortlessly, wraps my legs around his waist and props me against the door. We're at eye-level now, and it kills me to see that in addition to the fire in his eyes, there is hurt too.

"Rhys, I don't want Rich."

"When you're naked with me, I don't want you to even *remember* another man's name." He slides inside me with one fast thrust, making me gasp. How am I already so wet when he's doing nothing but pissing me off?

"You're being unreasonable."

His eyes narrow. "No, Gabby, I'm not." He begins to move, making me moan. "This right here? This is *mine.* You are *mine.*"

What?

"Rhys."

"That's right, me. Just me. Do you understand, Gabby? What we have is ours, and I'll be fucking goddamned if I'll share you with anyone else."

Jesus, the things this man does to my body are insane. But even more than that, what he does to my heart is out of control.

How can I be mad when he just wants me?

"I want you too, Rhys."

"I want you, yes, but I fucking *need* you. Do you have any idea how damn terrifying that is?" He tips his forehead to rest on mine. "Seeing another man come on to you, and you *not* shoot him down right away was a knife to my chest."

"I'm sorry. I was about to shoot him down."

He shakes his head, unable to speak any more as he thrusts in and out of me, harder than he ever has. His fingers are gripping my ass so hard he's sure to leave marks. Not pink ones: bruises.

I've never seen him this intense. This...*needy*.

And it's all because of me.

"Mine," he mutters again, and reaches between us to press his thumb on my clit. "Come. Now."

My whole body clenches as I come, caught between him and the door, my entire world breaking apart and coming back together again, all centered around this amazing man holding me up.

"Did you just *mark* me?" I ask breathlessly.

"Literally or figuratively?"

"Both."

"Yes."

CHAPTER FIFTEEN

~Gabby~

"Gabby, I heard you hired some help," Mama says as she stirs the red beans and rice on her stovetop. We're all at her house for a Sunday dinner, as usual.

"About six weeks ago, yes," I reply and smile as Rhys leans down to kiss me on his way to help set the table. He's been very affectionate with me in front of my family. My brothers are all a little twitchy because of it, but Van, Charly and Kate just wink and smile.

Mama simply pats my shoulder.

He makes me happy.

"And how is that working out?" Declan asks and picks a carrot out of the salad bowl. "You're such a control freak."

"It's my business," I reply with a shrug. "I should be a control freak. But it's working out great. Eva comes in for me in the mornings and takes care of breakfast, and helps check guests out. She leaves by about noon each day."

"I'm glad you took Rhys's advice and hired Eva," Kate says, ignoring Eli's glare. "You were taking on too much."

"It was beginning to be a lot to handle," I admit softly. "But I love it. It's not work for me, you know?"

"But it *is* work," Rhys says and plants his lips on my head. "You work your ass off, sugar."

"She comes by that honestly," Mama says with a smile. "Every one of my children are hard workers."

"Just like our parents," Van says.

"There's nothing wrong with hard work," Beau adds. "But there is also a time to admit that you need help, and I'm glad you did."

"It is nice to have some flexibility in the morning," I reply with a nod. "And Eva seems to love it. She caught on quickly, doesn't piss me off, and is happy to have the job."

"Perfect," Charly says with a grin and pulls the pork chops out of the oven. "There is nothing worse than an employee who pisses you off."

"Of course she's happy to be there," Mama says as she pulls me in for a big hug. "You're very easy to love."

"You're my mom. You're supposed to say that."

I glance up at Rhys, who winks at me then resumes a conversation with Kate and Beau, and I can't help but remember an evening in bed with him not long ago, when after we'd made love, he smiled and said, "You're so easy to fall for."

Yet, he's never said he loves me. But he shows me he does in so many little ways. The easy affection he shows me, the way he jumps in to help me whenever he thinks I need it.

And I'm beginning to hope that maybe, just maybe, he's not going to disappear from my life. He seems so content here. Maybe he'll stay.

I wish I wasn't so fucking scared to just *ask* him what he wants. But Daddy always said don't ask a question that you don't want the answer to.

And if the answer is that he's having fun with me for now, but he'll be returning to Chicago soon, well...I don't want to hear that.

So, I'm basically a coward.

"Earth to Gabby," Declan says, waving his hand in front of my face. "Where did you go there, baby-doll?"

"Sorry." I smile and shake my head. "Daydreaming."

"About what?"

"Dessert." I glance longingly at the pecan pie Mama made for dessert.

"Can we have pie now?" Sam asks, just as he does every Sunday. And every Sunday he gets the same response.

"I know you're not gonna try to eat my pie before dinner," Mama says, shaking her finger at him. Sam's shoulders droop and he lets out a long sigh.

"No, ma'am."

"Dinner is just about ready," Charly says, plating all the dishes, and passing them to me to put on the long table in the dining room. Charly and Mama are the best cooks in the family.

"Why doesn't Gabby ever help cook?" Beau asks. "You're a great cook."

"I do well enough at the inn, but I don't love it the way Mama and Charly do." I shrug and set a bowl of salad on the table. "And I helped chop the salad."

"I like your cooking," Beau says.

"Does that mean you'd like to join us for more dinners?" I prop my hands on my hips as a smile slips over my eldest brother's lips.

"Well, since you invited me so nicely, sure."

"Uncle Beau wants mac n' cheese," Sam says as he sits in his chair. "Every night."

"I think that's what Sam wants," I reply dryly. "And you already get it at least twice a week."

"That's hardly *ever*."

"Yes, you're incredibly abused," Charly says with a roll

of the eyes. "I'm so very sorry for you."

"Well, maybe not *abused*," Sam says, thinking it over. "Maybe mac n' cheese abuse!"

I ruffle my son's hair and help him dish up his plate before I dish up my own. But when I turn to do so, Rhys has already loaded it up, dropping scoops of everything when he scoops his own.

"Thank you." I lean over and kiss his bicep, then look up to see Declan's eyes on me. Of all three of my brothers, Declan is the most laid back. He's the typical artist; very sensitive and easy going, but he can be just as fiercely protective as Beau or Eli, in his way.

But right now, his eyes are smiling, and his lips are quirking, and I know that I'm in for a conversation outside with him before we leave Mama's house today.

And that's okay because sometimes Declan gives the best advice.

"Mom, I don't feel great," Sam says softly. When I lay my lips on his forehead, it feels warm to the touch, but he's not burning up.

"Do you think you got too much sunshine today?"

"Maybe."

He's picking at his food, and that's not like him.

"Does your belly hurt?"

"No."

"Have you felt like this for very long?"

"No, ma'am." He takes a bite of rice and swallows, and he looks okay to me.

"I'll give you some medicine when we get home," I murmur and kiss his head. "Just eat what you want. You don't have to clean your plate."

"Do I still get dessert?"

"Yes, baby, you can still have dessert."

"I think it's just because you didn't hug your Nannan when you came in," Mama says and kisses Sam's head as she passes him to her seat. "You don't feel warm."

"He might have overdone it today," I say, a little worried. But my boy plays hard, and sometimes he just wears himself out.

"Charly," Kate says, "I need some new shoes for fall."

"Oh, sugar, I have you covered." Charly tucks her hair behind her ear and rubs her hands together. "I have a whole slew of new shoes coming in later this week, and they are *to die for*."

"Perfect," Kate says with a grin.

"We'll be there," Van agrees.

"You should come with us," Kate says to me. "You hardly ever come into the city."

"Well, now that I have an employee, I might be able to do that," I reply happily. "I'll let you know."

Suddenly, Rhys leans down and whispers in my ear, "Snag a pair of new fuck-me shoes."

I grin over at him and feel my cheeks flush. "Yeah?"

"Yeah."

"Done."

***

"So talk to me about Rhys," Declan says as he leads me into Mama's back yard. We're wandering through her gardens, on brick paths. As summer is coming to an end, the evenings are cooling off a bit.

Not *cool* by most people's standards, but it's not stifling.

"What would you like to know?"

"Everything." He sighs and drags his hand through his longer hair. "How are you? How does he make you feel? Is he good to you?"

"Being the big brother."

"And your friend." He takes my hand in his and squeezes it lightly. "Always your friend, baby-doll."

And that just brings tears to my eyes. I love that all of my brothers and sisters are also my dear friends. My best friends.

I don't know what I would do without them.

"I'm doing very well," I assure him immediately. "I'm happy. He makes me feel happy."

"You look happy," he says. "You look like you're in love."

"And I suppose I am."

He nods, then frowns, as though he's trying to find the words.

"Just say it."

"It's not that easy, Gabs." He sits on a bench and leans his elbows on his jean-covered knees. He's in a blue T-shirt, showing off the muscles in his arms.

Despite them being my brothers, I'm not stupid. I know they're all good looking men. And I tend to be a bit protective of my Declan because his heart is softer than the others, and I'll be damned if anyone is going to hurt him and live to tell about it.

"I love you, Dec."

His head whips up, surprised.

"Where did that come from?"

"I just don't get to see you often enough, and I miss you. I love you."

"I love you too." He rubs his fingers over his mouth, studying me. "Okay, so this is how I see it, as an outsider looking in. And keep in mind that I'm your brother too, so there's that."

"Oh boy."

"You're clearly in love with each other. The way he looks at you is how Daddy used to look at Mama."

Oh. My heart goes all gooey and I bite my lip.

But then he keeps talking.

"And frankly, it worries me."

I blink at him. "Wait. What?"

"It worries me, Gabs. What happens when he goes home?"

"I don't know."

My honest statement stops him cold. "But you've thought about it."

"Of course I've thought about it. I know he's not going to be here forever."

"And your home is here."

I nod. "I know."

"I am so happy that you've found someone who makes you happy," Dec says with a smile. "But I see this ending with you broken-hearted and that hurts me too. I don't want to watch you go through that again."

"He might stay," I say optimistically. "I mean, yes, he plays baseball, but, you never know."

He nods, his eyes sober and maybe a little sad. "Just be smart, Gabs. And if he does break your heart, I'm here."

"You're not going to threaten to kill him?"

"No, Beau and Eli will do that." He grins. "I'm the more passive of the three of us."

"You know, for a big brother, you're not so bad."

"And for a snot-nosed, baby sister, neither are you."

I laugh as he stands next to me and hug him tightly around the middle. He's so tall, I feel small next to him. "I'm gonna wipe my snot nose on you."

"Wouldn't be the first time."

"Or, I have a feeling, the last."

***

I have a very sick little boy on my hands.

"I'm gonna throw up again," Sam says pitifully. He's kneeling on the floor of our bathroom, his head hanging in the toilet.

"Okay, buddy, go ahead." I'm rubbing his little back and holding a cold, wet cloth to his neck. I feel so helpless.

"But I don't want to."

"I know, but you'll feel better after."

Rhys pokes his head around the doorjamb. "Need me?"

More than anything.

"No, we're okay."

Just then, Sam loses his pecan pie in the toilet.

"I'll bring a bottle of water," he says and disappears. I had no idea how nice it was to have someone with you when your baby is sick. He hands the water to me, and I take it gratefully.

"Okay, baby, have some water," I croon to Sam as he sits back on his haunches. He's breathing hard and sweaty.

Throwing up takes a lot of energy.

Sam cautiously sips the water, looking up at me with water-filled brown eyes.

"I'm sorry you don't feel good, sweetie."

"My tummy hurts."

"I know." I wipe his face off with the wet cloth and help him brush his teeth, then take him into his room and get him settled in bed. "How do you feel?"

"Tired."

"Do you feel like you're going to throw up again?"

He shakes his head no. "Will you stay here until I fall asleep?"

"Of course." I lean in and kiss his head. He's warm.

Not burning up, but warm. He must have caught a bug from somewhere.

So I sit and sing our song to him, gently stroking his face and hair. His eyes are closed, his cheeks just a little flushed, and his lips are rosy red.

He looks like my baby.

But suddenly, he sits up and throws up, all over both of us and the bed, and immediately bursts into tears.

"What's happening?" Rhys asks as he runs into the room.

"He got sick again," I reply grimly, trying to soothe my boy and avoid the vomit. "We're a little messy here."

Without missing a beat, Rhys gathers us both into his arms and carries us into the bathroom.

"We're going to get you messy too. And we stink."

"You're fine," he replies as he sets us down on the closed toilet. "I'm going to go take care of the bed linens. You guys clean up. I'll bring fresh clothes."

And with that, he marches out and leaves us to strip out of our clothes, down to our underwear. I toss the soiled pajamas into the hamper, and Rhys passes me fresh ones, not even taking a second to stare at me in my mostly nakedness, and Sam doesn't even care that Rhys has seen us half naked as I help him into the fresh clothes, then pull mine on too.

"Feel better?" I ask him.

"A little. I'm just tired now."

"God, you're heavy," I mutter as I lift him into my arms and carry him into my bedroom and settle us both into my bed. Rhys will just have to sleep in "his" room tonight. My boy needs me.

Sam is lying in the dead center of the bed and I'm lying on my side beside him, playing with his hair and whispering to him.

"Where's Derek?" he asks.

"Rhys is getting him all settled for the night."

"Can he sleep with us?"

"Sure," Rhys says as he comes into my room and lifts the puppy onto the bed. "I just took him outside, and he's good to go for tonight."

He holds my gaze as he strips down to just his T-shirt and underwear and slips into the bed with us.

"Are you sick too?" Sam asks as Derek curls up next to Sam's legs and with a big, gusty sigh, settles in to sleep.

"No, I just want to hold you and your mom," Rhys says as he pulls us both against him, Sam between us. "I'm kind of worried about you both, and this makes me feel better."

"But Mom isn't sick," Sam says with a yawn, and I hold my breath, praying that the vomiting is over. But he doesn't throw up again; he just snuggles against Rhys's chest.

"No, but she's worried about you, and that makes me worry about her."

"Oh," Sam says with a frown. "But Moms are strong."

"Your mom is very strong," Rhys agrees, still holding my gaze with his over Sam's head. He reaches up and tucks a loose strand of hair that has fallen out of my ponytail behind my ear. "But even moms need someone to look after them."

"What about you?" I ask softly.

"I have everything I want in this bed," he replies and I have to lower my eyes so he can't see the tears that come at that statement.

Ask him if he's going to stay! Tell him you love him! Stop being a pain in the ass and torturing yourself!

But instead, because I'm an idiot, I simply kiss Sam's head and settle in next to him, not saying anything.

"I love you, Rhys." Sam's voice is sure and unwavering as he says those words that I find impossible to say. Rhys simply smiles softly and kisses Sam's head.

"I love you too, buddy."

He loves my son.

"I love you, Mama," Sam says softly.

"I love you too, baby boy."

"I'm not a baby boy. I'm a man," he says with as much indignation he can muster, given how crappy he feels. Rhys and I both chuckle.

"Well, I think that when you're sick like this, you're still my baby boy," I reply. "You were so tiny when you were born."

Rhys tilts his head to the side in curiosity.

"He loves hearing the story of how he was born."

"Tell me again," Sam says, his eyes closed now. Derek is snoring loudly, snuggled between Sam's legs.

"It was a really hot summer night," I begin the way I always do. "And I was in my room at Nannan and Pawpaw's house, when suddenly, my water broke."

"That's gross," Sam says.

"It was scary because you weren't supposed to come for six more weeks." I bite my lip as I think back to how terrified I was at the thought of having Sam so early. "But, I've come to learn that you're just an impatient boy."

"Am not," he mutters.

"Okay." I chuckle and kiss his head. "So, I woke Pawpaw up and he took me to the hospital while Nannan called all of the others, and they met us there later."

"And Uncle Beau and Aunt Charly were in the room when I was born."

"That's right. You took your time, though. Twenty-six hours of labor was a long time, but then suddenly, there you were, all pink and tiny, and angry as could be."

"Well, I was getting crowded in your belly," Sam says logically.

"I see. Well, we got you all cleaned off, and the nurse laid you on my chest, and you looked up at me and just stared at me as I talked to you, as if you already knew that I was your mama."

"It's because it's just you and me, against the world," he whispers softly, making more tears spring in my eyes. God, I'm so damn emotional tonight!

"That's right," I whisper back, and glance up to see Rhys watching us, listening intently. "And you were as healthy as could be, even as tiny as you were."

"I eat all the gross vegetables you make me eat," he says. He's so sleepy, he's going to drift off any second. So, I stop talking and just stroke my fingertips over his forehead, his cheeks, through his hair.

"I hate that you went through that alone," Rhys says softly when Sam is finally asleep.

"I didn't. I had my family with me."

"I know, but it's not the same. That's not how it's supposed to be."

I bite my lip, thinking about that night not so long ago, and how loved I felt.

"Honestly, I didn't feel like I was missing anything in that moment. My family was there, loving us so much, and I had him. At the end of the day, he was all that mattered."

Rhys nods and leans over Sam to kiss my lips gently. "You should sleep too, baby."

"I know. Are you staying?"

"Do you mind if I do?"

I glance down at my son and his sleeping puppy, then back up at this strong, sweet, loving man. "I don't mind at all."

"Good, because you were going to have a very difficult time getting me out of here."

Chapter Sixteen

~Gabby~

I haven't just laid in bed and enjoyed the quiet in…I don't remember the last time. Eva's been with me long enough now that I feel comfortable leaving the inn in her hands. I heard Sam get up with Rhys about an hour ago, and it sounded like they were headed to the barn to work out.

That Sam enjoys *working out* with Rhys makes me smile. It's been two days since he had the nasty bug, but it was gone by morning, and he was back to his old self yesterday.

And now, lying here, I feel like I'm catching it.

Figures.

I haven't thrown up yet, but I feel a bit queasy. Thankfully, his only lasted about eight hours.

I hope I'm that lucky.

I'm scrolling through my phone, pinning recipes on Pinterest, when it suddenly starts to ring.

Unknown number.

"Ugh, give it up already," I mutter as I accept the call. "Hello."

There's a pause and I'm about to hang up when a

man's voice says, "Gabby?"

"Yes. Can I help you?"

"This is Colby."

My mouth drops open, and a cold sweat immediately breaks out over my skin. "What do you want? Are you the idiot that's been hanging up on me lately?"

"I don't know what you're talking about," he mutters, clearly lying. "Did you get my email a couple months ago?"

"I did."

"Why didn't you respond? I want to see my child."

"I didn't respond because you signed your rights away, Colby." I swallow hard and close my eyes, determined to stay bad-ass during this conversation. "There was no need to reply to your email."

"Look, this doesn't have to be difficult, Gabby. I was young when I did that, and now I'm curious to meet him."

"How do you know it's a him?"

"Because I'm not an idiot. I've kept tabs over the years. He should know his father."

"No. He shouldn't. His father wanted to have him killed before he was born."

"We were children, Gabby." He's raising his voice now, and I'm simply seeing red.

"We were old enough to have sex, Colby. I was adult enough to get pregnant and raise that baby by myself for seven years. Sam doesn't ask about you. He's fine, and you have no legal right."

"I'm going to see him."

"No. You're not."

I end the call and drop my phone on the bed, cover my face with my shaking hands, and take a long, deep breath.

What I said is true; Colby has no legal right. My father's lawyers made damn sure that the documents he signed were airtight. He can't hurt me, and he can't get to Sam.

But damn it, I haven't heard his voice since that day in the garden. Back then I couldn't get enough of his voice.

Today it makes me ill.

In fact, I think I'm going to be sick.

I run for the bathroom and lose last night's dinner, and then dry heave for long minutes. My eyes are watering, and my stomach muscles are screaming when it's finally over.

It's just a combination of the adrenaline from the phone call and this bug that Sam had, and it attacks once more. Jesus, there's nothing left in me, but I keep heaving uncontrollably.

I lean against the toilet seat, and my boobs cry in protest. Holy hell, they are *sore.*

When the heaving stops, I drop back on my haunches, breathing hard, and feel the sides of my breasts. Oh my God, they hurt. I must be about to start my period. It's surely due, I haven't had a period in...

Holy fucking hell.

That can't be right.

I stand, rinse my mouth out, splash cool water on my face and stare at my reflection as I mentally count back again. I don't think I had a period last month.

How in the hell did I miss that?

My phone. I need my phone. It's still on the bed. So I run out and grab it, then run back into the bathroom, lock the door and call Van's number.

But it goes straight to voice mail.

Shit.

So I call Charly.

"Hey, sugar."

"I know you're probably super busy, but I already

called Van and I got her voice mail."

"Gabby?"

I glower at the phone. "Of course this is Gabby."

"Why are we whispering?" she asks in a loud whisper, matching my tone.

"Because I need help."

"Are you in danger?" she screeches.

"No. I need a pregnancy test, and I don't have one, and I need you to go get one and bring it here. But don't tell anyone."

"Gabby, are you kidding me?"

"Shhh!" It's too damn hot in here. I'm starting to sweat. "If you're too busy, I understand."

"Fuck that, I'll be there in one hour."

She's here in thirty minutes.

"It's Charly," she calls through the door. "Open up."

I unlock the door, let her in, then close and lock it behind her and take the white plastic bag out of her hand. "Are you going to watch me pee?" I ask as she perches herself on the edge of the tub.

"I did the first time," she reminds me with a shrug. "Might as well this time too."

"It's weird to have you watch me pee."

"Sugar, I've seen everything on you there is to see. Just pee on the fucking stick."

I open the box and smirk. "You got the fancy kind that actually says *pregnant* or *not pregnant.*"

"I don't want there to be any doubt of the outcome," she replies and crosses her legs, as though we're talking about the weather.

When I'm finished, I snap the cap back on the end and set it on the countertop to let it do its thing.

"Now talk to me," Charly says. "We have, like, three

minutes to waste."

"My boobs hurt, I threw up this morning, and when I did the math, I haven't had a period in about six weeks."

Her jaw drops. "Gabby, you know how this happens."

"Clearly," I reply dryly. "This isn't planned."

"You know, you've always been a planner. Why didn't that flow over into the pregnancy arena as well?"

"I guess I like to keep things interesting," I reply and pick the stick up, stunned when I see *Pregnant.*

"Charlotte Boudreaux!" I exclaim and throw the stick in the sink, as if it's a snake and it's going to bite me any second.

"I guess that means it's positive? And I'd just like to clarify, I'm not the one who got you pregnant, despite the way you just yelled my name, as though it's all my fault."

"What in the hell am I going to do?" I sit on the toilet and hang my head in my hands, and I'm suddenly nauseous again, but I don't even have time to turn around and get it in the toilet. I grab the trash can and heave in it for what seems like forever. "I'm dying."

"Not today," Charly replies with too much cheer in her voice. "But you *are* going to be a mommy again."

"Oh, my God."

"Tell me you've been using protection."

"Of course we do," I reply and wrinkle my forehead as I try to remember back. "I'm not an idiot. There was *one time* that we forgot, but he pulled out."

"Well, you didn't forget to ovulate." She sighs and shakes her head. "Van and I really failed you when it came to sex education, sugar. I *knew* we should have had that talk with you."

"This isn't funny," I reply softly. "What am I going to do?"

"You're going to tell the man you've been having an intimate relationship with that you're pregnant and go from there. You're not in this alone, Gabby."

"I don't want him to think that I'm trying to trap him."

"He'd be an idiot to think that."

I nod, but I'm not convinced. "I need some time to think. I just need to get my own head on straight before I dump this on him."

"The longer you wait to tell him, the more it'll feel like a betrayal when you finally do."

"How about if you tell him and I go to Tahiti?"

She laughs, then rubs her hand over my back in a big circle. "It doesn't work like that. If anyone's going to Tahiti, it's me."

"Killjoy."

***

"Mom, I don't want to go to bed."

I sigh and look up toward heaven, already exhausted and not in the mood to play the bedtime game with Sam.

"You were supposed to be in bed an hour and a half ago, Samuel Beauregard Boudreaux. I don't want to have this argument."

"But I didn't tell you yet that I love you."

I narrow my eyes on his angelic face. Angelic my ass. "Yes you did."

"But I didn't whisper it so the ghost couldn't hear me."

We are in the sitting room. I'm setting out fresh brownies for the guests to have with their wine. Only a few have come down for the wine hour. Rhys is sitting with them.

"There are no ghosts," I inform Sam with a shake of my head.

"You don't know that."

I bite my lip. I have never yelled at Sam over bedtime, and I refuse to start now, but I'm reaching my limit.

"I do know, Sam. I love you, too. Now, go to bed."

"But I'm not sleepy."

Rhys and the two guests are watching us like it's a tennis match.

"Count sheep."

"But I don't like to count sheep. They make me puke."

The guests chuckle. Rhys smiles, the traitor. And I simply hang my head.

"Sheep don't make you puke."

"Yep, they do."

"I don't care what you count, Sam. Just go to bed."

"But I—"

"Come on, buddy." Rhys stands and takes Sam's hand, then winks at me. "Let's go find something to count that doesn't make you sick."

He leads Sam to his bedroom, and I breathe a sigh of relief.

"I'm sorry about that," I say to the kind couple who are enjoying brownies and wine. "He's fought me over bedtime since he was small."

"Ours did too," the wife replies with a wave of the hand. "He'll eventually turn into a teenager, and then all he'll ever want to do is sleep."

"I'm looking forward to that day," I reply with a grin.

"Let him be small," her husband replies with a kind smile. "It's over in the blink of an eye."

I nod and leave them in the sitting room. I'm feeling a little better this evening, but now I'm just full of nerves. Rhys has been his usual happy, affectionate self all day, and all I can think is, once I tell him that I'm carrying his baby, is he going to go running in the other direction?

Because why wouldn't he? He has no ties to me. He doesn't owe me anything. He's already gone above and beyond where Sam and I are concerned.

And I'm not even sure that he won't be leaving to go back to Chicago any day.

Because I'm too much of a pussy to just ask him.

I finish cleaning the kitchen and prepare the food for Eva tomorrow morning. That will save her some time.

Finally, about an hour later, Rhys finds me in the kitchen. He moves up behind me, grips my shoulders in his hands and kisses my head. "You okay?"

I nod and turn in his arms, wrap my arms around his torso, and hug him close. His heartbeat is strong and sure against my cheek. God, he feels so damn good. Safe. Familiar.

He feels like home.

"Come on," he murmurs and leads me out of the kitchen, flipping off lights as we go to my private quarters. But instead of walking into the bedroom, he sits on the couch and turns on the TV. "Lie down. Put your head in my lap."

Well, that sounds like a little slice of heaven. So I do. As soon as my head meets his thigh, Rhys's fingers are in my hair, combing it softly, rhythmically.

"I wish you'd tell me what's wrong," he murmurs. I look up at him, surprised to see so much worry in his bright green eyes.

"I just don't feel well," I reply quietly. And it's the truth; I don't feel well. "I probably caught whatever Sam had the other day."

"Do you need to throw up?"

"No." I smile, and without thinking about it, I cup his

cheek in my hand, enjoying the way his light stubble feels against my skin. "You are so handsome."

"You say that to all the guys who play with your hair when you don't feel well."

He always makes me laugh. "Only the ones who have green eyes and sexy arms."

"You like my arms, do you?"

I nod and sigh as his fingertips scrub my scalp. "You're good with your hands."

"I love your hair."

I love you.

"What do you want to watch on TV?" I ask instead.

"I don't give a fuck about the TV."

"Well, you turned it on," I reply with a frown, and he clicks it off. "What's wrong?"

"Nothing's wrong. I'd just rather look at you than watch TV."

"Are you going to stare at me in a creepy way?" His lips twitch, and then tip up in the corner in that way they do when he finds me particularly cute.

"If you think lust is creepy, then yes."

I laugh out loud, unable to stop the snort that comes along with it. "No, there's a difference between creepy and lustful."

"Okay then, just lustful."

I rest my hands over my belly and the tiny baby sleeping there. I need to tell him. Now is the perfect time. We're alone, and we're comfortable.

But instead, I close my eyes and enjoy the way his fingers feel in my hair. No one in my life has ever touched me the way Rhys does.

"What are you thinking?" he asks softly.

"I was just thinking that no one's ever touched me the

way you do."

His hand pauses for a moment, and then resumes. "I should hope not."

"Does it bother you that I don't have a lot of experience with men?"

Why did I just ask him that?

"Why would it bother me?"

"I mean, I'm twenty-seven. Shouldn't I have had more partners?"

"I don't think so. It's been a lot of fun to show you new things. To watch you experience new feelings. It's been a privilege, Gabby."

I nod, but don't open my eyes.

"How old were you when you lost your virginity?" I ask suddenly.

"Sixteen," he replies immediately. I open my eyes to find him looking down at me with a grin. "No need to lie about that. Or anything else, for that matter."

Direct hit.

"I was nineteen," I reply. "And I got pregnant at the same time."

"That's crazy," he replies.

"How many partners have you had?" *Don't ask questions you don't want the answer to, Gabrielle!*

"My fair share." He narrows his eyes on me. "You're acting very strangely tonight."

"I'm just getting to know you better."

"Okay." He tosses his head back and forth. "I guess there have probably been about a dozen women."

A dozen.

"I guess that's not bad for a professional athlete. I mean, what's the average? Fifty?"

"I have no idea," he replies with a laugh. "Probably

more than a dozen, yes."

"So you're not a man-whore."

"No."

"What's your favorite flavor of ice cream?"

"Wow, your brain is on fire tonight." His fingers drift down my cheek to my neck. "Cherry Garcia."

"Favorite sexual position?"

"Any position that includes you in it," he replies immediately.

"Good answer." I grin up at him, and try to think of more questions. "What's your shoe size?"

"Sixteen."

"Holy shit! That's a big foot."

"I have to special order shoes."

"Do you like to read?"

"I'm a Clive Cussler fan," he replies and shakes his head. "I think we're playing twenty questions."

"I think it's fun."

"When is it my turn?"

"Go ahead." I shift my hips so I'm lying on one side, but I'm still looking up into his handsome face. "Ask away."

Just don't ask me if I'm pregnant.

"Are you comfortable?"

"That's an easy one. Yes."

He chuckles. "What's your favorite flower?"

"Magnolias."

I close my eyes and enjoy the feel of his fingers in my hair.

"What's your favorite dessert?"

"Hmm, that's a hard one. I guess it's a tie between Mama's pecan pie and key lime pie."

"Favorite alcoholic drink?"

"Margaritas."

"Are you getting sleepy?"

I grin as he brushes a fingertip down the bridge of my nose. "Yes."

"Do you want to go to bed?"

"Not yet."

"Okay. Tell me about the best concert you ever saw."

"That's an easy one too. I saw Nash a few years ago, and those guys put on one hell of a show. Also, Leo Nash is my boyfriend."

"I think he got married."

"Yes, we're fighting because he got married without asking me if it was okay, but he's hopelessly in love with me. I'm pretty sure that the whole time he was singing at the concert, he was singing just for me."

"I'm sure he was. What's the appeal of Leo Nash?"

"Have you seen him?" I open my eyes and lift my head, looking at Rhys like he's grown a new nose.

"Of course."

"Well, there's the tattoo thing, and the playing guitar thing, and the man can sing like crazy."

"Declan can sing like crazy."

"Declan is my brother," I remind him. "Declan will never be sexually attractive to me."

"Point taken."

"Speaking of celebrity crushes, who's yours?" I ask.

"I don't know."

"Lies! Of course you do. We all have our hall pass list."

"The list of people we get to sleep with without any repercussions?"

"That's right."

"So, you mean there's more on your list than just Leo Nash?" He's frowning, but I can tell that he's fighting a smile.

"Maybe. Who's on yours?"

"I don't think I have any," he says after giving it a moment of thought. "There are some beautiful women out there, but I don't think I want to have sex with any of them."

"If you don't want to tell me, just say so."

He suddenly stands and lifts me into his arms, walking toward my bedroom.

"I'll show you who I want to have sex with, Gabrielle."

"Oh, okay then."

CHAPTER SEVENTEEN

~Rhys~

She hasn't been herself for days and it's making me crazy. She won't tell me what's wrong, and when I ask, she just says she's tired. Or she doesn't feel well.

But it seems that she's backing away from me, and no matter what I do, it doesn't change. Even during her silly twenty questions game on the couch the other night, I could feel the coldness from her.

But when I took her to bed, she let go, and it was normal, *she* was normal.

I need to sit her down, right now, and have a heart to heart. I need to know if she's done with me, because I'm sure as fuck not done with her.

I'll never be done with her.

My phone rings and I answer without looking at the display.

"Hey, Rhys, this is Eli."

"Is Kate okay?"

"Yes, she's fine. I'm calling because I'm just hanging out here with Beau, Declan and Ben, and we'd like for you to join us."

"Now?"

"Now."

"Is this an emergency?"

"No, this is a guys' night in, and you're one of the guys. We're at Ben's house. I'll text you the address."

And with that, he hangs up, not even giving me a chance to turn him down.

So much for that talk with Gabby.

Gabby's in the kitchen with Sam and Derek, just finishing up dinner.

"Did you get Eli's call?" she asks with a smile.

"Yeah, we just hung up. They want me to go into the city for a while, but if you're not feeling well, I'll definitely stay."

"I'm fine." She waves me off and sets a bowl of mac 'n cheese with hot dogs in front of Sam. "Eli called me to get your number, and told me that you have to go. If y'all sacrifice a virgin or something, I don't want to know about it."

I chuckle and pull her into my arms, kiss her head, and just enjoy having her against me for a moment. She's been pulling away from me lately, which also has me on edge.

I need to touch her.

"Are you going to kiss and do gross stuff?" Sam asks while shoveling pasta into his mouth.

"Not right now," I reply and back away from Gabby. She won't look me in the eye, and I'm done playing this game. I tip her chin up so she has to meet my gaze. "We're going to talk later. Something is up with you, and I want to know what it is. I won't be late."

Before she can answer, I leave through the back door and head into the city. One way or the other, I'm going to know the score with Gabby before I fall asleep tonight.

***

Ben's house is in a nice neighborhood in New Orleans. All of the homes are large, surrounded by massive green oaks and tall wrought iron fences.

And Ben's home is simply impressive. I have no idea what the man does for a living, but whatever it is, he does well at it. I pull into the driveway behind a black Mercedes and cut the engine. I'm not stupid. I'm well aware that this is most likely an ambush.

I'm just hopeful that I can take at least one of them before the others kill me.

I can probably take Declan.

"Hey, man, come on in," Beau says when he answers the door and leads me through the house and down to the basement, where the others are shooting pool and watching a baseball game on a big screen TV.

Mariners are playing the Angels.

Eli is leaning over the pool table to take a shot. Declan is staring down at this phone while perched on a bar stool and Ben is pulling beers out of a fridge behind the wet bar. They all wave and say hello, looking nonchalant and innocent.

Not one of these fuckers is innocent. I like them all, but they're not innocent.

"Welcome to impromptu guys' night," Ben says as he passes me a beer and claps me on the shoulder. "Sorry for the short notice."

"It's totally fine," I reply calmly. Ben is as tall as the Boudreaux brothers, but a little leaner, less broad in the shoulders. He's also a solid brick of muscle, and from the stories I've heard, he's no one to fuck with. And he may not be a brother by blood, but he's been friends with all of them since they were small kids. "Thanks for the invite."

"Here's a picture of her!" Declan says and holds his phone up for all of us to see. "Blonde, leggy, pouty lips."

"Who is this again?" Eli asks as he examines the photo.

"She owns one of the clubs in the Quarter," Dec replies and sips his beer.

"And she doesn't fall for your charms?" Beau says with a wide grin. "Good for her."

"Yeah, it's a love-hate relationship." He shrugs as if it's of no consequence, but I can see that it's not. He likes her.

And it sounds like she doesn't like him much.

"Damn it, I'm off my game tonight," Eli mutters as he walks away from the table and Beau steps up.

"You're out of practice," Beau says mildly.

My eyes are on the game on the TV. Mariners are up, three to one, at the bottom of the sixth.

"I can see if the Cubs are playing," Beau offers. I simply smile and shake my head.

"No, it's cool. Are you a Mariners fan?"

"Nah, this was the first game I found," Ben replies. "Would you like a tour of the house?"

"Are you going to kill me and bury me in the basement?" I ask. Declan snickers and Beau and Eli exchange glances, but Ben's face remains perfectly calm and sober.

"Not right away," he replies and then a smile slowly slides over his face.

"Not that that's terribly reassuring, but sure, I'd love a tour. Your place is beautiful."

"Thanks." Ben turns to the brothers, nods, and leads me out of the room.

He's a man of few words.

"The house was built in 1875," he begins. "By one of

my great-grandfathers."

"So you inherited it."

"I did."

He leads me upstairs and shows me around the first floor, then leads me through the rest of the house. Finally, he gestures for me to follow him outside and to a guest house out back.

He really is going to kill me.

"So, you're not going to bury me in the basement. You're going to bury me in the back yard."

He simply smiles back at me. A cold smile that would make most men's blood run with ice.

I simply raise a brow and follow him into the building, then whistle at the sight of the exercise equipment and fighting ring. "This is impressive."

"This is where I find my balance," he replies quietly. "Look, the other guys might want to kill you, and if you fuck up, I will too, but I just wanted to talk to you alone."

"Fair enough." I cross my arms over my chest and wait for the other man to speak. Ben frowns and looks down, then looks back up at me with pure possessiveness.

"I'm sure you've already received a few *fuck with my sister and I'll kill you* talks."

I nod, but I don't smile. It's not funny.

"So I want to give you mine. Gabby is as much my little sister as she is the others. I've known her since the day she came home from the hospital. She's amazing."

"No lie."

The door opens behind me and the other guys walk in.

"We didn't want you to kill him without us seeing it," Declan says to Ben calmly. "He's a big guy. It could be a good show."

"I want to help," Eli says.

"You do realize that without me, you and Kate wouldn't *be*," I remind him. "Don't make me regret encouraging her to forgive you for being an idiot."

Beau lays on a bench and begins doing bench press.

"As I was saying," Ben says, glaring at the other guys. "Gabby is important to all of us. She's sweet, and she has an innocence about her that makes her vulnerable."

"She's the strongest person I know," I reply. *She's not weak.*

"She's been through a lot," Ben continues. "I wanted to kill the fucker who knocked her up and left her high and dry, but no one would let me."

"I would have let you," Beau says. "If I could have helped."

"I'd like to kill him myself," I add.

"Let me put it this way," Ben says as he steps closer to me. I stand my ground, looking him unblinkingly in the eyes. I'll be damned if he's going to intimidate me and scare me away. "If you fuck with her and break her heart, I'll kill you and no one will ever find the body. I may go to jail, but it won't be because they found your body."

"I'm not going to hurt her," I reply and shake my head. "Hurting her is the farthest thing from my mind. I *love* her, for fuck sake."

I push my hands through my hair and pace. "Why does everyone always assume that I'll break her heart?"

"Because you're not permanent," Declan replies. "You're here for a while, but then you're leaving again, and Gabby's home is here."

"I am gone a lot for my job," I agree. "But that doesn't mean that Gabby and Sam can't join me in the summer sometimes, or that I can't make New Orleans my home base."

"You'd do that?" Beau asks, not looking convinced. "You'd uproot your life for her?"

"I'd do anything for her," I reply honestly. "She is all that matters."

"There's Sam too," Eli says. "They are a package deal."

"Absolutely. Jesus, do you all think I'm such an asshole that I don't know that Sam is, and will always be, a part of it?"

"We don't think you're an asshole," Declan says. "We've seen the way you look at Gabby, the way you treat both of them, and if we thought it was with anything less than love and kindness, we'd have killed you already."

"But kids complicate relationships," Ben says. "People put up with someone's kid for a while, and then get tired of them."

Now I'm just getting pissed.

"Those people are assholes," I reply coldly. "Sam is a great boy. He's smart and loving, and I love having him around. He's not an add-on or something for me to tolerate."

"Gabby's young, and she's been through a lot," Eli begins, but I whirl, cutting him off.

"You're pissing me off with this whole *Gabby's innocent and weak* shit you keep flinging at me. She's not fucking weak. She's the strongest person I know, and if you had any respect or love for her at all, you'd see that too. If she didn't want me around, or if I did something to piss her off, trust me, she'd be the first to kick my ass.

"She's the most amazing mother I've seen, and I was raised by one of the best there is. She loves that boy more than anything. She'd die before she ever let him come into harm's way. But you know what? She'd do the same for any of you, or anyone else she loves. She's fiercely loyal, and she loves so big for someone so small.

"Just because she's a little thing doesn't mean that she's *weak*."

I stop pacing and ranting to find all four men standing with their arms crossed and smiles on their faces.

"You're right," Beau says. "So what are you going to do?"

What am I going to do?

"I'm going to make sure she knows how magnificent she is, and I'm going to beg her to have mercy on me and be with me forever."

"There better be a ring in there somewhere," Beau says.

"She can have anything she wants," I reply. "You guys do know that I do quite well at baseball."

"If we didn't think you could take care of her, you wouldn't be here," Ben says quietly. "But the money is only one piece of it. No woman we love will ever be hurt by a man again, not if we can stop it."

"I get it." I rub my hands over my face, and then meet Eli's eyes with mine. "You know I get it. Kate was hurt more than any human being should be, and I couldn't stop it. It's the most helpless, fucked-up feeling there is. No one deserves that. You have to know that I'd kill anyone that ever tried to hurt her that way again."

"I do know," Eli says with a nod.

"And I'd die before I ever let Gabby be hurt. I don't want to hurt her, I want to love her. I want to make sure she and Sam are safe and happy, always."

.Beau, Declan, and Ben are much more relaxed. Almost...*jovial.*

"Did I miss something?"

"Nope, we're just happy with your response," Beau says. "Shall we go back in so I can continue to kick Eli's ass at pool?"

"Fuck that. I have a woman waiting at home," Eli says with a grin. "I'm out of here."

Gabby is waiting at home, too, and she hasn't been feeling well. Not to mention, she and I need to have a talk.

"I'm out too," I reply.

"I'll play," Declan says. "Come on, Beau. We can take Ben."

"You can't take me at anything," Ben replies with a laugh. "But you can sure as fuck try."

"I was fucking winning," Beau says with a scowl.

"Come on, take it like a man," Ben says.

***

It wasn't terribly late when I got back last night, but Gabby was already asleep, and now I feel her trying to quietly slip out of the bed without waking me.

She's fucking avoiding me.

And it's pissing me off.

I let her slide out of the bed, and when she's a few feet from the bathroom, I say, "We need to talk, Gabby."

She stops in her tracks and her shoulders sag as she turns around and stares at me with sleepy eyes. "About what?"

"About why you're avoiding me."

"I'm not," she says and pushes her hand through her hair as I climb out of the bed. "I was trying to let you sleep. Sam and I are heading into the city for the day."

She doesn't say it out loud, but *without you* is obviously at the end of that sentence.

"Did I do something to piss you off?"

She frowns and looks down at her feet, then up at me. "No."

"Then what's wrong, baby?"

She shakes her head, but before she can deny that anything is going on, I grip her shoulders in my hands and kiss her forehead. "Something is wrong, and I need to know what it is."

She steps back out of my grasp. "I've told you a hundred times, nothing is wrong."

"You're lying."

She shakes her head stubbornly. "Stop this. I told you. Nothing. Is. Wrong. Now drop it. I don't need this from you, Rhys. If you don't like my answer, that's your problem."

She stomps into the bathroom and slams the door, and I decide to give her space for now before I say something I'll regret.

Like *stop fucking lying to me and just tell me what the fuck has crawled up your ass.*

That won't help anything.

So I return to my own room upstairs, and take a shower, answer some emails, and waste a bit of time, and when I'm sure that Gabby and Sam are gone, I head downstairs.

Eva, the new employee, is in the kitchen getting breakfast ready for the guests. Eva is in her fifties, recently widowed, and wealthy. But she's also lonely, and this job was right up her alley.

She smiles as I walk in the kitchen.

"Can I get you anything, Mister Rhys?"

"No thank you, Miss Eva," I reply with a smile. She raises the spatula and points it at me, a smile on her pretty face.

"You're too skinny. You need to eat."

"I'll keep that in mind." I wave and leave out of the back, heading for the road. I need to work off some of this frustration. I plug my earphones in my ears and jog, then work my way into a run.

Something is very wrong with Gabby. When I pulled her into my arms last night, I could tell that she'd been crying. Why won't she just talk to me? I can't fix it if I don't know what's wrong.

I run for thirty minutes, then turn around and head back toward the inn.

I have no idea where she and Sam went this morning. Not that she needs to check in with me, but she usually lets me know if she's not going to be around. It's just a matter of consideration for each other.

And, goddamn it, I miss her.

I run around the inn to the barn and spend another hour working on stretches and weight training. The music is still pulsing in my ears when it suddenly stops and my phone starts ringing.

"Hello."

"Where the hell are you?" I frown and stare down at Melanie's name on my phone.

"What are you talking about? I'm in New Orleans."

"You're supposed to be in Chicago, *today,* to film the Children's Hospital commercial." She sounds very shrill, and very pissed. "I can't believe you forgot, Rhys!"

Fuck.

"I'm sorry. I can be there today. Charter me a plane and I'll be on my way to the airport in less than thirty minutes."

"Make it fifteen," she growls and ends the call.

"Damn it," I mutter and run for the house. I don't have time for a shower, but take a quick one anyway, throw some clothes on, and then simply scoop up my things and throw them all in my duffel.

I have no idea what I'll need, so I just take it all. I didn't have much to begin with anyway.

Gabby's phone rings and rings, and finally sends me to voice mail. Where the fuck is she? I don't want to leave without explaining to her what's happening.

I run past Eva and out to my car, then peel out of the driveway, headed to the airport.

I try to call Gabby again, but it's no use. So I send her a text.

I'm needed in Chicago. I had to leave.

I'll call her when I get there and explain it all to her. I already miss her. I've been missing her for days. I wish I'd had a chance to kiss her and hold her in my arms before I left.

I wish she'd fucking talk to me.

CHAPTER EIGHTEEN

~Gabby~

"Mom, I'm hungry." Sam's shuffling his feet as he follows me out of the mall toward our car. We've been shopping for school clothes and new linens for the inn all morning, and I admit, I'm hungry too, which is a relief because food hasn't set well on my stomach for days.

"I know, buddy. Let's go get some lunch."

"But it's not even eleven. It's too early for lunch."

"Okay, let's go get a second breakfast," I reply with a laugh and pull my phone out of my pocket to check it. I've missed three calls from Rhys, and one text from an hour and a half ago.

I'm needed in Chicago. I had to leave.

I read it three times, hoping the words will change, but each time they're the same.

He's gone.

He's gone.

And why am I surprised? I knew this day was coming. He's never been permanent, but I thought that he would have at least said goodbye in person.

I try to call him back, but it goes directly to voice mail. Seriously? How could he have caught a flight in less than two hours?

I guess he was in a hurry to leave.

"Mom, it's getting hot in here," Sam whines from the back seat. I meet his eyes in the rearview mirror and want more than anything to fall apart.

How am I going to explain this to him? He loves Rhys just as much as I do.

"Sorry, buddy," I reply and turn the car on, blast the air conditioning, and chew my lip while I try to figure out what to do.

What do I do?

I can't fall apart in front of Sam. And I'm not ready to tell him that Rhys is gone. I just don't know how I'm going to do that.

I need my mama.

The ten-minute drive to her house seems endless.

"Why are we going to Nannan's?" Sam asks.

"Just because," I reply and pull in her driveway. Sam follows me up to the front door of the massive house, and when Mama answers, she smiles and hugs us both.

"This is a nice surprise. Come on in."

"I need a favor," I reply immediately, and Mama's shrewd eyes narrow as she pats Sam on the head.

"Sam, why don't you go pour yourself some sweet tea?"

"Yes, ma'am. Do you have any food? I'm starving!"

"You can help yourself to a cookie, and I'll make you something in a minute."

"Thanks, Nannan," he says with a grin and heads out to the kitchen.

"What's wrong?" she asks immediately when Sam is out of earshot.

I shake my head, still not ready to fall apart. "I have a lot on my mind. Would you mind keeping him overnight? I know it's short notice, and I'm sorry."

"He can stay as long as you need him to, but you didn't answer my question."

"I think I might be heartbroken," I whisper and find myself immediately caught up in her arms, held close.

"He's a fool," she says simply, then pulls away and pats my cheek. "And you're worth more than that."

"You don't even know what happened."

"I don't need to; I'm your mama. Go ahead and go. I'll keep Sam."

"Thanks, Mama."

Once in my car, I immediately drive into the Quarter and park in front of Charly's shop. She's the only one who knows *everything*. I need her.

I push inside and find Charly arranging a hat on a mannequin. There are no customers in the store. She glances up and smiles, and then sobers when she sees my face.

"What's wrong? Are you okay?"

And now the tears come, hard and fast, swooping over me like waves on the shoreline, and I'm lost under them. I can't breathe, I can't think, I can only cry and cry. Charly wraps me in her arms and rocks me back and forth, murmuring in my ear, but I can't hear the words.

All I know is that another man that I cared for is gone. But even worse, the only man I ever loved just walked out of my life.

Without saying goodbye. Without even a backward glance.

"He's gone," I whisper when the worst of the sobs have subsided.

236 | KRISTEN PROBY

"What?" She grips my shoulders and pushes me back so she can see my face. "Are you kidding me?"

"No, I got this text this morning." I show her the message and begin crying again.

"He sent a *text?*" she asks.

I simply nod and take a deep breath.

"So, you told him you're pregnant and he cut out of here? What the fuck is wrong with men?"

I glance down, embarrassed, and Charly shakes her head adamantly.

"No. No, Gabby. Don't tell me you didn't tell him!"

"I didn't tell him."

"Why the hell not? You've had *days* to tell him!"

"Because I was just starting to get my own head wrapped around it," I reply and pace away from her, touching the pretty shoes she has displayed throughout the store. "And then he went to hang out with the boys last night. I was surprised he came home without any bruises."

"What did the boys do?" she asks, surprised.

"I don't know. Eli said they wanted to include him in a guys' night with Beau, Dec and Ben."

"Ben?" Her eyes go wide and she swallows hard. "And Rhys returned alive?"

"I know. I was a little surprised."

"Why didn't you tell him when he got back?"

"I pretended to be asleep." I wince. If I'd known that it would be the last night I'd have with him, I wouldn't have done that. I would have embraced him and let him make love to me. I would have talked to him all night, and I would have savored every smell, every sound, *every moment.* "I know, Char. I know I should have told him, but it didn't exactly work out well for me the last time I had to tell a guy that I was pregnant."

"Rhys isn't that piece of shit Colby, Gabs."

"No," I agree and sigh. "I understand that not all men are Colby. But he still left. He didn't even say goodbye to Sam. How am I supposed to tell Sam that he's gone, and we weren't important enough to say goodbye in person?"

"Where is Sam?"

"With Mama."

She nods and leans on her counter, demolishing a paperclip as she thinks.

"And Eva is taking care of the inn?"

I nod. "I brought Sam into the city for school clothes and some new things for the inn. Eva's taking over all day."

"Wow, you took a whole day off that isn't a Sunday."

"I needed to get away and think."

"You've been doing a lot of thinking, Gabby. It was time to talk."

"It doesn't matter. He's gone."

"You have his phone number."

"Stop, Charly. I don't know what I'm going to do." I shake my head and feel the tears want to start again. "I need to *not* think about this for a while. I need to clear my head."

"Okay." Charly grins and points to a stack of shoe boxes. "You can display those. And wait on customers when they come in."

That dries up the rest of the tears. "You want me to *work* for you?"

"Yep."

"So much for a day off."

"It'll take your mind off of *he who shall not be named*, and I can keep my eye on you. Win-win."

"What are you going to pay me?"

"Lunch." She grins as a customer walks in and begins browsing through the shoes. "There's your first customer."

"I really wanted to spend the day wallowing in self-pity."

"Too bad," Charly says. "I don't have time for that. We will work, and then we'll wallow."

"Why are *you* wallowing?"

"Because you are," she replies, as though I'm just being stubborn. "Women wallow together, sugar. Now, go greet your customer."

And with that, she walks through a curtain to the stock room.

I turn and smile at the blonde wandering among the shoes. "Good morning. Can I help you find anything?"

"Well, I'm not sure," she replies and glances up to smile back at me. She's beautiful with long, loosely curled hair and big blue eyes. She's in a tank top, showing off some of the most amazing tattoos I've ever seen on her right arm, and she's got a great rack.

"What are you in the mood for?"

"I'm in the mood to kick a man's ass," she replies and then laughs. "And shoes always make me feel better."

"I know that feeling," I reply with a nod. "Men are jackasses."

"Amen."

"I'm Gabby."

"Callie," she replies and picks up a pair of sexy red stilettos. "These are hot."

"Super hot," I agree. "And designed to make a man's tongue fall out of his mouth."

"Hmm, that wouldn't be a bad thing." She turns them over in her hands. "I'll try an eight, please."

"Sure thing." I fetch the shoes and return to Callie, dying to ask her lots of questions. "Are you from here?"

"Yes, ma'am," she says and slips her feet into the shoes,

then struts around the shop expertly. "Oh, these are amazing."

"They make your legs look six feet long," I reply with envy. "And that peep toe shows off your pedicure."

"I'll take them."

"Perfect." Callie joins me at the register. "So, who are you trying to kill with these shoes?"

She laughs and hands me her debit card. "A man that makes me crazy. I either want to deck him or climb him. There doesn't seem to be an in-between."

"Well, these shoes are badass."

"And I can wear them to work," she says with a nod.

"What do you do?"

"I own a club just a few blocks over. I've walked past this store dozens of times and I'm addicted to shoes, so I had to come in."

"Isn't it in our DNA to be addicted to shoes?" I chuckle and bag her purchase add tissue paper, and walk around to pass her bag to her. "Thanks for coming in."

Callie smiles and waves as she leaves the shop, and I mentally thank Charly. I need this distraction.

I didn't think about Rhys at all for about ten minutes. The mental picture of his amazing arms and abs never once entered my brain. Or the way he would smile that smile that he reserved just for me. Or the way his eyes would drift closed every time he first pushed inside me, then whisper *fucking hell, Gabrielle* because it felt so damn good.

Nope, didn't think about any of that.

Baby steps. That's the key.

"I talked to Mama," Charly announces as she joins me. "She's going to keep Sam until Sunday's dinner."

"She doesn't have to do that," I insist, but Charly shakes her head firmly.

"They'll have fun. And this way you can figure some stuff out and hang out with me for a few days."

"You're going to hang out with me?"

"Again, not letting you wallow alone, sugar." She winks and sets a hat on my head. "That's a good color for you."

"I love you, you know."

"I love you more."

***

"I'd forgotten how nice it is out here," Charly says as she swings opposite from me. She's in a pretty sundress, lazily swaying back and forth. I'm in my usual spot, paging through the reservations coming up this week on my iPad, thanks to the cops for returning it to me. Cindy was fined and spent a night in jail for grand larceny.

And I'm just petty enough to find the thought of Cindy sitting in a jail cell very satisfying.

"I love how the trees make the house so cool," Charly says with a sigh.

"Me too."

"Have you heard from Rhys?"

"No." I don't look up. The sting of not hearing from him at all is still sharp. It's like he left and immediately forgot about me. And I miss him, damn it. I got so used to having him here, laughing with him, being in his arms, feeling him next to me while we slept.

And now he's just *gone*. And it hurts so fucking bad.

"Maybe you will," she says optimistically.

"I doubt it."

"Why?"

"Because he's a jerk."

"Oh, come on, sugar. It's not like he knew you were pregnant and jetted. He *didn't* know."

"I *trusted him*, Charly. I trusted him with my son, with my heart. I let my guard down, and I don't *do* that. I let myself feel something so big for him it consumed me. I knew he would leave eventually, so I put that on me. He didn't make me love him, but I did all the same. He never said that he wanted to stay, but regardless, he didn't say goodbye. He didn't say *anything*. And I can deal with it when it comes to me, but not when it comes to Sam. Sam idolizes him and Rhys left as if Sam doesn't matter at all. And that's bullshit. So he can rot in hell as far as I'm concerned."

"Gabby, you don't know why he was called to Chicago, or even if he intends to stay there."

"Why wouldn't he stay there? That's where his team is, his doctors, everything."

"But until you talk to him, you don't *know*. What if there had been an emergency with one of the other players or the coaches? Maybe someone died, or got hurt? Maybe he didn't have a choice."

"He hasn't called *once*. All he had to do was pick up the phone and explain. He hasn't. And he took all of his stuff."

"Your phone has been off for the better part of two days, Gabby. You only turn it on to check messages, which is *very* unlike you. How do you know he hasn't tried to call?"

"He hasn't left a message."

"Maybe—"

"Look, I appreciate that you're playing devil's advocate, but I don't want to try to guess what he's thinking. I'm not a mind reader, Charly. And if he's not going to communicate with me, well, things aren't going to work out anyway."

"All I'm suggesting is that you should keep an open mind."

"So noted." Keeping my eyes pinned on the iPad, I hear a car driving up the driveway.

"Are you expecting anyone?" Charly asks.

"No. It's Sunday. The guests are all gone. Someone's probably lost. It happens all the time."

The car stops and a man climbs out of it, and my whole world stands still.

"Oh shit," Charly mutters next to me and is immediately on her feet, pulling her phone out of her bra. "Beau, we need you on the front porch *now*."

"Hey, Gabby," Colby says as he saunters closer. It's been almost exactly eight years since I saw Colby, and little has changed about him, but as I stare at the man I once foolishly believed I loved, I can't for the life of me figure out what I found attractive about him before.

"You need to get the hell out of here," Charly says, her voice hard and mean. But Colby doesn't even glance at her. He just watches me and continues talking to me.

"You look fantastic. You haven't changed at all. Your body's still smokin', even after having a kid."

"You're such a piece of shit," Charly growls, and suddenly, Beau is with us, coming through the front door.

"Call the police," he instructs Charly, who steps to the side and does as Beau asks. Without taking his off of Colby, Beau turns to. His face is blank, but his whole body is tight with anger. "What the fuck are you doing here?"

"It's nice to see you too, Beau," Colby replies, but he's still watching me. He's trying to intimidate me, and eight years ago, it would have worked.

Today, he's just pissing me off.

"There's no need to call the police," Colby continues.

"I'm not doing anything wrong."

"This is private property," I reply, speaking for the first time. Thank God my voice sounds strong and unwavering, because I'm pretty sure my stomach is in my throat. My hands are shaking, so I clench them into fists. "*My* property. And I want you off of it."

"Yeah, I heard you made this old place into a hotel." He looks around and nods, as though he needs to give me his approval. "It's real nice."

"Cut the shit," Beau snarls. "What the fuck do you want?"

"I want to see my kid." Colby smiles innocently.

"You signed your rights away," Beau replies. "You have no legal right to be here."

"Yeah." Colby nods thoughtfully. "I did sign that contract, but I was pretty young, and didn't understand what I was doing. Especially with you and your bully of a father standing over me. I think I felt threatened. Coerced." He smiles again, all innocence gone, replaced with nothing but menace.

"Bullshit," Beau spits out between clenched teeth. "Your own lawyer was with you, you piece of shit."

"Well, I saw a new attorney," Colby begins and my blood runs cold. "And he seems to think that I have a case here. That I might be able to appeal and have that contract thrown out."

"You're out of your fucking mind," Charly cries. "You weren't coerced into anything. In fact, it was probably Gabby who was coerced into having sex with you."

"Oh no, she was more than willing." He winks at me, making my stomach roll.

I'm going to throw up.

"I'm going to kick your ass," Beau says calmly.

"Again."

"I should have pressed charges the first time," Colby replies. "You broke my fucking ribs."

"You deserved worse," Charly says. "I'd like to kick your balls into your fucking nostrils."

"Wow, violence must run in the family." Colby smirks. "I wouldn't want my child to be raised in such a volatile situation. That can't be good for him."

"Oh, I'll show you volatile, you slimy piece of shit."

I can hear another car approaching, but all I can see is Colby and his cold eyes as they bore into mine.

He's going to try to take my child from me.

It'll be a cold day in hell before that ever happens. My family has enough money to destroy him, and Beau and Eli would do it without batting an eye.

A car door slams shut, and Charly whispers next to me, "Oh, shit."

Now what?

I turn to my left and my gaze collides with bright green eyes.

Shit.

CHAPTER NINETEEN

~Rhys~

I can't reach her. Now Gabby's phone is turned off, sending me straight to voice mail.

It pisses me the fuck off.

Chicago has been a flurry of activity since I got to town, and I just got to my hotel. I don't know anyone else's phone number, so I call Kate.

"What's up, buttercup?" she asks as she answers the phone.

"I'm in Chicago," I reply dryly.

"What?" I hear her chair creek as she sits up straight. "Why are you in Chicago?"

"I forgot about a charity thing I was signed up for and couldn't back out, so I had to rush out of town, and Gabby wasn't home when I left so I couldn't explain."

"Uh oh," Kate mutters.

"I mean, I did text her, but now I can't reach her."

"What did you say in your text?"

"That I was needed in Chicago and I had to leave."

She's quiet for a long moment, and then she sounds

246 | KRISTEN PROBY

exasperated as she says, "That's it?"

"I've been trying to *call her,* Kate."

"Idiot," she mutters, making my jaw tick. "What do you want me to do? Do you want me to go out and see her, tell her what's up?"

"No, that should come from me."

"I agree."

"I'm going to have some groveling to do, aren't I?"

"Oh yeah. Are you sure you don't want me to go let her know what's up?"

"I'm sure. I just want to freaking talk to her, and I was frustrated, so I needed to vent. I'll be back on Sunday and I'll grovel."

"Flowers. Flowers work. And things that sparkle."

Things that sparkle.

"That's an excellent idea."

"Flowers are always an excellent idea."

"No, the things that sparkle."

There's another pause, and then my phone is suddenly buzzing. Kate has switched to FaceTime mode.

"Hey."

"Are you talking about a necklace, or earrings or something?" she asks with narrowed green eyes.

"Or something."

"Define *something.*"

"I love her," I begin and rub my hand over the back of my neck. "She's mine, Kate. Forever. There is no one else out there for me."

"You're going to buy a *ring?*" she shrieks.

"Damn right."

"Rhys, I adore Gabby, and I love you more than almost anyone, but it's only been a couple of months." She's frowning the way she does when she's particularly worried that I'll do something to screw up, but I know in my heart of hearts that this is right.

"I knew the minute I saw her," I admit softly. "It was like I was hit with a jackhammer. She's everything I've ever wanted, Kate. She's all I'll ever need. The thought of being without her makes me fucking panic."

"Wow." Tears fill her pretty eyes and she gives me a goofy smile. "I'm so happy for you."

I glance at the time and calculate the couple of hours I have before I have to be on set for the commercial.

"I have to go shopping." I grin at the woman who's always been more of a sister to me than anything else. "Love you, kiddo."

"I want photos, Rhys O'Shaughnessy. You'll need my input."

"Good point. Okay, I'll send photos from the jewelry store."

"Tiffany," she insists, pointing at me. "If it doesn't come in a blue box with a white bow, we don't want it."

"Yes, ma'am."

"Oh my God, you're buying a ring!" She does a little happy dance in her chair.

"This is our secret, Mary Katherine."

"Call me Mary Katherine again and I'll slash your tires."

"Promise me you won't tell. Not even Eli."

She sighs, blowing her lips together in a raspberry, but finally nods. "Okay, I won't tell Eli, or anyone else. But make it quick."

"I'll see her on Sunday."

I end the call and rush out of the hotel, catch a cab to Tiffany, and spend the next several hours searching for the perfect ring for my girl. I send several photos to Kate, but each time she replies with a simple *no*.

And I agree, none of them are right. Finally, the saleswoman, who has been exceedingly patient and kind, says, "Wait, I just saw something come in this morning that might be perfect." She leaves for several minutes and then returns with the perfect ring.

Perfect.

"It's vintage inspired," the saleswoman begins. "That means it has an older feel, almost like an heirloom. As you can see, there is etched scrollwork on the sides, with diamonds, and the stone on top is a princess-cut. It's three total karats."

It's so Gabby. She has such a love for tradition, for older styles. I can just see this on her hand.

"I'll take it."

"I didn't even tell you how much it is," she says with a chuckle.

"It doesn't matter. It's hers."

***

It's the second day of filming. I've had lunches and dinners and other meetings crammed between shooting short scenes for the commercial for the children's hospital. And in between it all, I've taken time to actually sit with the kids.

They're the best part.

And they make me miss Sam, and so damn thankful that he's healthy and whole. Having a very sick child must be its own special kind of hell. I didn't like it when Sam had the flu. I can't imagine having a child with cancer.

I can feel my phone buzzing in my pocket, but can't take the time to answer it as I'm once again surrounded by fans and parents of the patients, wanting to say hello and get their baseballs autographed.

When the crowd thins, a petite woman about Gabby's age approaches me with a shy smile.

"I'm sorry to bother you. My name is Fiona. My son is a huge fan of yours, and I was wondering if you'd be willing to say hi to him?"

"Of course," I reply with a grin. "Where is he?" I glance around, but I don't see any little boys nearby.

"He's in room 432. He's not well enough to come out here." She bites her lip, looking hopeful.

"No problem." I catch Melanie's attention. "I'll be back. I have a fan to go see."

"We're done here," Melanie replies with a smile. "No worries."

I nod and follow Fiona to her son's room. He's lying in the bed, hooked up to IVs and other machines that I'm not smart enough to know what their function is.

He's completely bald. No eyelashes or eyebrows. But he's smiling widely, and his dark brown eyes, rimmed with dark circles, are overjoyed.

"You talked him into it!" he exclaims.

"I wasn't a hard sell," I reply and shake his hand. "I hear you're our biggest fan."

"I'm *your* biggest fan," he says and tries to sit. "Mom, will you push me up?"

"Sure, buddy." She pushes a button and his bed inclines. "But you know you can't stay this way for long."

"Just for a little while," he says. "Are you coming back next season?"

"Absolutely. I wouldn't miss it."

"Thank God! They suck without you!"

"Andrew!" Fiona narrows her eyes on her son. "Be nice."

"It's okay." I chuckle and shrug. "I don't know what

to tell you, kid. But I will be back in the spring."

"Good."

"How old are you?"

"Seven," he replies. "I have osteosarcoma in my legs."

Same age as Sam.

"It means I have bone cancer."

The fact that a seven-year-old even knows the meaning of the word osteosarcoma makes me sick to my stomach. I sit with Andrew for a long time, talking about baseball and TV shows, and when his eyes are so heavy he can hardly keep them open, I say goodbye, then walk out of the room with Fiona.

"Thank you for that," she whispers. "He'll talk about that for the rest of his life."

"Here's hoping that's a very long time."

She nods, but looks sad when she shrugs. "They're doing everything they can do. Now we wait and hope it works."

"Will you keep me posted?" I ask without even thinking. "I'll give you my email address. I'd like to know that he's okay."

She tilts her head to the side, and suddenly she's in my arms, hugging me tight.

"I will gladly let you know how he's doing."

"Thank you."

When I'm out of the hospital, I pull my phone out of my pocket and find that I missed a call from a Louisiana number that I don't recognize. When I check my voice mail, I hear Charly's voice.

"This is Charly. Call me back."

She doesn't sound particularly happy with me.

I sit in the rental car and dial her number.

"It's about time."

"It's been a busy day. What can I do for you?"

"You can go straight to hell," she replies, her voice full of ice. "You're a real asshole, Rhys O'Shaughnessy."

"Hold up."

"No, *you* hold up. You left without even saying goodbye to either Gabby or Sam. That was an asshole move, Rhys. We all trusted you with them. We believed that you'd be good for them. My brothers let you *live*."

"Nice of them," I mutter, but she doesn't even hear me; she just keeps going. She's in über protective sister mode, and she's on a roll.

"But even more than that, *Gabby* trusted you. Do you know how hard it is for her to do that? Because *she doesn't do that*. And she let you in. She and Sam both fell for you, and you just walked right out of their lives without even a backward glance. I sure as fuck hope you're a better father than you are a fuck buddy, I'll tell you that right now."

"Wait. What?"

Better father?

"Because she doesn't deserve what she got last time this time around."

"Charly, stop taking."

"Don't you tell me to stop talking! You're not the one who's been consoling her since you walked out. How could you do that?"

"I didn't leave for good! Jesus, is that what she thinks?"

"Of course that's what she thinks! What do you mean you didn't leave for good?"

"I had to come to Chicago for a charity thing, Charly. I forgot about it, and had to leave unexpectedly. I'm coming back down tomorrow."

"Well, thank God. You need to work on your communication skills, Rhys."

"So does your sister," I reply. "And what did you mean about the father thing?"

"Oh." There's a long pause, full of her mumbling about being stupid, except I think she's talking about herself this time. "Look, you need to just get back down here as soon as possible."

"Charly—"

"Seriously. This isn't my story to tell, Rhys. But you *need* to be here."

"I have a breakfast thing tomorrow that I can't get out of, but I'll be on a flight right after it's done. I'll be there by early afternoon."

"Good."

"Is she okay, Charly?"

"She will be," she replies, her voice much more calm now. "And she would be without you, too. Trust me on that. But I think she's better with you."

I'm so much better with her too.

***

It's a beautiful day in Louisiana. I've driven this road a hundred times now, yet it feels like it's taking me forever to get there.

I need to see her.

When I finally pull into the long driveway, I see Gabby standing on the porch with Charly and Beau, and a strange man standing just off the porch, his hands on his hips, talking to them.

Beau's hands are fisted, his face tight. Charly is simply scowling.

And Gabby looks terrified.

What the fuck is this?

I rush out of the car and around the house to the porch, my eyes immediately on Gabby. She raises her face to meet my gaze, and she freezes, her eyes widening. She looks shocked to see me.

And not exactly happy.

"What's going on?" I ask as I climb the stairs and stand next to Gabby.

"That's the sperm donor," Charly says, nudging her chin toward the stranger.

"What are you doing here?" I ask, glowering. Beau is almost quivering with rage.

"Who are you?" Colby asks.

"None of your fucking business," I reply calmly. "But I can be your worst nightmare if you don't tell me what the hell you want."

"So many threats around here," he replies with a smirk. "The judge will love hearing about it when I go to get custody of my kid."

"What is he talking about?" I stare down at Gabby, then Beau and Charly.

"He's talking out of his ass," Beau replies.

"I don't know why everyone is so surprised I'm here," Colby says with a shake of his head. "I've been telling Gabby for two months that I was coming to see my kid."

We all stop cold and turn to look at Gabby, who looks ready to tear Colby's head off.

"You emailed me *one time*," she says, pointing her finger at him. "You called me *one time*, three days ago. I told you to stay away, that you're not welcome here. *Why* for the love of Moses would I expect you to show up here? You aren't welcome here!"

"Wait. You've been corresponding?" Beau asks incredulously. "You were told to never contact her again. It's in the fucking contract!"

Colby shrugs as if it's all of little consequence to him.

254 | KRISTEN PROBY

I can't stop looking at Gabby, wondering what the fuck is happening here, and why she never said anything to me.

Two cop cars pull into the driveway and Gabby visibly relaxes when four officers approach.

"What's going on here?" one of the officers asks.

"This man is trespassing," Beau replies. "This is private property and he's not welcome here."

"Is he acting in a threatening manner?"

"He's not welcome here," Beau repeats.

"Looks like you need to leave," the officer says to Colby, who points at Gabby.

"She's keeping my son from me."

"That's a lie," Gabby says, hysteria on the edges of her voice. "He has no right to my child."

"Is he the father?"

"He's the fucking sperm donor," Charly says again.

"Do you have a court order saying you can see the child?" the officer asks Colby, who shakes his head.

"No. We were just kids when she got pregnant, and then her brothers and father made me sign away my rights. I mean, they're rich and really big, and made sure I knew that they'd make my life hell if I didn't sign."

"That's a fucking lie," Gabby repeats and Beau looks ready to jump off this porch and kick Colby's ass.

I'll happy join him. *This* is the loser who knocked Gabby up? What was she thinking? He's a smarmy idiot.

"Without a court order, you have no business here. You need to leave."

"Fine. I'll go, but I'm taking you to court." He points at Gabby, glaring at her, and I growl low in my throat. I want to pull his fucking balls out. "I want my kid."

"You'll never lay your fucking eyes on him," Gabby replies firmly. She tilts her chin up, throwing daggers with her eyes. "He's not your son. He's nothing to you."

Good girl.

Colby is escorted off the property and the policemen wait until he's driven away. When everyone is gone, Charly breathes a huge sigh of relief, and Beau whirls on Gabby, his face furious.

"What. The. Fuck. Gabby."

"This is *not* my fault," she insists, going toe-to-toe with her brother. God, she looks magnificent. I've missed her so damn much. I want to carry her inside and protect her from all of this. I want to scoop her up and never let go.

"He *emailed* you!" Beau yells. "Months ago!"

I tuck Gabby behind me and confront Beau myself. "Don't fucking talk to her like that. Ever."

"It's my *job* to protect her!" His eyes find Gabby's, and as angry as he is, he also looks hurt. "I told you to tell me if he ever tried to contact you."

"I know," she says.

"Well, why didn't you?"

"Because I'm not a baby!"

CHAPTER TWENTY

~Gabby~

I can't believe this is happening. Between Colby showing up, Beau being pissed at me, and Rhys coming back, my nerves are shot.

And I'm royally pissed.

"That's it?" Beau asks and shakes his head. "You didn't tell me that asshole was contacting you because *you're not a baby?*"

"Stop trying to fix my life!" I stomp away, then back again. "I love you. I know that you think that you have to always swoop in and save the day where I'm concerned, but I'm a grown woman, Beau! I'm not the young girl who got in trouble. I'm a mom. I'm a business woman. I have my fucking shit together."

"No one said you didn't," Beau replies as I walk past Rhys again. He's leaning against the railing, watching the show. He looks almost casual, but his eyes are narrowed and every muscle in his body is tense, as if he's ready to spring to my defense any second.

Another man who thinks I need to be rescued.

"Gabby," Charly says, always the peacekeeper. "We're a family. We handle these things together. That's why we're upset that you never told us that Colby had contacted you."

"It was nothing." I tip my head back in exasperation. "It was one email and one phone call. I ignored the email, and when he called I told him to stay the hell away from here. There were no threats."

"I told you," Beau begins, his voice calmer now, but he's *so fucking pissed.* "I told you to tell me if he ever so much as breathed in your direction."

"Beau—"

"No. Stop talking and *listen to me.* Yes, you're strong. And independent. And you're a fantastic mom. But Gabby, you can be those things and still allow the people who love you to help you. To have your back."

I shake my head and look down at my feet. Why don't they understand?

"I'm so tired of being treated like a baby," I murmur.

"We're not treating you like a baby," Beau says and shoves his hands in his pockets, reminding me of Daddy and Eli. "We would do the same for Charly or Eli. Hell, when Savannah's world was turned upside down a few months ago, we all rallied around her. We didn't treat her like a baby. We *loved her.*"

I blink at him, pissed to feel tears filling my eyes. He's right.

"Don't you understand that with one phone call, I can make Colby and all of his bullshit *disappear?*" Beau's face is stone-hard. And not a little scary.

"I don't think he needs to be killed," I reply with a chuckle and wipe tears from my cheeks.

"We have the best lawyers money can buy," Beau replies without blinking an eye. "This is nothing but an annoyance. There was no need for you to worry about this all these weeks."

"I wasn't—"

"We know you," Charly says, shaking her head. "You've worried. And it wasn't necessary."

"We talk to each other," Beau adds and finally pulls me in his arms for a tight hug, making me cry all over again. Jesus, I'm so fucking emotional when I'm pregnant.

Fuck, I'm pregnant.

"I get it," I whisper. "I'll let you know if he ever contacts me again."

"Thank you." He kisses the top of my head, sighs, and finally lets me go. "We love you, Gabby. And that has nothing to do with you being the youngest and everything to do with the fact that you're our sister and one of the best people we know."

"When you're not a pain in the ass," Charly adds. "I'm heading out. I'll go check on Sam and Mama. I'm assuming you won't be over for dinner." She raises a brow and glances toward Rhys, who still hasn't said anything.

I shake my head quickly. "Thanks."

"I'll go in with Charly." Beau doesn't move, he simply stares between me and Rhys, and finally says, "Do I need to kick his ass before I go?"

"No," I reply and roll my eyes. "Just go."

"Damn, I really wanted to kick someone's ass today. I should have pummeled Colby before the cops showed up."

"Goodbye, testosterone man," I say and push him off my porch, then wave as he and Charly leave.

Rhys silently moves up behind me, but I can feel him. I'm always aware of exactly where he is. He grips my shoulders in his hands, then turns me around.

"We need to talk."

"I'm all talked out." I try to walk around him, but he grips my arm and spins me back to face him.

"We need to talk," he repeats. "About several things.

Let's start with Colby. Why didn't you tell *me* he'd been contacting you?"

"Not you too." I roll my eyes and pace away. "Because when it started, I barely knew you."

"You knew me pretty well when he called the other day."

"I had other things on my mind then."

"Gabby—"

He looks...*pissed.* "I don't know why this pisses you off, Rhys. He's just some idiot from my past."

"I'm not angry, I'm hurt. Trust me, there's a difference."

"Look, I don't know why you're back, but I'm not doing this with you right now." The tears are threatening again, and God, he looks so good I just want to jump in his arms and have him hold me for about a week.

But I'll be damned if I do that.

"Yes, you are." His voice is tender now as he cups my face in his big hands and smiles down at me gently. "Fuck, I missed you."

"Then why didn't you call me?"

Damn it, I hate that I sound so fucking needy.

"I called you over and over again and I went straight to voice mail. Either your phone was off or you blocked me."

I shrug and pull out of his reach, not ready for him to touch me yet. "You left."

"Didn't you get my original text?"

"Oh yeah, I got it. And then when I got home all of your things were gone. *You left.*" The mad returns, boosting my confidence, and making me feel better. "You didn't even say goodbye. You didn't even say goodbye to *Sam.* What am I supposed to tell him? He loves you!"

"I love him too."

Why does he sound so damn calm?

"Well you have a shitty way of showing it," I reply.

"What about you, Gabby?"

"What about me?"

"How do you feel?"

I love you so much I can't see straight.

"I'm fucking pissed off at you."

"Obviously. Baby, why did you think I wasn't coming back?"

"Don't call me *baby.*" I glare at him, and the hurt in his eyes from my words makes me feel like a piece of shit. "Your things were gone, Rhys. You left. And men..." I shrug and look down.

"And men?"

"Men leave." I raise my head and look him right in the eyes. "Men leave. I don't trust that any man is going to stick around for any significant length of time, Rhys. Because they don't."

His eyes narrow.

"And you know what? I'm fine."

"No, you're not."

"What?"

"I call bullshit," he says and walks toward me. Slowly. Menacingly, and yet so fucking sexy I can hardly stand it. He's tall, his light brown hair is messy from his fingers, and his green eyes are on fire.

I step back, just as slowly.

"You can call bullshit all you want, but it doesn't make it false. I was fine before you got here, and I'll be fine after you leave."

"I'm not leaving."

I stop and blink rapidly. "What?"

"I never left for good, Gabrielle. I had a charity thing that I totally spaced because I've been so wrapped up in *you*. I told you, you've pushed everything else out of focus for me. I had to rush out of here, and it absolutely fucking frustrated the hell out of me that I couldn't reach you before I left. And then your phone was off, all fucking weekend."

Oh. So, pregnancy hormones make me a tad bit dramatic.

Fuck.

He keeps advancing on me, and I continue to back away until my back hits the railing on the far end of the porch, and I have nowhere else to go.

Rhys props his hands on either side of me and leans down until he's nose-to-nose with me. "I'm so fucking in love with you, Gabrielle."

"You weren't leaving?" I whisper, still processing the words that just came out of his mouth.

"That's all you got out of that?" he asks softly, his eyes searching my face. He's not touching me yet, and I *so* want him to touch me. "I'm not leaving you. Ever."

"Say the other part again, please." My voice is rough with unshed tears.

"I'm in love with you."

I bite my lip as one tear falls down my cheek.

"Are you going to say anything?" he whispers and catches the tear with his thumb. All I can do is shake my head. *He loves me.* "Good, because I have more to say."

He takes my hand in his and leads me to my swing, gestures for me to sit, then sits beside me. "I've done a lot of thinking this weekend. Hell, I've been thinking since I got here."

He smiles tenderly and pushes his fingers into my hair behind my neck, then begins to comb it. God, I've missed his touch.

"I really hope you want to stay," I whisper, so softly I can barely hear it myself. Why am I so scared to tell him what I want?

"I think *stay* is the most beautiful word there is," he replies and kisses my forehead.

"But I feel so selfish too," I admit.

He cocks his head to the side. "Why?"

"Because you'd be changing where your home is, just for me. You'd be changing your life."

"Gabby, *home* is wherever you and Sam are."

I blink at him, stunned. Has anyone ever loved us so fiercely? And how did I miss this over the past few weeks?

"What about baseball?"

"What about it?"

"You'll be gone a lot of the year for it."

He nods thoughtfully. "Yes, but the majority of the season is in the summer when Sam is out of school. We are fortunate in that we can afford for you to go with me a lot of the time." He drags his finger down my temple, then hooks my hair behind my ear. "All you have to do is tell me what you want, and it's yours," he continues.

"I want—"

"What?"

I shake my head and look away, but he tugs my chin back, so I have to look him in the eyes. "What do you want, baby?"

"I just want you. And I don't want you to get mad when I tell you this next thing."

He exhales slowly, still looking me in the eyes. "I'm not going to be mad."

I nod and take a long, deep breath. *This so didn't go well the first time.* I'm scared to hope that it'll go better this time, so I clench my eyes closed, terrified to look him in the eyes.

"I'm pregnant."

"Look at me."

I simply bite my lip.

"Look at me, Gabrielle."

I comply and feel the breath leave my body. His green eyes are soft. Tender. And if I'm not mistaken, a little misty.

And his voice is so damn soothing.

"Why in the world would that make me angry?"

"This conversation hasn't gone well for me in the past," I reply. "It scares me."

He pulls me into his strong arms, holding me close, and kisses my forehead, then my lips. "No one wants this baby more than me," he says. "You're the best mom I've ever seen."

"But it ties you to me forever," I reply. "And I don't know if you want that."

"Well, that leads us to the next thing." He clears his throat, then smiles widely, almost the way Sam does when he's giddy. "I'm gonna be a daddy."

"Yes, you are."

"So fucking amazing." He clears his throat again, and then his face sobers. "I love you, Gabby. You're every hope, every dream I've ever had, and I didn't even know it until I met you. No matter what happens in our life, every day I get to be with you is the greatest day of my life."

Tears are now rolling unchecked down my cheeks. I can't take my eyes off of him.

"You make me believe that love isn't hard because you love everyone in your life so effortlessly." He cups my jaw in his hands, his fingers mingle in with my hair, and his thumbs brush the tears from my face. "When you smile in that sweet way you do just for me, I swear I can see the next fifty years of my life."

I smile and drag my fingers down his cheek. "I always think that you smile at me in a special way too."

My heart stalls in my chest as he reaches in his pocket and pulls out a blue box with a slightly smashed white bow and places it in my palm. With shaking fingers, I unwrap the box and gasp at the gorgeous ring winking up at me.

"Rhys."

"I need you with me, beside me, as my partner and my love, for the rest of my life, Gabrielle. Please tell me that you'll be my wife. Have more babies with me. Let me give you and Sam my last name."

Is this real?

"I love you so much," I whisper through my tears. "I was so scared that I'd lost you."

"Never."

"I would be honored to marry you."

"Oh no, sweetheart. The honor is all mine." He lifts the ring from the box and slides it on my finger. It's a perfect fit.

And suddenly, I'm in his arms and he's carrying me into the house.

"Where are we going?"

"I can't do what I want to do to you on the porch."

"What do you want to do to me?"

His grin is slow and naughty as he carries me into my bedroom, lays me on the bed, then covers me with his body. "I'm going to make love to you."

"Mmm," I moan. "That sounds like a good plan."

He kisses my lips sweetly and drags his nose down my jawline to my neck as his hands make quick work of shedding my summer dress and panties.

His hands are *everywhere.*

"I missed this," I whisper before kissing his shoulder.

"I was going crazy in Chicago," he says as he nibbles his way down my torso, paying special attention to my nipples on the way. "These are sensitive," he murmurs.

"They've been sore," I agree.

"Am I hurting you?"

"No." I push my fingers into his hair, loving how soft it is. "I don't think you'd ever hurt me."

"Never intentionally," he agrees and slides his hand down my stomach and into my already wet folds. "God, you're so damn wet."

"You're doing sexy things to me," I reply with a giggle, then sigh as he pushes two fingers inside me. "You're so good at that."

His thumb is wreaking havoc on my clit, making me writhe and moan beneath him.

I need him inside me!

"Rhys."

"Yes, baby, sigh my name like that again."

I smile. "Rhys, I need you inside me." I'm yanking at his shirt, trying to get it over his head. "You're seriously over-dressed."

Finally, he rears up and sheds the shirt, works his jeans off, and I cup his impressive hard-on in my hand, pumping it firmly, wiping the bead of precum with my thumb.

"You're going to be the death of me," he whispers.

"What a way to go," I reply with a satisfied grin, and then he's suddenly nudging inside me, pushing slowly.

So fucking slowly.

I try to tilt my hips up to meet him, but he's holding me down, making me feel every incredible inch. And then he keeps the torture going with long, slow strokes, filling and emptying me, watching me with those amazing green eyes.

"I love you," I whisper, holding his face in my hands. "I'm sorry I didn't tell you before."

He kisses my palm and lowers himself over me, resting on his elbows. His lips are against mine, my arms and legs are wrapped around him.

I've never felt so physically and emotionally connected to anyone in my life.

"I should have told you too," he whispers against my lips. "There aren't words sufficient enough to explain to you how amazing you are. I promise you, I'm going to spend every day making sure you're happy."

"You do make me happy," I reply. "You make me feel things that I don't even have a label for, it's so big."

"That's my cock, baby," he replies with a naughty grin.

"You're such a man." I giggle and clench down on him harder. "You know what I mean."

He pushes even deeper inside me, making us both gasp.

"Sex and love all at the same time is a powerful thing," he whispers. "A very smart woman I know once said that. I had no idea just how powerful until you."

His hands are in my hair, just as they always are. I hope he never stops loving my hair.

With his eyes on mine, he sets the pace, increasing the tempo, pushing harder, until finally we can't stand it anymore, and fall apart at the seams, exploding into a million pieces, then falling back together again.

He collapses on top of me, panting and sweaty.

"I'm so fucking hungry," he growls in my ear.

"I'll go make you something to eat."

"Oh, you think you can still walk?" He pulls back to

stare down at me with a raised brow. "Then we're not done."

"How are we going to get food?" I ask.

"We'll worry about that later. For now I'm going to make love to the mother of my children."

My children.

I blink up at him in surprise.

"Yes, Sam is mine, just as much as this baby is mine." His hand covers my belly. "Just as much as *you* are mine."

"We're all yours," I agree. "And you're ours. Always."

He smiles at me, in that way he does that makes my toes curl.

"Always."

CHAPTER TWENTY-ONE

~Gabby~

Two Months Later

"Thank you for having dinner with us, darling," Susan Waterbury, the wife of Rhys's coach, says as she hugs me tightly. "And if you have any other questions, please don't hesitate to call me. We baseball wives have to stick together."

"Thank you so much," I reply with a smile, enjoying Susan very much. "It was so nice to meet you."

"Goodnight," Rhys says with a wave, and with his hand linked with mine, escorts me in the opposite direction of the Waterbury's toward our hotel room.

"That was nice," I say and lean my head on Rhys's shoulder. "Thank you for bringing me to Chicago to meet your team. Everyone has been very nice to me."

Rhys kisses my head and squeezes my hand. "I needed the two most important parts of my life to finally meet each other. And Coach's wife has been a baseball wife for more than half of her life."

"She'll be a great source of information," I agree. "She's sweet."

"She'll also be a great source of gossip," Rhys says with a chuckle as he leads me into the elevator and presses the button for the penthouse. "Are you tired?"

"No, I'm feeling good."

After the first trimester was over, my energy seemed to come back in full force. Morning sickness is gone. I feel great.

He pins me in the corner of the elevator and his lips tip up in that sexy smile of his. "I'm glad to hear that, because I have some plans for you tonight."

"That sounds promising."

He nods and kisses me soundly, passionately, until the bell dings and the doors open to our floor.

He takes my hand and leads me through the penthouse to the master bedroom. His body is tense. He's been broody and intense all day. For the first time in a long time, I'm having a hard time reading him.

"Are you okay?" I ask.

"Fine."

Hmm.

I kick my shoes off and reach for the zipper on the back of my dress, but Rhys turns me away from him and unzips it himself. He kisses down my spine as he slowly lowers it, then kisses his way back up as the dress falls around my ankles and I'm left in a black bra and matching black panties.

"You're beautiful," he whispers against my ear. "And mine."

"Yes," I agree.

"On the bed, please."

I glance back at him, still not able to read his mood,

but I comply, crawling into the middle of the enormous bed and lying on my back.

"On all fours."

"Rhys, are you okay?"

He raises a brow. "I'm fine. I've had a lot on my mind today."

Okay.

"What do you need?"

"I need you to turn over, please."

I'm watching him, his deep green eyes, his face. He's still tense, but he's also watching me with the love-filled eyes I just can't get enough of.

So, I turn over onto my hands and knees, already wondering what he has planned.

"Do you trust me?" he asks. I can hear him shucking his clothing, and then the bed dips when he joins me, kneeling at my side.

"Of course."

"Grab onto the headboard," he whispers into my ear, sending shivers all over my body.

Oh, this is going to be so damn fun.

I grin and stretch out, the way I did when we were still learning each other, and grip onto the headboard. His hands are *everywhere,* rubbing down my back, my hips, my thighs, then up between them so he can tickle my folds with his fingertips.

"I have something I need to get off of my chest, baby." His palm is circling over my ass. Gently, lazily, in big wide circles around the cheeks, up my center and crack, then around the opposite one.

It's freaking *amazing.*

"What is it?"

SMACK.

I gasp and look back at him, my mouth gaping and eyes wide. "You just *spanked me!*"

"You let go of the headboard."

His face is sober, but his eyes look...*hurt.*

I lean back down and grip the bed and Rhys resumes caressing my body, turning me on, making me sweat.

"You say you trust me, but you *didn't* trust me before, Gabby. You immediately assumed the worst about me, believing that I'd left you for good."

SMACK.

I bite my lip, caught between the sting of the slap and the pure pleasure of his hands and mouth all over me. I'm sopping wet. My hips are rotating, begging for more.

"You say you trust me, but you didn't tell me that Colby had been harassing you the *entire* time I was with you."

SMACK.

Oh my God.

I thought I liked being spanked before, and that was *nothing* compared to this.

"My actions speak for me, Gabby. I did nothing but support you. Care for both you and Sam. And you devastated me by jumping to the most horrible conclusion there was."

SMACK.

"I'm sorry," I whisper and bite my lip. He's right. I told him I trusted him, but I didn't. Not when it counted.

Not when he needed me to the most.

"Is it going to happen again?" His voice is raw now, full of what sounds like unshed tears, but I can't move my hands from the headboard long enough to look at him.

I need to look at him.

"Rhys—"

"Not yet. Is it going to happen again, Gabby? What if there's a misunderstanding again? What if I can't communicate with you as often as you'd like when I'm on the road? Are you going to automatically assume that I don't want you? Or that I don't love you?"

SMACK.

"No, never."

I can't stand it now. I move my hands and flip around so I can take his face in my hands and look him in the eyes.

"You moved."

"I don't care. You can spank me again later. Rhys, I'm so sorry. Why did you wait all of these weeks to tell me how hurt you were?"

"I don't think it hit me until we were here in Chicago and Susan was telling you about the number of marriages that don't work, for all of the ridiculous reasons that they fall apart. And Gabby, jumping to conclusions is a *big one.* There will be times that I have to travel without you. I couldn't handle it if I didn't think you trusted me. And based on what happened before, you said you trusted me, but obviously that's not true."

"So you spanked me?"

His eyes flash. "Yes."

He pushes me back on the bed and covers me gently, wraps my legs around his waist and slowly slips inside me.

"I thought you'd want to fuck me hard to go along with that spanking."

"I don't want to hurt you," he replies and kisses me softly.

"You didn't hurt me. Even the smacks didn't hurt."

"You're pregnant," he reminds me, as if I'm likely to forget. "And you like spankings, so it really wasn't much of a punishment."

"I love you so big," I whisper against his lips. "I trust you with *everything I am,* Rhys. I will never, ever doubt you again."

"It almost killed me, Gabrielle. I'm your constant. I'm what you can depend on. And you're that for me. You can trust that, I promise you."

I smile and wrap my arms around this amazing man. "I love you."

He grins and moves so slowly that I have to bite my lip. "I love you too. Let me show you how much."

***

Ten Months Later

"Look, Mom! There's Daddy!" Sam points at Rhys, who has just taken to the pitcher's mound in Wrigley Field. The crowd is going wild, as they always do when their pitcher enters the game.

God, my husband is fucking sexy in that uniform. And he loves it when I wear his jersey and nothing else to bed.

In fact, I think I'll do that later tonight.

Ailish, our two-month-old daughter, squirms in the baby carrier I have strapped around me and lets out a little squeak, then settles down again, sleeping peacefully.

This baby girl has red hair, just like her aunt Kate, and I hope it stays that way.

"What is she doing?" Sam asks and peeks in on his sister.

"She's just getting comfortable."

He smiles up at me. "She's cute."

"You didn't say that the other day when I suggested you change her dirty diaper," I remind him with a chuckle, then lean down and kiss his head. "I think you said she was gross."

"Well, yuck," he says, sticking his tongue out. "For

such a little thing, she sure makes a big mess."

"True."

Very true. This little bundle of joy runs on her own timeline. Where Sam was super early being born, Ailish was two weeks late. Rhys almost didn't arrive in time to see her be born because he had to be in Philly for games that week. But as soon as I called him, letting him know that I was in labor, he jumped on a chartered plane, and walked in the hospital room just in time to hold my hand while I pushed and cursed him for *doing this to me,* and then he held both me and Ailish while all three of us cried.

He's an awesome dad to both of our kids. The same day we married, Rhys adopted Sam, and thanks to the iron-clad contract my father made Colby sign before Sam was born, Colby had no case, and is officially out of the picture, again.

Sam couldn't be more proud to call Rhys his dad.

"Mom! Look!" Sam is jumping and pointing at us on the big screen, and I'm suddenly shy.

"Ladies and gentlemen," the announcer bellows, "we are excited to introduce you to our Cubs pitcher's family! This is Gabby, Sam and Ailish O'Shaughnessy!"

Sam and I wave at the board, and when I glance down at Rhys, he blows me a kiss, then waves.

I'm a lucky woman. Actually, no, luck has nothing to do with it. I deserve this life. I deserve this man and these amazing children.

I deserve this happiness.

"Let's play ball!"

EPILOGUE

~Declan Boudreaux~

I don't know why I'm still here. My set ended a half an hour ago, and I passed up a sweet piece of ass to stay.

I wasn't even interested in the petite brunette that made it very clear that she'd be happy to share her bed with me tonight.

Instead, I can't take my eyes off the owner of this club, Odyssey, as she bustles about, giving orders to the wait-staff and bartenders, getting the place closed up for the night.

"You're still here," Callie says as she approaches the bar. Her platinum blonde hair is up in some sort of complicated-yet-messy-looking knot on her head, showing off her slender neck and shoulders. Her lips are red, and her eyes are ice blue as they look me up and down.

So I pay her the same courtesy, taking in the white halter crop top and black leather pants, showing off a navel piercing and a nice handful of tits, not to mention her sexier than fuck ink.

But it's those fucking hot red shoes that make my cock twitch. Jesus, what she'd look like, bent over, wearing those shoes and nothing else as I take her from behind, pulling her hair just enough to make her gasp.

"Still here," I confirm.

"Why?" She cocks a brow and saunters behind the bar, gathering dirty glasses and placing them efficiently in the sink.

"Thought I'd grab a drink before I head home."

"Okay." She nods and slaps two shot glasses on the bar, then fills them both with Patron. We clink glasses and throw the shots back. She doesn't even flinch.

"Nice piercing." I point to her navel and watch her red lips twitch. "What else do you have pierced?" *And can I take you home, strip you bare, and find out for myself?*

"Wouldn't you like to know?" she replies and laughs before throwing back another shot.

"I would, yes."

She sobers and watches me with those amazingly blue eyes. I love how tall she looks behind this bar. She's a beautiful woman, and in those spectacular fuck-me heels, she's only a few inches shy of my six-foot-four.

"You'll only get a drink out of me," she replies. "What'll it be?"

"Do you have Chivas Regal Scotch?" I ask and her eyes instantly go cold. Her shoulders tense. Her jaw ticks.

"I do. Want it on the rocks or straight up?"

"Straight up."

She pours the drink and slides it over to me, then turns to walk away.

"What did I say?"

"You didn't say anything important," she replies and walks away without looking back, her hips swaying with each step, those shoes clicking on the hard wood.

I usually like my women sweet, curvy and docile. Soft.

There is nothing soft, sweet or curvy about the woman walking away from me. She's all sharp edges.

She's going to be work, and she just might kill me.

I grin and sip my drink. It's going to be one hell of a ride.

The End

Don't miss Declan and Callie's story, EASY MELODY, releasing in the fall of 2015!

ABOUT KRISTEN PROBY

New York Times and USA Today Bestselling Author Kristen Proby is the author of the popular With Me in Seattle series. She has a passion for a good love story and strong characters who love humor and have a strong sense of loyalty and family. Her men are the alpha type—fiercely protective and a bit bossy—and her ladies are fun, strong, and not afraid to stand up for themselves. Kristen spends her days with her muse in the Pacific Northwest. She enjoys coffee, chocolate, and sunshine. And naps. Visit her at KristenProby.com.

OTHER BOOKS BY KRISTEN PROBY:

The Boudreaux Series:
Easy Love

The With Me In Seattle Series:
Come Away With Me and on audio
Under the Mistletoe With Me and on audio
Fight With Me and on audio
Play With Me and on audio
Rock With Me and on audio
Safe With Me and on audio
Tied With Me and on audio
Breathe With Me and on audio
Forever With Me and on audio
Easy With You

The Love Under the Big Sky Series, available through
Pocket Books:
Loving Cara
Seducing Lauren
Falling for Jillian

Baby, It's Cold Outside
An Anthology with Jennifer Probst, Emma Chase, Kristen
Proby, Melody Anne and Kate Meader

CPSIA information can be obtained
at www.ICGtesting.com
Printed in the USA
LVOW10s2020140318

569840LV00012B/854/P